PRAISE FOR

TRUE ALLEGIANCE

"Meet our new Ayn Rand."

—Salon.com

"*True Allegiance* is a terrifying read that brilliantly lays bare the chilling future we all fear is headed right for us."

—Brad Thor, #1 *New York Times* bestselling author of *Code of Conduct*

"Provocative, intense, and about five minutes from becoming reality, Ben Shapiro's *True Allegiance* is a riveting thriller about what happens when America falls apart. It's not just a phenomenal thriller, it's prophetic."

—Ann Coulter, author of ten *New York Times* bestsellers

"We all know Ben Shapiro for his keen intellect and his impeccable ability to articulate the principles that made America great. Now Ben has delved into the world of fiction in his book, *True Allegiance*—but is it really fictional? This is a must read novel in which we must ask ourselves, will we make a stand?"

—Lt. Col. Allen B. West (US Army, Ret.),
Member, 112th US Congress

"A gutsy and gut-wrenching vision of an America coming apart at the seams—an America not so different from the one we're living in right now. Ben Shapiro has used his deep understanding of current events to create a fictional world that could well be our world the day after tomorrow. It's a scary story and just a little too real for comfort."

—Andrew Klavan, screenwriter, Edgar Award-winning and *New York Times* bestselling author of *True Crime* and *Don't Say A Word*

"Ben Shapiro's strong, elegant writing moves from journalism to fiction with grace and impact. His famous insights into the characters and institutions of our times now present in razor sharp delineation of characters and their gripping progress, each with their own arc that draws you tightly into his remarkably well-told story. *True Allegiance* cuts no corners and makes no easy choices in unfolding its tale of the great challenges of our times and the perilous way they're being managed. Shapiro's view, through the eyes of those who become captives of history, finds them all, those who seek greatness only to becoming unwitting pawns, and others upon whom destiny is thrust. This is a wonderful novel, a brisk and enjoyable read."

–Lionel Chetwynd, Emmy Award-winning screenwriter

"Hard to put down. Ben gleefully serves up a combustible mix of real-life anecdotes, dramatic license, comically precise details and conservative worldview—and a jaw-dropping, I-can't-believe-he-wrote-that climax!"

–Jim Geraghty, senior political correspondent, *National Review* and author of *The Weed Agency*

BEN SHAPIRO

A POST HILL PRESS BOOK

True Allegiance
© 2016 by Ben Shapiro
All Rights Reserved

ISBN: 978-1-68261-077-0
ISBN (eBook): 978-1-68261-078-7

Cover Design by Christian Bentulan
Interior Design and Composition by Greg Johnson/Textbook Perfect

Post Hill

PRESS

Post Hill Press
275 Madison Avenue, 14th Floor
New York, NY 10016
posthillpress.com

Published in the United States of America
1 2 3 4 5 6 7 8 9 10

PROLOGUE

NEW YORK CITY

BY THE TIME JENNIFER COLLIER hit the George Washington Bridge, it was already almost 9:00 a.m. Rush hour. The bridge had turned into an enormous parking lot.

Jennifer looked out at the sea of red lights before her, stretching all the way into New York, and sighed. There had to be thirty thousand cars on this bridge, all of them moving two miles an hour.

Jennifer glanced at her watch and sighed.

She was on the west side of the bridge, and she could see its two enormous steel-encased towers looming before her. In the passenger seat, her daughter, Julie, breathed softly, sleeping.

Jennifer glanced at her watch again. 9:03. "Come on," she muttered.

Which is when she heard it.

The bridge groaned.

It was a loud, low groan that made the car vibrate.

Julie woke up. "What was that?" she asked drowsily.

The groan died away.

"Nothing," said Jennifer. "Probably just a plane overhead. Go back to sleep."

"Mommy…"

The bridge groaned again. This time, it was longer, more drawn out. Jennifer felt the brake pedal vibrate beneath her foot.

"Mommy, that's not a plane," said Julie, wide awake now.

The groaning continued, booming from beneath them.

The bridge was undulating slightly up and down now. Jennifer could see the cables of the suspension bridge oscillating like the strings of a guitar.

"Mommy, *what's going on?*" Julie cried.

Cars ahead were honking now, urgently pleading for those at the front of the bridge to hurry up. A few cars were trying to ram their way through the traffic, pushing other cars toward the edge of the bridge. The honking and crashing, combined with the burgeoning low roar, made Jennifer's head ache, pound, the driving rhythm of her blood surging through her temples.

Then the bridge's roar stopped again. The people ahead of Jennifer kept honking, panicking, trying to get off the bridge. After about thirty seconds, the honking seemed to die down a little bit. Julie's wide eyes grew wider. She was staring at a crash on the other side of the divider, the flames leaping from the engine of a smashed Toyota. Jennifer could see a man's arm hanging, lifeless, out the window.

Jennifer reached out and gripped Julie's arm. "It's okay, baby," she whispered, wetting her lips.

Then time seemed to stop.

The noise of the traffic went silent.

Jennifer's eyes opened in horror.

The bridge before Jennifer tilted sideways. The 604-foot tower before her began to lean, almost gracefully, to her right.

Jennifer screamed, but it was drowned out in the ear-splitting cracking noise, hundreds of thousands of tons of steel twisting and bending and grating on each other, the sound of a million airplanes all crashing at once. Jennifer looked to her left as she heard the steel cables shriek, stretch on the other side of the bridge. She locked eyes with an elderly man driving a silver Lincoln Continental. Behind him, she saw one of the enormous metal cables snap clean and slither wildly back and forth like a beginning fly fisherman's messy cast.

"Look out!" she shouted at the man. He couldn't hear her, but he turned to follow her eyes.

The cable ripped through the Lincoln, slicing its occupant in half vertically, a jet stream of red following in its wake, splattering Jennifer's windshield.

She opened her mouth to scream and realized that she was already screaming so hard, no sound was emerging.

In front of her, the road itself began to tilt. Cars slid horizontally toward the railings, bath-time playthings of an angry god.

The first tower buckled.

Jennifer felt herself fall as the top level of the bridge dropped. For a moment, she was weightless—the peculiar memory of jumping inside an elevator when she was a little girl flitted through her brain—and then the second level of the bridge slammed down on top of the first level at a twenty-five-degree angle. The tower stopped, bending but holding grotesquely, the metal shrieking and moaning, smoke emerging from below.

Jennifer could hear the screams and cries of the wounded below her, the carnage of metal and bone. An awful crematory smell burned her nose as cars exploded beneath her, one by one, muffled by the tons of cement and steel, sounding for all the world like popcorn. Julie was screaming uncontrollably. In the distance,

3

sirens sounded eerily, and over the river, she could see emergency helicopters approaching.

Jennifer fumbled for her purse and dug through it for her cell phone. She threw aside her wallet, her makeup, poured out the contents on the floor of the passenger seat. Grabbed her cell phone. Speed-dialed Bill.

It rang once. Then twice. Finally, it went to message.

"I love you," she whispered into the phone.

As she did, Julie pointed through the front windshield, her lips quivering in silent horror.

The second tower was tilting, too.

Like some sort of horrible snake, the bridge responded to the tower. It tilted and keeled over, the road peeling away before Jennifer as it leapt up and to the side. Jennifer saw thousands of cars turn on their sides, rotate like clothes in a washing machine.

Jennifer heard the awful roar, the unnatural screaming of thousands of voices, as the stream of red lights before her began to disappear.

There was nowhere for her to go. She turned to Julie, her eyes round with terror. She grabbed her hand.

"It's going to be all right," she whispered. Julie nodded slowly. Jennifer clasped her by the face and looked into her eyes. "I promise you," she said. "It's going to be all right. Now, just close your eyes, darling."

Julie closed her eyes. Jennifer didn't. She looked into the river below her, saw the disappearing taillights of the thousands of cars descending into the depths of the Hudson.

"God," she whispered. "Oh, God."

PART 1

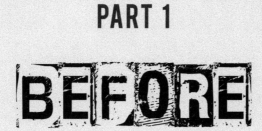

BRETT

KABUL, AFGHANISTAN

Brigadier General Brett Hawthorne looked at his M9 magazine and cursed to himself. Empty.

He was sat up against a mud-brick hovel in the city's poor part of town—even in Kabul, there was a large income gap—and felt the sweat trickle down cold between his shoulder blades. He hadn't been alone for years—generals always had a personal security detail—but things had gone hellishly wrong.

Hawthorne was a bear of a man, six three in his bare feet and two hundred fifteen pounds in his underwear, with a graying blond crew cut and a face carved of granite. But he had plenty of smile lines. He just didn't like showing those to people unless he knew them.

He looked up at the Hindu Kush. The city was romantically placed in full view of the mountain chain, a bizarre, large cyst at the bottom of the grandiose peaks. The Kabul River, which once passed lazily through the city, slicing it in half and providing it with an anchor, had dried up to a series of puddles, leaving the city afloat on the steppes.

It was freezing, just like every other December day. What wasn't like every other day was the silence.

It was quiet, except for a few scattered screams and the occasional rapid-fire rounds. Hawthorne sucked in the smell of smoke with every breath; he could see the Kabul Serena Hotel burning. The new coalition government had bragged about the hotel as the standard-bearer for the modernization of the city, with its historically imitative Islamic architecture, satellite TV, and wireless Internet. Now the flames licked at the windows as ashes floated down on the city.

It wasn't the only building burning. It seemed as though half the city was on fire.

Well, Brett thought to himself, *at least I can tell those stupid bastards, "I told you so."*

A few short years ago, Afghanistan had seemed to be on the upswing. The Taliban had been on the run, hiding in the mountains of the Tora Bora region, sallying forth every so often to hit a supply chain, but mainly holing up waiting for the invaders to leave. The coalition forces had been systematically rooting them out from local areas, empowering Afghan forces to hold the areas, and funding local governance in those areas.

Hawthorne knew all of this because he had designed the strategy. And now that strategy had gone to shit.

Brett Hawthorne was the youngest general in the American military. He'd grown up lower middle class in Chicago, his mother a teacher, his father a salesman for the local phone company. When his dad lost his job, the family moved from the more expensive North Side to the South Side of Chicago—poorer, industrial, and heavily black.

He'd been a shy kid, gentle, quiet, built like a reed. But he learned one skill pretty quickly at Thomas Edison High: how to talk his way out of a bad situation.

That, he learned from Derek.

On the second day of school, Brett was sitting by himself at lunch. He wasn't one of the Irish kids, and he wasn't one of the Italian kids, so he couldn't sit with those cliques. And he'd made the mistake the day before of trying to befriend a couple of the black kids. That hadn't gone well. He'd ended up with a black eye and a few new vocabulary words to add to his dictionary.

So today, he sat alone. Until he made the mistake of looking up. Standing above him, glaring at him, was a behemoth, a black kid named Yard. Nobody knew his real name—everybody just called him Yard because he played on the school football team, stood six foot five, clocked in at a solid two hundred eighty pounds, and looked like he was headed straight for a lifetime of prison workouts. The coach loved him. Everybody else feared him.

If Brett hadn't looked up, everything would have worked out just fine. But then again, he didn't have much choice, given that Yard grabbed him by the shirt and pulled him out of his seat like a rag doll.

Then Yard mumbled something in his face.

"What?" said Brett.

"I said," Yard growled, "did you just call me nigger? Because I just heard you call me nigger."

The entire room turned to watch the impending carnage.

Yard's hand came down on Brett's shoulder, heavy as doom. Brett could feel his bowels begin to give way when a smallish hand emerged on Yard's shoulder. A black hand. Yard swiveled ponderously to face down the person connected with the hand.

A small person, slim, wearing glasses and a wide smile across his face.

9

"Yard, man," he said, "he didn't call you nigger."

"What you talking about, Derek?" rumbled Yard.

"It was me, man! I called you nigger."

Yard looked puzzled. "No," he said slowly, "it was the white boy."

"Oh, yeah, man," said Derek. "It was. I'm white. You just mixed us up." He moved around to stand next to Brett. "See? We're twins. Identical. Anybody could mix us up. Even though I'm more handsome."

Yard's eyes glazed over with confusion. The giggling started at the back of the room. Yard's hands clenched and unclenched as the wave rose over the room, until the kids were slapping each other on the back. Yard's fists closed tight.

But as they did, Derek leaned forward, reached out, and lightly tapped Yard's hands—and then started singing at the top of his lungs that Paul McCartney and Stevie Wonder song, "Ebony and Ivory." "Come on, sing with me, Yard! You be ebony, I'll be ivory!"

But Yard was backing away now, a look on his face asking, *who is this nut job*?

Derek turned to Brett and continued singing.

And Brett smiled and crooned back, in warbled harmony.

That's how Brett met his best friend, and learned how to talk his way out of violent confrontation. He'd become a master at it over the years, learned to stick and move with his words, disarm the enemy, keep him laughing rather than fighting. It was a tool that he'd deploy with soldiers and presidents.

It also brought him Ellen.

Between junior and senior years of high school, Brett finally hit his growth spurt. Like his dad, he bloomed late—but when he did, he put on muscle and height like a racehorse. He sprouted five inches, to six foot two; he broadened through the chest, filling out to a healthy two fifteen. The coaches had ignored him in high school, but at The Citadel, he quickly became their favorite. He didn't pick the college because of its military background. He picked it because he read a Pat Conroy book, and because South Carolina seemed gothic and romantic compared to the South Side of Chicago.

It was. But the college was brutal, especially for a kid lacking discipline. He bridled at the orders, bridled at the system. He bucked it whenever he could, and found himself on the wrong end of a lot of forced runs and extra burpees and early morning wake-ups. Fortunately, the extra meat on his bones helped.

On one of his rare off days, Brett found himself at Charleston's bustling City Market. The shops were heavy with traffic; rain outside had forced everyone into the covered complex of artists hawking their pictures and crafts. He was wearing his Citadel uniform, standing out conspicuously among the women in their summer dresses and the men in their jeans and seersucker sport coats. Reluctant to run back out into the rain, he leaned back against a bookcase.

"No loitering, cadet."

The voice was musical—for some reason, the image of a woodwind came to mind. A southern woodwind, since her accent sang of long summers and lemonade.

Brett didn't care about that. He turned, irked—and found himself face-to-face with a beautiful young woman, about seventeen, staring aggressively at him.

"No," she said, "I expected better from a cadet. Hanging around here, driving away all the customers."

"And what if I *do* drive them all away? What if I was the last man left on earth, standing right here, at this shop?" He couldn't believe his mouth was moving this well, considering his tongue had turned to glue against his molars. "Would you do me the honor of letting me take you for a walk along the pier?"

He flashed what he hoped was his most charming smile.

"I've been asked by cadets before, and I'll be asked by cadets again," she shot back, without hesitation. "And if you'll wipe that grin that looks like you're eating tacks and manure off your face— and if you buy one of these here pictures—I'll think about it."

The smile disappeared. His hand flashed to his wallet. He took out a $20 bill, fingered it, then handed it over, pointing at a watercolor of a palmetto-lined road along the shore. "I'll take that one." She handed it over. "So, how about it?"

She raised an eyebrow in mockery. "No. I think I'll pass."

He felt the frustration rise in his chest. "But I just bought the picture!"

"I'm not *that* cheap a date," she laughed. This time, the musicality of it pierced him.

So maybe his way with words didn't win Ellen. But his persistence did. By the time he bought his fifth picture, she agreed to a walk. By the tenth, they were going steady. Two years later, they were married.

After college, Brett and Ellen moved to Quantico for Brett's Marine training. He hadn't liked The Citadel, but it had wormed its way into him—the need to serve, the belief in discipline, the recognition that somebody had to stand between the barbarians and the gates. The uniform. The camaraderie.

Although he'd graduated top of his class at The Citadel, at Quantico his star truly began to rise. The brass's eye settled on him as he bust record after record in training. By the time of the Gulf War, he'd been promoted to first lieutenant. He had also learned Arabic.

He was just twenty-two when they sent him to Saudi Arabia; the war was already winding down. Operation Desert Sabre had been a full-fledged success, and the famed left hook had already busted the Iraqi defenses wide open. But he heard the promises;

he heard the broadcasts in February 1991 promising that those who rose up against Saddam would be liberated. And he watched in horror as those promises were abandoned, as the Kurds were gassed in the streets.

When he returned to the United States, he talked with Ellen about getting out. The mission shook him. Yes, they'd saved Kuwait from Saddam, saved the Saudi oil fields. But what about the children, spittle flecking from their mouths, spasming to death? What about the Kurds fleeing their homes, forced into Turkey, dying all along the way? He'd seen the images on television, and he'd heard the broadcast; he knew that those people had risen up, hoping that the United States would stand with them.

Eventually, the decision became simple: he could stay in and try to wield influence on the inside. Or he could leave.

Ellen wanted him to leave. She told him she was tired of the military life; she'd traveled enough. She was tired of losing him for months at a time, tired of him coming home with that empty look in his eyes, tired of the formality and the cheap military hole-ups. She also told him she was pregnant.

For the first time since Iraq, she saw the light come back into his eyes.

"Okay," he finally told her. "When the baby is born, I'll let them know. The timing works out just right." Then he kissed her, felt the softness of her lips, and knew everything would be all right.

Three weeks later, in the middle of the night, Ellen woke him, screaming. Her voice cracked as it reached the apex, shrieks over and over in the night, blood on the sheets, her hands clawing at her face. He picked her up in his powerful arms, held her tight, so small against him. He rushed her to the car, foot to the floorboard, one hand gripping hers—and her hand gripping his so tight he thought she might break his fingers.

Afterward, the doctors told them children were out of the question.

Whether it was unwillingness to leave the life, principled practicality, or a cowardly need for something to cling to—or a mix of all three, Brett eventually came to suspect—he stayed in.

And he rose.

By Kosovo, he was a captain. By September 11, he was a major. A major who, by simple coincidence, knew Pashto. He'd thought it prudent when, after the bombings of the US embassies in Kenya and Tanzania in 1998, he first heard of some piece of shit named Osama bin Laden, holed up somewhere in Afghanistan.

That little fact made him one of the first men on the ground in Afghanistan. He knew little of the country's culture, but his knowledge of the language made him a valuable commodity. They assigned him to a unit working in direct contact with the heads of the Northern Alliance, the band of horse-riding tribesmen tasked with taking down the Taliban. It was all very *Lawrence of Arabia*, Brett thought. Except that Peter O'Toole never had to deal with roadside bombs or donkeys laden with explosives or the lure of the opium trade. And T. E. Lawrence hadn't missed his wife, either, of course.

And he missed Ellen.

After the quick victory over the Taliban, CENTCOM in Afghanistan ordered his promotion to lieutenant colonel—the youngest in the Marines—and assigned him to the security team for central Kabul. That Pashto was really paying off.

It also put him in direct contact, on a daily basis, with the president of the new Islamic Republic of Afghanistan. It turned out that Afghanistan's new president didn't trust the US ambassador to Afghanistan; soon, the only American he'd talk with was Brett.

Brett saw the man as a corrupt tribal leader thrust into national leadership. He also told the American ambassador as much, and his superiors. It seemed to have no impact. All those issues were ignored; too much money was changing hands, too much politics shaping the game. The Afghan president wanted permanent US military bases, but a blind eye turned to his own corruption; the Americans wanted permanent US bases, but a guarantee of more participation by the Afghan military to help transition away from the use of US forces; the ambassador just wanted to be left alone.

Daily, he missed Ellen more and more. He was thirty-seven now; they'd spent nearly a decade in this on-and-off relationship. It was, he had concluded, inhumane.

One night, he unloaded it all to Ellen. She told him that he'd worked too hard to give it up—that he could still make a difference. He heard the musicality of her voice, her lips kissing him through the phone.

"It'll be okay," she said. "It always is."

"Okay," he grumbled half-heartedly. "But let's keep thinking about it."

"Take a bullet for you, babe," she said.

"Take a bullet for you, sweetheart," he replied, their usual sign-off.

He still wanted to go home. More than ever.

Then, all at once, things changed.

It started in May, when *Newsweek* reported that US interrogators had desecrated a Koran by flushing it down the toilet at Guantanamo Bay, Cuba. They later retracted the story, but the damage was done. Riots broke out across the Muslim world; at least seventeen people were murdered in the streets of Afghanistan, and more than a hundred brutally injured. Mullahs in the northeast of the country threatened a new *jihad* against the United States if the interrogators weren't turned over for *sharia* prosecution.

The deal for the military bases was all but dead. The administration was scrambling. The Afghan president, in an attempt to appease his inflamed population, demanded that US troops change their rules of engagement to avoid civilian casualties—in the process, endangering more American soldiers.

Then Colonel Brett Hawthorne saved the day.

He'd been ushering a CNN crew around—"Gotta keep these schmucks from reporting that we eat Muslims," he told Ellen—showing them Kabul. He handed candies to the children, spoke Pashto with the shopkeepers. The marketplace was crowded at this time of day, vendors hawking their wares; the security presence was heavy, too.

All of this fell within the normal spectrum. But Brett *felt* something was off. He had developed a sixth sense about these things, spending all these years in-country. The market normally buzzed with activity, but now it seemed just a tick too quiet.

The members of the CNN crew were yawning. One of them leaned up against the pole of a stall, camera still fixed to his eye. "Colonel," he said lazily, "I think we've got about enough footage." Brett turned to speak—and from behind the cameraman, he saw a child on a donkey, about three hundred feet away.

His service weapon, a Beretta M9, was in his hand before he even felt it leave his holster. That motion became smooth after thousands upon thousands of repeats. The cameraman perked up, then swiveled to see what Brett was looking at. Other Marines began to pay attention now, brought their M4s to their shoulders. Vendors swept up their goods, ran from the square, emptying it almost instantaneously.

One of the soldiers moved toward the donkey. "Get away from it!" Brett barked.

The child began to cry. The cameraman zoomed in eagerly. This was absolute gold: a crying Afghan child, frightened to death by the awful Americans. Brett shouted to the kid in Pashto. "They're watching us, aren't they?"

The child nodded, tears streaming down his face.

If the soldiers got too close, the Taliban fighters would detonate the donkey, Brett knew.

"Stay back, boys," Brett shouted, his voice carrying in the still air.

Then he saw it. Because the bomb was mobile, the terrorists couldn't use one of their hard-lined IEDs—they'd rigged it with a cell phone. Brett could see the phone glowing on the side of the donkey. They were planning to detonate the bomb remotely by calling a number.

And if he called in an EOD team, he knew, the terrorists would simply detonate the bomb, taking the kid with it.

And so he leveled his weapon. The cameraman zoomed in on his face, sweat pouring down his forehead. His thumb fingered the grip, caressed it.

"Come on, baby," Brett said to himself.

The donkey was now about waddling toward him, the cell phone bouncing in its cloth pack. The child's eyes went wide.

He fired.

The bullet smashed into the cell phone at an angle, shattering it completely.

The donkey panicked, took off at a dead run right at Brett. Brett fired his handgun two more times into the dirt, forcing the donkey to rear—and then Brett reached up and grabbed its bridle, using his full body weight to pull it to the ground. Then he untied the kid, picked him up off the donkey, and muttered a few comforting words in Pashto.

The kid hugged him around the neck fiercely.

When he looked up, the lens was in his face.

What the hell, he thought.

And he winked.

The video went viral, of course. His face graced the cover of *Time*—"THE NEW FACE OF THE GOOD WAR," it touted.

The military put him on tour. He became a recruitment tool, the purest example of American military might combined with American caring.

Then Mark Prescott was elected president.

By that time, Brett had been back in the United States for several years, doing cable news, pumping up the war effort. Prescott's election, however, sent a shock wave through the military infrastructure. Prescott had campaigned on ending the war in Iraq and getting out of Afghanistan as soon as possible. He said the wars had dragged on too long, that military spending could be slashed and the money rededicated to domestic concerns.

As an active military member, Brett couldn't say anything, of course. Once again, he talked with Ellen about quitting—and this time, she seemed more amenable to it, given the latest break-downs in Afghanistan. She knew it was a matter of time until they called Brett back there, and with both of them pushing forty, she wanted her husband home.

Then Prescott called.

The election was still two months off. But Prescott, a genius for campaigning, knew that he lacked military credentials—and his opponent, General Harold Hart, had those credentials stacked up. If he could somehow finagle Brett into his camp, he'd have a public relations coup on his hands. Brett patiently explained that he couldn't be involved in campaigning. Nonetheless, two days later, an anonymous source somehow told *The New York Times* that Senator Mark Prescott had spoken at length with Colonel Brett Hawthorne—and that Hawthorne would be an integral part of any Prescott administration.

"Asshole," Brett cursed to Ellen.

"Boss," Ellen corrected him.

Prescott bumped three points in the polls. By the time of the election, a slim lead had turned into a blowout.

The day after the inauguration, Prescott called again.

"Colonel," he said, "I'm gonna violate military protocol. I'm bumping you to general, effective immediately."

Brett was stunned. The youngest general in the Marines was in his mid-forties. Brett had just turned forty-one.

"Sir, I'm flattered, but that's against all the regulations…"

"I'm the commander in chief, son," said Prescott genially. "Congratulations."

The announcement came at the White House. The president beamed as he introduced Brett; Brett shifted uncomfortably, his bulk imposing beside the slim and tailored Prescott. When he stepped to the microphones, for the first time in a long time, his mouth felt dry.

"Why do you deserve this promotion, general?" shouted a reporter.

"I don't," he answered truthfully. "There are men ahead of me who deserve it more. But I promise to do my best." Then he glanced at his commander in chief. Prescott grinned and gave him the thumbs-up.

The newspaper headline the next day said it all: "THE KID TAKES CHARGE."

Prescott immediately tasked Brett with trotting out his new Afghanistan strategy on national television. He asked him for his advice peremptorily, of course—Brett told him in no uncertain terms that Afghanistan would be lost without a major counterinsurgency surge, akin to the one the British had used in Malaya in the 1950s. Prescott dismissed that possibility out of hand.

"No," he said. "We're pulling out. I promised."

"Sir," Brett protested, "we'll lose the country."

"I have more faith than that, son," said Prescott.

For six months, Brett followed orders. He kept his mouth shut.

Then, as the casualties mounted, Prescott told Brett that he'd be pulling another ten thousand troops from the country by the end of the year.

"With all due respect, that's a bad idea, sir," said Brett.

"It's happening," said the president. "Get over it. And, by the way, get familiar with the policy. I need a uniform on television defending this thing."

Perhaps it was the snide reference to the uniform—the old piece of clothing Brett had once hated, then learned to love. Perhaps it was the casualness with which Prescott perused the casualty reports.

But sitting across from NBC's Sunday morning anchor, Brett began to feel the pressure and heat build up behind his eyeballs. And suddenly, he began talking. In a wave, he explained all the flaws with Prescott's policy. He slammed Prescott for precipitously putting American and Afghan lives at risk, for creating a vacuum that could only be filled by al-Qaeda or a similar renewed terror group. He told the news anchor that the president would need to send no less than eighty thousand troops to Afghanistan, and that there could be no timetable for withdrawal. Timetables, he said, would lead the enemy to bide their time, to wait them out, and then to strike.

When he walked off the set, he knew he was finished. It was only a question of when. He knew he'd been insubordinate; he knew the president was the commander in chief. But Brett Hawthorne had worked for better men than Mark Prescott, and his main charge, he had always believed, was not to the president but to the Constitution and to his men. He had to obey the orders of the president, true.

"But," he later explained to Ellen, "screw those orders. I've got men dying over there."

Three days passed. Then, Prescott hit back.

First, a report appeared in *Beat* magazine, with anonymous quotes describing Hawthorne as a young gunner, a career military man interested only in bulling his way through china shops and making rank. Prescott himself did an interview defending Hawthorne from such charges, although he admitted—grudgingly, of course—that he hadn't always seen eye to eye with his new boy, but appreciated Brett's willingness to speak his mind. After all, hadn't Lincoln had a team of rivals?

Then, a week later, the real bomb: a report appeared in *The New York Times*, filled with anonymous accusations of a sexual liaison between Brett and a young reporter, Dianna Kelly. Kelly had requested an interview with Brett a few months before; she'd been studying at Harvard's John F. Kennedy School of Government, and wanted to write her thesis on counterinsurgency. She was thirty, sexy, and extremely sharp. She'd taken to running with Brett on his morning jogs, quizzing him, questioning him. They spent long nights huddling over maps of the country, with Brett explaining in minute detail how the insurgents would plot their counterattacks.

Brett couldn't honestly say he was surprised when he saw Kelly's face on the cover of the *New York Daily News*, tears in her eyes. In the article by muckraker Jack Blatch, she said Brett had slept with her, that he'd promised to leave his wife for her. She said she'd been in love with him, had made love to him in his office.

Ellen didn't even ask him about it.

The next day, Prescott called him to the White House. "General," he said, a sad smile on his face, "I think it would be best if you resigned. We'll give you a big send-off. You'll go out a hero."

Brett looked at the president incredulously. "What do you take me for, Mr. President?" he said.

Prescott's eyes narrowed. "A smart man."

"Then I'm a damn fool," Brett said. "I've got men in the field, and I'm not going to abandon them just because some floozy is telling purple stories."

Prescott laughed. It sounded tinny in the carpeted room. "That's what I like to hear, General. A fighter. That's what you've always been, right?"

Brett didn't answer.

"Good," the president continued. "You're dismissed."

At 1:00 a.m. the next morning, the phone rang.

"General Hawthorne," the president said, "you have been reassigned, back to Afghanistan. Thank you for your service."

That was last January.

Prescott played the situation beautifully, at least politically. He acknowledged that more troops would be needed, but slashed Hawthorne's recommendation from eighty thousand to twenty thousand. He placed a six-month timeline on the surge, and pledged openly that Americans would be out of the country totally by the end of the year.

By June, the president accelerated his timetable and began withdrawing troops. Some had served just a few weeks on the ground before being pulled back to bases in Europe. The pace escalated. Week after week, more troops came out. By the end of the month, Prescott's redeployment was nearly complete, with just a couple thousand troops scattered around the capital city itself.

The result was predictable—the Taliban assumed that they had the US on the run.

They were right.

Safe areas shrunk in Helmand Province and Kandahar. Afghan troops went AWOL, melting into the Taliban ranks, recognizing that once the US was gone, they'd have no protection. If there was one thing Brett had learned about the Afghan population, it was that they could shift their political allegiances on a dime. It was how they had survived so long.

They stationed Brett in Kabul, told him to make nice with the locals, smile for the cameras. They told him to follow the lead of Ambassador Beauregard Feldkauf—a major donor to the president, who for some reason had requested Afghanistan as a post. He then proceeded to bungle the job so badly that none of the local Afghan warlords would even talk to each other. Hoping that he'd be able to influence local policy on behalf of the troops, Brett complied.

Meanwhile, the Taliban moved.

Then, yesterday, everything went to hell all at once.

At 9:13 a.m., the Taliban launched three simultaneous raids on the outskirts of Kabul. The raid kept US troops and their sparse allies occupied for just a few precious minutes—long enough for a fuel truck to drive into the center of the city. The driver approached the crowded Kabul *furushgah*, parked the vehicle, and then whispered to himself, "*Allahu akhbar!*"

The explosion of his suicide vest blasted outward, through the cabin, into the enormous gas tank. Before anyone could react, six thousand gallons of fiery gasoline spewed into the center of the market. Troops rushed to the scene to find hundreds of burning human beings crying out for relief, the charred flesh of children smoking in the streets. The troops sprang into action, trying to administer aid, trying to save lives. They'd been hamstrung by the administration when it came to killing terrorists, but at least they could help victims. Dozens and dozens of troops rushed to the site.

They never saw the second truck, parked near a fruit stand.

Until it exploded.

Men and women screamed as white-hot shrapnel blew through their bodies. Brett could hear it all the way from the embassy. It was a classic technique, and Brett knew he should have seen it coming: use a first bombing as a magnet for help, then hit with a larger second bomb, taking out the relief force. He silently cursed himself.

"All troops back to the embassy, fall back to the embassy," he shouted at his aide. "They're coming…"

That's when Brett saw it.

Approaching slowly but steadily, bouncing along the poorly paved road, a white van. The big black letters "UN" marked its side.

The driver's mouth moved in a silent whisper. Over and over, over and over.

Allahu akbar.

The explosion rocked the building, blowing Brett off his feet, grabbing his lungs and squeezing the air out of them. He struggled to his knees as streams of Taliban fighters sprinted through the gaping, flaming hole in the fence.

Brett had just enough time to marvel in grim admiration at the planning—the Taliban had obviously infiltrated dozens of fighters into the nearby homes. And it wasn't just the fighters in the streets: women and children had now occupied the square, and were throwing rocks and Molotov cocktails at the embassy, providing civilian cover for the Taliban. If the Americans opened fire, they'd be blamed for a massacre.

When Brett turned back to give his men orders, he saw the ambassador in the corner, cowering under a desk, clutching his briefcase to his chest. He was screaming at Brett in his high-toned, Boston Brahmin accent, "*Your job is to keep me safe! So do your goddamn job!*"

"Shut the fuck up," Brett said.

The coldness in his tone stunned the ambassador into silence. Then, an odd, keening noise emanated from his mouth. It rose higher and higher, louder and louder.

So Brett punched him in the mouth. Not hard. Just enough to stun him.

"Get your pansy ass onto the roof right now," he said, slowly, glaring.

Now, Feldkauf nodded. Brett motioned, and the Marines pouring into the compound formed a phalanx around the ambassador, whose eyes had gone blank with fright and shock. The group moved toward the staircase.

The helicopter pad was on the roof. It was already overloaded— every staffer with an ounce of brains had rushed to the roof after the fence came down. Brett flashed back to the old videos of the last helicopter leaving Saigon, with all the wailing civilians attempting to climb onto the landing skids. Feldkauf took one look at the crowded helicopter, filled with civilian staffers.

Then he pointed at one woman. She was crying. "Off!" he cried. "I'm the ambassador."

She was crying, too. "Mr. Ambassador," Brett said, "we can get you out another way."

"Screw that!" Feldkauf was nearing hysterics again. "That's *my* helicopter, and I'm getting on it! And I'm in charge!"

The woman got off the helicopter, sobbing.

From the street, the noise rose, then fell silent. Her sobs echoed in the quiet, along with the *whop-whop-whop* of the chopper blades.

Brett moved to help the woman when the bullet struck her in the throat, tearing it open. She looked up at him, blood gurgling onto the roof. The blood pumped out, slowly. She tried to speak, grabbed Brett's hand hard. Then her eyes went cold.

Brett hit the deck as bullets began taking down the people on the roof, one by one. "Move toward the center of the roof," he yelled. "They can only spot you from the street."

The helicopter rotors went transparent, and the machine began to take off. Brett caught Feldkauf's eyes. *If I see you again, you son of a bitch,* Brett thought, *I'll make you pay for that.* But Feldkauf didn't see him. He was too busy smiling, a trickle of blood spilling down his split lower lip.

Brett heard the alarm go off. The compound had been breached.

"Men, gather up!" Brett shouted.

Bullets smashed through the windows and glanced off the cement facing of the building in unpredictable patterns. The courtyard was filling up again, new Taliban fighters taking the places of the old. From below, on the first story, Hawthorne could hear the whining strains of an Arabic melody—one of the Taliban fighters had apparently brought a boom box along. Hawthorne stifled a bitter grin. They'd been so comfortable with their plan that they'd even brought their primitive iPods.

Brett took quick stock of his men.

Thirty left.

Just thirty.

"You," he said, pointing to a dozen men. "Pin them down at the front of the building. The rest of you, come with me. We will see you all at the airport. Good luck."

Brett led his group downstairs.

When they hit the stairwell above the bottom floor, he turned to his men. "Okay, boys," he said, calm. "Here's the plan. We fight through these bastards. Then we flank them, and hit them from the east side of the courtyard. We'll catch them in a crossfire from the roof, then make our way to the airport. Got it?"

The men nodded.

"Go," Hawthorne barked.

One of Hawthorne's men, Sothers, a twenty-one-year-old private, burst through the door—and immediately took a bullet to the jaw. His helmet popped off like the top of a Pez dispenser, blood and brains pouring out on the floor.

Brett recognized the mistake immediately: the Taliban had cut off all the exits. The embassy was a death trap.

That's when he saw the smoke.

It poured beneath the door, waves of smoke, with fire licking around the hinges. He could smell the gasoline from the fire, so strong he almost choked on the stench. Brett cursed himself for his carelessness, picked Sothers up, slinging him over his shoulder.

"Back to the roof," he shouted, panting.

Then he sprinted back up the stairs, his sweat mixing with Sothers's blood, covering his face in ooze. He heard the sharp whizz of a bullet ping off one of the railings—he heard it sizzle as it approached—and then he heard it sink deep into Sothers's back with a sickening *thunk*. He bashed the second-floor door open with his forearm, and he found two of his men lying on the carpet, bleeding profusely.

"Report!" he shouted.

A sergeant yelled to him, "Sir, we've lost Martinez and Thomas. We can't hold them here. They're breaking down the door, and they've got snipers across the way firing at us continuously. We don't have enough cover."

"Get your asses to the roof, now!"

The men found the stairwell again and dashed up the metal stairs, their feet clanging.

Brett counted the men as they reached the roof, one by one. Only twenty-four left now.

And no place to go.

Except down.

Hawthorne recognized it right away. The building was surrounded on all sides by open space. It was at least a forty-foot drop to the ground. But that didn't change the situation.

"Men, listen up," said Hawthorne. "We're going over the side of this building. When you hit the ground, don't try to land on your feet. Let your knees buckle and roll. You'll be fine. We're all going to be okay."

He pointed at a young private, perhaps twenty-three. "You go first," he said.

The private was shaking. "I have vertigo, sir."

"Son, you don't get your ass over the side of that building, they're going to kill you."

The private's eyes were welling up with tears now. "I can't, sir."

Hawthorne ran over and grabbed him by the back of the uniform. "Come with me, Marine."

He stood him at the edge of the roof. Then, before the kid could protest, Hawthorne acted. "Buckle and roll," he said, then pushed him from the roof.

The kid plummeted faster than Hawthorne could have predicted. But the kid had enough brains to listen. He hit the ground and rolled forward, then stood up, shaken but alive. Hawthorne dropped the kid's weapon down to him.

The other soldiers formed a line, then rolled off one by one. "Hurry it up," Hawthorne kept muttering. "Hurry it up." The gunshots were close now, the smoke thickening around the outside of the building. Brett could hear the approaching whine of the Arabic singer. "Get your asses over the side of that building!"

One of the men landed awkwardly, and he shrieked as his ankle cracked. The other Marines silenced him. Hawthorne glanced down the side of the building, hoping nobody had heard. The area was still empty, and he could see his troops below. "Maybe," he thought, "just maybe, we have a shot."

Then, almost in slow motion, Brett heard the door behind him open. The big metal door creaked on its rusted hinges, and the Arabic whine blared through.

Brett moved his bulk quickly—more quickly than he had since high school—and opened fire on the Taliban fighter behind him, blowing him back down the stairs. The thought flashed across his mind that the Pentagon would be beside itself knowing it had a general officer in a close-quarter battle. Then he thought that Prescott probably wouldn't care, so long as it didn't make too much news.

Brett didn't have time to think about what he did next—he just did it. He rolled toward the opposite edge of the roof, away from the enemy soldiers, and fell off the roof forty feet toward the ground.

Time slowed as he fell, the wind brushing his blood-smeared cheeks. He had time to think that he'd fallen in the wrong position, that his arm was awkwardly stretched behind him. Then he hit the earth, and the searing pain in his arm told him that he'd broken it. Worse, the smashing noise from his waist told him his comms were dead. Above, he heard the Taliban men running toward his side of the building.

He struggled to his feet, his nerves shrieking in excruciating agony, and staggered toward a nearby alley. He didn't even hear the bullet coming—when it hit him in his broken arm, he didn't even feel it.

It had been three hours. Brett sat in another alley in the slums of the town, separated from his men—if any of them were still alive—listening to the silence of a city at peace. A city in the enemy's hands.

He gripped the empty pistol tighter.

PRESIDENT PRESCOTT

WASHINGTON, DC

"WE SIMPLY CAN'T PAY FOR it, sir."

White House chief of staff Tommy Bradley was standing over the president's desk in the Oval Office, a sheaf of budget papers in his hand. Crumbled, wrinkled papers covered in red notes. The numbers just didn't add up.

And President Mark Prescott didn't care.

"Listen to me, Tommy," said the president. "My reelection relies on our ability to secure funding for this action. You know that. I know that. The polls show it. We don't have a choice in the matter."

Tommy gritted his teeth. He knew Prescott was right. The president had been dropping precipitously in the polls—his critics blamed his policies for widespread inflation and unemployment. Prescott was deathly afraid of becoming Jimmy Carter, and he was right on the precipice of having his worst fears realized.

When Mark Prescott ran for president, he didn't know what he'd be inheriting. He was no babe in the woods—he was a hardened ideologue, a product of the Chicago machine, the handpicked protégé of the power brokers—but he hadn't quite contemplated the nature of the country he'd be handed once elected. He campaigned on great blustering clouds of rhetoric, his boyish good looks, and a record obscured by a complacent media. He came out of nowhere, they said, an inspirational figure unlike any candidate since John F. Kennedy. He answered no difficult questions, evaded all the exposés about his early political career, his rocky marriage, his connections to some of the more shady characters in town. He brushed off all the attacks on him as the cynical manipulations of a tired opposition.

It didn't hurt that his opponent, General Hart, had been a militant and boring old man; it also didn't hurt that his presidential predecessor had been an unpopular member of Hart's party. Prescott linked Hart to the president, and the country bought into it.

Once Prescott entered office, however, he soon realized that the stock market crash had been a mere symptom of the nation's economic ills. The country was running a massive national debt and a trade deficit beyond reckoning. The unemployment rate had climbed beyond 10 percent and was headed toward the 15 percent mark—if you counted those who had stopped looking for a job, the real unemployment rate was closer to 25 percent.

So Prescott did what Prescott knew how to do: he survived.

The easiest way to survive: end his predecessors' wars, no matter what the cost, then pump up the spending at home. There was no glory to be won on the poppy fields of Afghanistan. Everlasting glory didn't come in the form of military victory in this day and age—it came in the form of everlasting social programs that grew and inured to the benefit of all Americans. FDR was worshipped not because of World War II, but because of Social Security; LBJ had lost Vietnam, but he'd won the Great Society.

Big men, Prescott knew, required big governments. And big governments required big spending.

So Prescott spent. He spent on green technologies, on education programs, on food stamps and highways and medical mandates. He spent on vacations and dinners and public works projects. Every dollar spent, he told the American public, created five dollars—no, ten!—in commerce. The money could either be hidden in the mattresses of the rich, or it could be shared with everyone.

His poll numbers went up initially. He waited for the inevitable economic bump that would enshrine his legacy and assure his reelection.

And nothing happened. The economy sputtered and spluttered along, not quite collapsing, but certainly not booming. Even members of his own party wondered whether Prescott would win a second term.

Then, a miracle.

In the middle of the night, Prescott woke up with a phrase ringing in his brain. Over and over. It was as though a higher power had placed them in his mind. He grabbed a pen from his bedside drawer and wrote it down: Work Freedom.

The Work Freedom Program.

Prescott's Work Freedom Program.

Everyone recognized the value of freedom. But what did that mean other than the right to a job? Freedom meant nothing if you couldn't put bread in your children's mouths at night. And America was a country of workers. Freedom was work, and work was freedom. Work Freedom. Simple. Easy. Repeatable.

Genius.

It was the program that could save America. More than that, it was the program that could save Mark Prescott's presidency, and put him in the pantheon of American greats.

Prescott didn't know what the WFP would entail, but it would have to be big. He had his advisors draw it up. It looked like a cross between FDR's Works Progress Administration and the child tax credit. The government would raise taxes on certain corporations—those were indirect taxes that wouldn't lose Prescott votes, particularly with anticorporate sentiment at fever pitch—and then offer tax incentives to other corporations that hired more employees. Meanwhile, for those who couldn't get a job, the government would offer direct hiring in certain key industries: the automobile industry, the banking industry. All the industries the government had either nationalized or heavily regulated in the aftermath of the stock market crash. The program could be expanded by executive fiat, too, so if the economy stagnated, he could always move to correct market failures.

It would be expensive. Massively expensive.

And now his chief of staff, Tommy Bradley, was telling him they couldn't afford it.

"Don't you tell me we can't afford it!" insisted Prescott. "We can't *not* afford it. Do you understand? This country rides on the ability of its people to work. And no one is hiring. No one. What am I supposed to do about it if we can't put through this program?"

Bradley stood silent. Then, after a pause, he noted softly, "Mr. President, the Treasury is *empty*."

"Don't you see, goddamn it?" Prescott yelled. "That's why we need it so bad. We have no money because we have no jobs. We need jobs in order to create wealth. A happy population, a working population, is a population that boosts our economy."

Bradley nodded curtly. Then he reiterated, more slowly for the three-year-old, "We don't have the money." WHAT DOES IT MEAN, "FOR THE THREE-YEAR-OLD"?

"So we raise it."

Bradley let that sink in. Then he responded. "*From whom?*" The European Union had descended into chaos several years beforehand as a result of their debt problems. They weren't lending—not after the Greek collapse, the Spanish collapse, the Italian collapse. Russia couldn't be trusted. Nobody else had that kind of cash. Well, almost nobody.

"China," said Prescott.

It was the right answer, and Bradley knew it. And he knew the president wouldn't budge on this Work Freedom Program. It was his baby. Anyway, who was Bradley to question him? Maybe Prescott wasn't the brightest guy in politics, but he was one of the cleverest. How else had he risen to the presidency from relative obscurity in a matter of a few years? How else had he beaten a well-established military hero despite a lightweight résumé?

Prescott was Bradley's man, and Bradley knew it.

"I'll set up the call for later today."

The president nodded. Then he smiled, rose from his desk, and clasped Bradley on the shoulder. "Tommy," he said seriously, "tomorrow we're going to make history. All we need is the money. Don't let me down."

Bradley took a deep breath. "I won't, Mr. President."

Prescott had always enjoyed this part of the process—the part where a pretty girl hovered over him with a makeup brush and her palette spread before her. He could finally relax. Everything would be on the teleprompter. And nobody knew how to read from a teleprompter like Mark Prescott.

Prescott smiled wryly as Tommy hovered around the set like a mother hen. Tommy had done yeoman's work. This morning, he had spent two hours on the phone with the Chinese government, trying to convince them to buy more US debt. He'd achieved his purpose. And it had been surprisingly easy. Shockingly easy, actually.

All that was left was to ram through the legislation.

Which is where the camera came in. Republicans in Congress, and some Democrats from red states, were skeptical of the plan. They'd cave eventually, Prescott knew—they always did. They just needed a push. A good, hard push.

"Mr. President," said Bradley, "you're on in two."

Bradley shooed away the makeup artist, a hot number in her mid-twenties, exactly the kind of girl Prescott's wife hated. As Bradley was about to push her out the door of the Oval Office, Prescott laughed. "Tommy, just calm down. We've done this a thousand times," he said. "Let the young lady stay." Then he winked at her. She fluttered her eyelashes.

"Ten seconds," said the cameraman. "Nine, eight, seven, six, five, four..." Then he motioned silently, three, two, one. He pointed at the president and the little red light went on. Prescott was now speaking to three hundred million Americans on every major network. That had been a tougher sell than the debt to China—a prime time slot on all the networks would have cost an advertiser millions. For the president, all he had to do was threaten a bit of FCC scrutiny, and promise a few cash payouts from advertisers who would quickly pay up when threatened by the executive branch.

Prescott gazed into the camera and opened his eyes innocently. The wide-eyed look spelled sincerity. He'd learned that from a speechwriter a decade ago, and it worked wonders.

"My fellow Americans," Prescott intoned in his sonorous baritone. "Today we decide whether or not every American truly has the right to life, liberty, and the pursuit of happiness.

"That was the promise of our founding fathers. And the key to realizing that promise lies in the right to work. Life cannot be sustained without work. Liberty cannot be attained without income. And happiness is a distant dream to those without a job.

"Our country is too great, our economy too powerful, our mission on this planet too important, for us to continue to tolerate the growing gap between rich and poor, between those who are lucky and those who are less fortunate. For generations, our parents and grandparents have told us that this was the land of opportunity. Coming from the Soviet Union or from Nazi Germany, they were right—compared to those places, America *was* a land of opportunity.

"But that did not mean that American opportunity was open to all. African Americans were denied work based on the color of their skin. Women were prevented from entering the workplace based on sexism. Minorities of all stripes were subject to discrimination at the hands of an unfeeling and uncaring majority."

Prescott's lower lip trembled—his pain at such evil was palpable.

"We still live with the vestiges of that system. A system that allowed some to exploit their privileged status to bully others, and to build their own wealth from the backs of those they could chain to low-paying jobs. A system that sucked workers dry, then tossed them to the ground in contempt. A system that assumed that some would prosper while others would succeed, that some people *deserved* to work while others did not. There are still those in Congress who advocate for such a system, who say that if we reject that system, we reject America."

Prescott shook his head in disappointment and disbelief. Then he stared into the camera, determination in his eyes. That meant not blinking, as he'd learned while playing the Henry Fonda role in *12 Angry Men* in high school.

"The critics and cynics are wrong. That old system's time has passed. We are better than that system. We are stronger than that system. Together, we can fix the imbalances that plague our society. We can ensure that everyone in this country has equality of opportunity by ensuring that everyone has the right to work. Our corporations must no longer line their own pockets and pad their bank accounts at the expense of the workers they refuse to hire. Our companies must no longer tell us that the free hand of the market will solve everything, or that handing money over to the rich will allow it to trickle down to the less fortunate.

"We have seen the results of that philosophy firsthand. We have seen the skyrocketing unemployment, the fiscal mismanagement, the utter irresponsibility and its fallout. We have seen what happens when the market is left to its own devices—we have seen the injustices and wrongs that ensue.

"There is no such thing as a magical system that punishes wrongdoers and rewards those who do right when it comes to economics. God granted us the power of free will and the power of free choice; God granted us the intellectual power to overcome inequality. All we have to do is use that power to be our brothers' keepers."

Sympathetic face, he said to himself.

"We already know the consequences of turning our backs on our brothers and sisters. We see it in our daily lives: the young single mother who struggles to make the rent because she can't take care of her child *and* work a full-time job. The elderly man who can't hold down a job because he suffers physical and mental ailments. The middle-aged couple trying hard to feed their kids, but failing because either mom or dad can't get a job.

"Maybe it's your next-door neighbor, who has to ask you for a handout. Maybe it's your mom or dad. Maybe it's even you."

Then he grinned that famous Prescott grin.

"That time is over. A new day has dawned. A day when everyone can live with security, without fear. A day when everyone can wake up in the morning without worrying about the next paycheck."

Prescott launched into an explanation of the Work Freedom Program. He brought out charts and laid it out, point by point. He gave personal examples. He added the emotional touch he knew the pitch needed. It was a brilliant exposition.

Then he came to his coup de grace.

"I know," he said wearily, "that some of my political opponents would like to call this plan irresponsible. I know they sling around words like 'socialism' "—he framed the word with his fingers—"and 'Marxism' and 'redistributionism,' and they hope to scare you with those words. I also know that you are too smart for that. Because the fact is this: the Work Freedom Program will pay for itself.

"I promise you right now that you will not pay one additional dollar in taxes for this program. You will not lose your job. And if your employer should selfishly fire you, we are establishing a business trust fund to which all businesses will contribute, and which will pay your salary during rainy days. Businesses may try to scare you, but people are always frightened of what they do not understand. Selfishness must not be allowed to trump the vital liberties of the American people.

"And this action will not contribute to our national debt. It will contribute to our collective wealth. With the entire American population working, producing, creating—not just 80 percent or 90 percent or even 93 percent—we will boost our gross domestic product exponentially. Our economy will be the envy of the world. And at the same time, we will level the playing field for every American."

Prescott spread his hands on his desk in a sign of generosity and openness—he'd been taught that one by a body language expert. "All I ask is for us to join together and make this country what it was meant to be: a land of freedom, liberty, and opportunity for all. The sun is rising on a new America, a better, kinder, gentler, and fairer America. And we can all be a part of it."

He shook his head, grimaced. "But as we all know, Washington is broken. For years, Congress has refused to act on my agenda proposals. And that's why I'm using my authority to do what is necessary on behalf of the American people. All my predecessors have taken similar action in times of serious need. Today, it is time to stand together as one. If my opponents in Congress don't like what I'm proposing, let them pass a bill and send it to me. If not, I will do what I need to do in order to achieve the vision of our founders and of our fathers and mothers. For together we will stand, or we will fall apart.

"And we will stand. Stand with me, and together, we will stand for a brighter future.

"God bless you all, and God bless America."

The red light blinked off.

"How was that, Tommy?" asked Prescott, leaning back in his chair.

Bradley was staring at him with the stunned expression that so often crossed his face when the president spoke. "It was magnificent, sir," said Bradley.

"Good," said Prescott. "Now, miss"—he motioned to the makeup artist—"would you mind coming here and helping me scrape this shit off of my face?"

SOLEDAD

CENTRAL VALLEY, CALIFORNIA

THE SWAT TEAM DIDN'T EXPECT it the first time she brought them cookies.

Nobody brings the SWAT team cookies.

But Soledad Ramirez knew the value of good press, and she baked mean chocolate chip cookies. "No oatmeal raisin here," she said good-naturedly, handing out the meltingly hot treats to the men wearing full military gear and carrying M4s set to burst. "Don't worry, they aren't poisoned."

At first they doubted her, so she took one herself and tried it. Then, one of the boys—and most of them were boys, Soledad knew—reached out, grabbed a cookie in his gloved hand, flipped up his fiberglass riot gear face shield, and took a bite. "Mmm," he said, spilling crumbs down his chin. The crumbs were still there when his commanding officer stormed up, screaming, asking what the hell he thought he was doing.

"Try one before you knock it," Soledad said to him.

The papers loved that one. The *Los Angeles Times*, as much as they hated her, still ran the page one headline: "Smelt Ramirez Melts Hearts With Cookies."

But they didn't leave. And even though every night she sent a plate of cookies to the boys, and every night they cleaned it, they were still out there, at the corner of her property, gun sights trained on her home, on her workers. One of her workers told her they didn't even have the safeties on.

So it was no surprise when she got up this morning and her cattle were missing. They'd been warning about it for weeks, telling her they'd start by confiscating her property if she didn't cease and desist watering them. She hadn't abided by their orders, and they had taken the next step: they'd stolen hundreds of head of cattle. Poof, gone.

The Environmental Protection Agency had ruled—and Congress hadn't overruled them—that the smelt fish were threatened by water overuse from the river. She protested; she sued. It didn't matter, according to the government, that her husband's father had bought the farm, worked it up from nothing. It didn't matter that her husband had worked his heart out, almost literally, on the farm, keeling over at the ripe old age of fifty-two while grazing those damn cattle. It didn't matter that she had fifty-some employees and their families dependent on her.

All that mattered was the smelt. That damn fish.

They restricted her water supply. They told her that no amount of lobbying could change it; the rest of the state simply didn't care about the Central Valley, and the environmental interests refused to compromise. They'd won a great victory for the smelt, and they were satisfied with it.

For a while, she lived with the situation.

Then the land began drying up. The cattle began dying. She tried to sell them before they died of thirst. She tried to sell the land. But like the river, the market had run dry. No one would buy it. The listing agency kept dropping the price, but the land was worthless, and the mortgage on the land made it a financial deadweight for investors. The land was the water; without the water, the land meant less than nothing.

She joined a consortium of farmers working to overturn state and federal legislation protecting the smelt. She spent endless afternoons with her neighbors propping signs along the highway reading, "CONGRESS-MADE DUST BOWL." She wrote letter after letter to the State Water Resources Control Board, begging them to reconsider. In return, she received form letter after form letter thanking her for her interest, but informing her that the law required the current water distribution scheme. After a while, she stopped meeting with the other farmers. She knew that made no difference to the regulators. And she didn't have the money to give to the lobbyists to cut their backroom deals with the environmental protection agencies. All her money was gone.

She began laying off her workers. One by one, they left, taking their families with them. Her accountant told her that her best option was bankruptcy. She resisted it as long as she could; she bargained with her creditors, took out credit cards, begged for swing loans from friends. Then, when all of that failed, she told him to begin filing the paperwork.

She was a week away from filing when she received the letter. It came from one of her former employees, Emilio. He'd immigrated from Mexico decades before, crossed the border illegally. She'd paid him well, sponsored his citizenship, and brought his family over to join him. "He's a valuable employee," she told her skeptical friends. "And if you were living on that side of the border, wouldn't *you* jump it? He's not taking money from anybody except me, and I'm paying him for work."

He was one of the last men to be laid off as the ranch died. She cried the night she told him the cash had run out. He thanked her, hugged her, and moved his family to Los Angeles.

She clung harder to the land. It didn't produce anything anymore, but it was everything to her. She gradually sold off whatever was left of her cattle. She doggedly paid down the mortgage. She dropped her health insurance and her life insurance. Every last dollar went into buying the worthless, barren stretch.

Then, one day, she received her property tax bill. The state government, hard up for cash, had decided to raise the property tax—she owed a supplemental $15,000.

The same day, she received a letter from Emilio.

He and his family had been forced to take a small apartment in East Los Angeles. Emilio had gotten a job at a local factory. Their son, Juan, had enrolled at the public high school.

That's where he had been killed.

One of his classmates, apparently, had tried to recruit him into a gang. When he refused, several of the gang members found him in the bathroom. They began punching him. When he fell, they kicked him. And when he didn't get up, they fled.

An hour later, the janitor found him. The doctors tried to relieve the bleeding in his brain by drilling, but it was no use. Now Emilio was begging for money to bury the boy. He was fifteen years old.

That afternoon, Soledad took the supplemental property tax bill, nailed it to a wooden box, aimed her shotgun at it, and blew a hole in it the size of a fist.

That night, she emptied her last bank account, some $25,000, and signed a check for $5,000. She sent it to Emilio. She'd always wanted to pay for the boy's college—she'd told Emilio that. Now she paid for his coffin.

The next morning, she took the other $20,000 and converted it to cash.

Then she went shopping.

She had plenty of fertilizer, could obtain Tovex easily, and had her boys order nitromethane, supposedly so that they could race their hot rods around the area.

Weeks passed. At least a hundred times, she considered backing out, moving on. She knew she was doing something borderline insane—even though she'd taken all the precautions, no precautions could prevent the federal government from bringing all of its resources to bear. And if they were concerned enough about a fish to stifle the livelihoods of hundreds of thousands of people, what would they do if someone destroyed one of their offices?

She kept coming back to one image: Juan's coffin. That image would quickly merge with the image of the dead cattle and the dried-up land and the empty house.

They didn't understand, she knew. And they'd never understand, unless she made them understand.

The handoff went down in the middle of a Saturday night in an open field. Nobody noticed it, of course—this was the Central Valley, and nobody cared what went down in the Central Valley.

She didn't sleep much. When she finally fell asleep, an empty wine glass dangling from her hand, it was 3:00 a.m.

She woke up with the television blaring. Pictures of the blown-out side of the Water Resources Control Board offices on I Street in Sacramento led every news network. All of them. Even Soledad was somewhat shocked by the security video—it looked like something out of a Schwarzenegger movie, with cement and steel blasting into the night sky. Plumes of smoke and ash rose from the bombing site. Soledad was grateful that the truck had been completely eviscerated by the explosion, but she knew that federal investigators would check the camera footage—it was only a matter of time before they did proper forensic analysis and traced the truck.

There were no casualties—Soledad had insisted on a weekend attack to avoid any human toll—but the building itself smoldered, a gaping crater where the front door used to be. The news crawl scrolled: "MASSIVE BOMBING AT FEDERAL BUILDING… TERROR SUSPECTED."

The governor pledged to get to the bottom of what he termed a "brutal terror attack." He called on the federal government for emergency relief—after all, the Environmental Protection Agency shared offices with the Water Resources Control Board. The president pledged to do what he could. He agreed with the California governor, saying, "Such acts have no place in a democratic America."

Prescott pledged to enforce federal law, to investigate fully, to prosecute those who would assault the government. Anarchy, he said, could not be allowed to reign.

Two days later, the SWAT team showed up. They were fully militarized, driving MRAVs. They looked like they'd been redeployed directly from Afghanistan. Which, in fact, some of them had. Virtually every agency of the federal government had been given heavy weaponry—even the environmental agencies. You never knew, the lawmakers said, what kind of weapons American citizens had socked away in their basements.

When the SWAT team arrived, they set up a perimeter around the ranch. They didn't approach, presumably fearful of sparking a firefight. Soledad spotted at least two surveillance drones flying above the barren ranch, with its remaining cattle lowing hungrily at the empty creek.

She turned on the news to see an aerial shot of the ranch—her ranch. The scrolling caption on CNN read: "TERROR SUSPECT RANCHER SURROUNDED."

So she called in. After first convincing several producers that she was, in fact, Soledad Ramirez, and had no intention of screaming "bababooey" live on air, they let her through to talk to Wolf Blitzer.

The scroller on the TV changed to "BREAKING: TERROR SUSPECT CALLS CNN." They flashed a picture of her, looking surprisingly sinister, and plastered it across the screen. The producers must have pulled it from her Facebook page and then darkened it for effect, she thought.

"Ms. Ramirez," Wolf said in his faux shout—it's like the man never knew how a microphone worked—"do you have any intention of surrendering to the authorities?"

"Hello, Wolf," she answered. "No, I don't have any intention of surrendering to the Environmental Protection Agency over some damn fish. They've been starving out me and every other rancher for years. So they can come in and arrest me. They can jail me. I have no interest in spilling blood. But they already have blood on their hands as far as I'm concerned."

She told Blitzer about Emilio and Juan, about the dead cattle and the bankruptcy. She told him about the surrounding farms, all dried out, about how the breadbasket of the country had turned into a dust bowl. "You tell the governor and the president," she concluded, "that I'm happy to surrender and do my jail time if they just keep this water flowing. Because I'm not going to stand for *my government*—yes, it's my government, too—violating my God-given rights to water my land. I've never taken anything from anybody. And I don't plan to start now by giving up not just my rights, but the rights of my friends."

The media went absolutely berserk. The governor called her a domestic terrorist, put her on par with al-Qaeda. The president vowed to stop violations of law at any cost. "The rule of law," he intoned, "must not be held ransom by some crazed cattlewoman."

Commentators on cable television speculated that Soledad had stocked up for war, armed herself with bazookas and grenades and every form of weaponry outside of nukes. It would be Waco, they predicted. Waco times two. Times ten. Times one hundred.

They would have been surprised to learn that aside from the shotgun, Soledad's weaponry was limited to the cutlery in her pantry, and that her only allies were a pet cat and a mangy dog she'd taken in.

Soledad expected to be arrested that day. But through the night, nobody approached the house. The drones kept circling. The cameras kept rolling. They shut off her phone lines and her electricity and her water. But they didn't move toward her house.

When the sun rose the next morning, she realized why. The members of the SWAT team stood on the ridges overlooking her ranch, their guns trained on her home. But around them, in a wider circle, were dozens of armed men. Over a hundred of them, actually. Militia members. And *their* guns were trained on the SWAT team.

That morning, she brought the members of the SWAT team cookies.

And the standoff began.

LEVON

DETROIT, MICHIGAN

DETROIT WAS A SHITHOLE. BUT it was *his* shithole.

That's the way Levon Williams thought of it. He'd grown up in this shithole, right near Eight Mile Road—a long stretch of street separating Detroit from Oakland County. Detroit was 85 percent black, with a median household income of $27,000 per year. Oakland County was 77 percent white, with a median household income of $65,000 per year. End up on the wrong side of the street, you could wind up carjacked, mugged, or beaten and left for dead. The emergency response time measured twenty-five minutes from city hall to downtown Detroit.

The stores dotting Eight Mile Road itself formed a steady, depressing pattern: liquor store, auto parts store, burned-out hulk, boarded-up shop, hair salon. Repeat ad infinitum. Every once in a while, an auto lot broke up the monotony, or perhaps a music store. But that was about it. What idiot would open up on one of the least-policed streets in America?

Levon would.

Some might call it idealism. Others, community loyalty.

Of course, his shop wasn't exactly legal.

Levon ran a local gang. The gangs out here weren't particularly organized. They were mostly neighborhood stuff, a few buddies hanging out, running drugs, holding up the local stores. The stores basically took it for granted at this point, shrugged and sighed and let it go. It took twelve minutes for the cops to arrive at an emergency, and eighteen minutes for the ambulances to come. Better to pay up, keep your head down, and not get shot.

Unless you were Levon.

Levon's shop was a barbershop. It didn't stick out on the road. The clientele was mainly older black men—the younger men didn't like to hang out there, for fear they'd be sucked into Levon's orbit. But the older men knew what was happening in the community. More importantly, they knew where the bodies were buried. Often literally.

The clientele didn't spend a lot of money. Then again, they didn't need to. In the back room, behind the swivel chairs, Levon and his crew shuttled crack cocaine. That drug had gone out of style in the mid-1990s thanks to the federal crackdown on crack dealers—black politicians had been the biggest advocates of putting crack dealers on different footing than powder cocaine dealers at the time. Nobody wanted to deal crack anymore. But Levon catered to a select population.

He also ran a protection racket on the side. At six three and two hundred twenty pounds of shredded muscle, Levon cut an imposing figure walking into other stores on the block. They immediately went quiet when he came in. When he told them he'd graduated from the U of M, they got even quieter. This kid was brutal *and* smart, they knew.

Today, however, Levon had run into an apparent snag.

It happened every so often, usually with one of the older folks who didn't want to pay him. He'd usually head over to their shops and casually inform them that while he appreciated their situation, the last thing they wanted was an unexpected fire striking in the near future. He'd shrug, smile, and turn to leave. More often than not, they'd immediately open the cash register. On rare occasions, when that cash register didn't open, an unexpected fire would turn the business into a smoking husk by morning.

This time was different. The old man in question, Timothy Gardner, had seemed like every other holdover from the 1950s. But Gardner was connected, it turned out. He counted among his myriad cousins the Reverend Jim Crawford. Big Jim. Community leader. Talk show host. Friend to the street.

And now Reverend Jim was standing in Levon's shop, grinning his million-dollar grin, wearing his thousand-dollar suit, shaking his five hundred-dollar haircut. He sat in one of the swivel chairs. The shop was empty. Levon stood before him, arms crossed, biceps flexed.

"Mr. Washington," said the reverend, "I understand that my cousin has been causing you some distress."

Levon nodded.

"Because he is living in your neighborhood?"

Levon nodded again.

"Well, what can we do to rectify this situation?" Big Jim's grin grew.

Levon pretended to think. He'd known the answer to this question the minute he heard about Gardner's relationship with Big Jim. Actually, it's why he had targeted Gardner's shop.

Slowly, he approached Big Jim's chair, saw the fear creep into Big Jim's eyes, the way it did with everyone when he gave them the dead stare—that blank look he could wash over his pupils to cloud his intent. He put his hands on the back of Big Jim's chair.

Suddenly, he reached into the cabinet next to the chair, whipped out a barber shawl, and wrapped it around Big Jim's neck. Then, like lightning, he reclined Big Jim's chair. Before the famous rabble-rouser could react, Levon grabbed a can of Barbasol, foamed it in his thick, uncalloused hands, and covered Big Jim's neck and face.

Then he took out a razor and a strop. Slowly, he began sharpening it as he looked down at Big Jim.

"I want in."

Big Jim laughed, and Levon found himself admiring the man's rich baritone. "You're an uppity one, ain't you?"

Levon gave him the blank stare again. *Sklop.* He sharpened the razor. "I want in," he repeated.

Big Jim looked up at him comfortably. "And what if I tell you I don't have any jobs available for such as you?"

Levon shrugged. *Sklop.* "Well, then, your cousin might need a job. Can never tell what's gonna happen to his shop. And he's older than I am. And less educated."

"What can you do for me? I don't run rackets on our own people."

Levon moved behind Crawford and slowly began shaving him. His stare never stopped. "I have an idea. But you'll have to trust me."

Crawford's eyes narrowed. "But I don't trust you now, brother. That's why I'm here."

Levon's eyes suddenly cleared. He smiled wide. "There is nothing either good or bad, but thinking makes it so," he said.

Now Crawford looked confused.

Levon's smile never faltered. "It's Shakespeare," he said. "It means you'll *learn* to trust me."

Crawford laughed. Loudly this time. Then he looked at Levon curiously. "Quoting dead honkies," he twinkled. "You might be useful yet."

Two hours to the end of the shift. Ricky O'Sullivan looked down at his watch. *Two hours.* He hated this beat. The only white boy working the zombieland near the abandoned Packard plant. The plant, which once turned out luxury cars for the upper class, now covered forty acres of dead zone. Now it looked like something out of *Mad Max*, with shattered windows, rusted beams, and graffitied walls covering block after block. The city had tried to rehabilitate the site dozens of times. They'd failed every time.

Now it was a known drug hangout. There had been a dozen killings in the nearby area recently, and the new mayor insisted that police presence in the area increase. That, at least, was the right idea—or would have been, if it weren't for the department's use-of-force policies, which made it nearly impossible to do proper police work. Morale in the department had never been lower, and for good reason. After the latest consent decree with President Prescott's Department of Justice, every cop on the force walked gingerly.

O'Sullivan rubbed his hands together in the car for warmth. He was low on gas and didn't want to leave the engine running—his shift was almost over, given that it was nearly midnight. He couldn't wait to get home, back to his apartment, far away from the cold and the dark.

He'd joined the force just a year before. He wasn't a Detroit native, but he'd seen the recruitment ads. High pay, chances for advancement. On the force, he was a newbie. But in Detroit, that was as good as being a veteran, given the turnover.

The radio clogged with static.

"10-31, handle the 459 in progress, Iowa and Van Dyke."

O'Sullivan sighed. Nobody responded.

"10-31, handle the 459 in progress, Iowa and Van Dyke," the dispatcher repeated.

"10-4," O'Sullivan said into his radio. He turned the engine over, flipped on the lights. The siren sounded. He still got a thrill in his legs every time it did. Burglary in progress at the gas station. That sounded about right. He hit the gas, shot forward on East Grand. From the radio, he figured there should be a couple other cops on the way soon, but he'd be there first.

First. Response time in this city was awful.

He breathed heavily out of his mouth. "Calm down, boy," he said to himself. "Keep cool."

Still, he could feel the sweat popping on his brow. This wasn't his first robbery, but it was his first solo response. No senior partner to help out this time. Short-staffing and budget cuts.

The gas station looked empty when he pulled up. Grass had pushed its way through the cement of the lot. Graffiti marked the station—illiterate bubble letters; O'Sullivan had given up on trying to decode that shit long ago—and the lights on the street flickered eerily. Rows of broken-down townhouses marked the surrounding side streets. Across the Earle Memorial Highway, there was an abandoned church, covered in graffiti, a couple boarded-up brick buildings. An open field bordered the gas station to the east.

He didn't see anybody on the street as he pulled up next to the quick mart. A couple of those windows were boarded up, too. He peeked through the window—nobody was behind the counter. The place looked closed. But he couldn't be sure from the car.

The car door creaked as he pushed it open with his foot. O'Sullivan reached out for the secure feeling of the gun on his hip—it was warm to the touch, comforting. He took his hand off the butt of the pistol and pulled his flashlight from his belt, turned it on.

Nothing. Just dark and quiet.

He looked through the glass door, saw the racks of Funyuns and Doritos. The cashier's counter lay behind a thick pane of double-plexiglass. Nobody sat behind it.

Then he heard the voice.

"Hey, pig," it said. The voice wasn't deep. It was the voice of a child. And the kid stood outside the door of the quick mart, legs spread, arms hanging down by his sides. A cute black kid, wearing a Simpsons T-shirt and somebody's old Converse sneakers and baggy jeans.

On his hip, stuck in those baggy jeans, was a pistol.

It looked like a pistol, anyway. But O'Sullivan couldn't see clearly. The light wasn't right. He could see the bulge, but not the object.

O'Sullivan put his flashlight back in his belt and put his hand back on his pistol, the greasy handle still warm to the touch.

"Stop right there, pig," the kid said. His hand began to creep down toward his waistband.

O'Sullivan pulled the gun out of its holster, leveling it at the kid. "Put your hands above your head. Do it now!"

"Fuck you, honky," the kid shot back. "Get the fuck out of my neighborhood." Then he laughed, a cute kid's laugh. O'Sullivan looked for sympathy behind those eyes, found none.

Oh, shit, O'Sullivan thought. Then he said, "Hands up. Right now."

The kid laughed again, a musical tinkling noise. "You ain't gonna shoot me, pig. What, you afraid of a kid?"

O'Sullivan could feel every breath as it entered his lungs. "No, kid, I don't want to shoot you," he said. "But I need you to cooperate. Put your hands above your head. *Right now.*"

The kid's hand shifted to his waistband again. O'Sullivan's hands began to shake.

"Get the fuck out of my neighborhood," the kid repeated.

O'Sullivan looked around stealthily. Still nobody on the street. Totally empty. The sweat on his forehead felt cold in the night air. In the retraining sessions at the station, they'd told officers to remember the nasty racial legacy of the department, be aware of the community's justified suspicion of police. Right now, all

O'Sullivan was thinking about was getting this kid with the empty eyes to back the fuck off.

"Go on home," he said.

"*You* go home, white boy," said the kid. His hand moved lower.

Suddenly, O'Sullivan's head filled with a sudden clarity, his brain with a preternatural energy. He recognized the feel of the adrenaline hitting. He wasn't going to get shot on the corner of Iowa and Van Dyke outside a shitty convenience store in a shitty town by some eight-year-old, bleed out in the gutter of some city the world left behind. He had a life, too.

The gun felt alive in his hand. The gun was life.

The muzzle was aimed dead at the kid's chest. No way to miss, with the kid this close, just ten feet away maybe. Still cloaked in the shadow of the gas station overhang.

"Kid, I'm not going to ask you again. I need you to put your hands on top of your head and *get on your knees.*"

"Fuck you, motherfucker."

"I'm *serious.*"

The kid's hand was nearly inside his waistband now.

"Don't do that," O'Sullivan said.

The kid smiled, almost gently.

"Don't."

The kid's smile broadened, the hand moved down into the pants. "Get the fuck out of my hood," the kid cheerfully repeated. "I'll cap your ass."

"Kid, I'm warning you," O'Sullivan yelled. "Put your hands above your head! *Do it now…*"

The roar shattered the night air, a sonic boom in the blackness. The shot blew the kid off his feet completely, knocked him onto his back.

O'Sullivan reached for his radio, mechanically reported it: "Shots fired, officer needs help at the gas station on Iowa and Van Dyke."

"Ohgodohgodohgodohgod," O'Sullivan repeated as he moved toward the body, the smoke rising from his Glock. He pointed it down at the kid again, but the boy wasn't moving. The blood seeped through Homer Simpson's face, pooled around the kid's lifeless body. The grin had been replaced with a look of instantaneous shock. His hand had fallen out of his waistband with the force of the shooting.

In it was a toy gun, the tip orange plastic.

For a brief moment, O'Sullivan couldn't breathe. When he looked up, he saw them coming. Dozens of them. The citizens of Detroit, coming out of the darkness, congregating. He could feel their eyes.

Officer Ricky O'Sullivan sat down on the curb and began to cry.

ELLEN

EL PASO, TEXAS

ANOTHER DEAD KID.

He was the fourth in two days, his body so bloated that he was barely recognizable as a boy. His face was caved in, his nose smashed, his eyes blackened and swollen.

Another face no one would see. Or remember. Or care about.

"The coyotes really did a number on him." Vivian's voice sounded small behind her. Scared.

"Yes," Ellen nodded. She stood up straight, took a picture of the body with her cell phone, and then turned from it. "The governor will want the picture. Let's get it to him." Just another day. Just another fact-finding mission along the Rio Grande.

Just another dead kid.

Overall, the last year had seen a sudden upsurge in the number of children attempting to cross the border without papers. Not all were children—a surprising number of the unaccompanied minors were of gang age, somewhere between fourteen and seventeen. Some had tattoos. Many were missing fingers, eyes, ears. Law enforcement thought the smugglers had mutilated the kids and sent their body parts back to their parents for ransom.

The flood wasn't completely unexpected—after President Prescott's announcement of no deportation for young, unaccompanied minors, parents all across Central and South America began shipping their kids up to the border. Some of the children rode the so-called "Train of Death" from the southern border of Mexico, then waited for American Border Patrol agents to pick them up in the desert. Others paid coyotes to ship their children through Mexico. Many parents never heard from their children again.

But those who did make it swamped the available federal resources. Border Patrol spent their days trying to help doctors screen for disease, trying to dig up enough formula for babies, trying to patch up wounds and find blankets and keep the incipient gang members from knifing each other. That meant that the border had even *less* personnel.

Every day, Ellen heard complaints from ranchers along the border. They'd been finding bodies on their land. Or ripped panties from rape victims. Or drugs. Or live cartel members acting as lookouts for the coyotes. Some refused to ranch their own land, fearful of stumbling on something that would land them in the soup with the cartels: the murder rate by the cartels along the border scared nearly all of them.

Governor Bubba Davis had asked Prescott for help. Prescott wouldn't even take his call. He *did*, however, tell CNN that those who wished to deport these children were obviously driven by xenophobia. That bullshit didn't surprise Ellen one bit. She knew what Prescott would do to push forward his agenda. Her husband was stuck in Afghanistan and her marriage was a public joke. That was proof positive of that little proposition.

The governor tried using state resources to shore up the border. The legislature passed a law, at his recommendation, enforcing federal immigration law. Noncitizens of the United States found entering the country illegally, the law stated, would be detained by Texas state law enforcement, then handed over to Immigrations and Customs Enforcement for deportation. The governor announced that if the federal government wouldn't enforce federal law, the state of Texas sure would. After all, the state of Texas was absorbing the cost of the feds' inaction.

So Prescott's attorney general, Jim Ballabon, sued Texas. And won. If the federal government didn't want to enforce the law, the Supreme Court found, it didn't have to do so. And if the state of Texas attempted to enforce that law, the court continued, it would be usurping federal authority. "Damned if you do, damned if you don't," the governor had muttered angrily to Ellen.

Ellen looked once more at the body of the dead child, then turned and walked away. It wasn't until she reached the black Ford F-150 that Ellen bent over and threw up. Then she primly took out a handkerchief and wiped away the vomit from her mouth.

"You ready to go, Viv?" she said.

Ellen first noticed the helicopter following her truck a few minutes after leaving the Rio Grande. It wasn't a news helicopter, Ellen knew—it was too decrepit for that, obviously a 1980s model. Cheap. Black. She could see it through her rearview mirror in the distance. And it was gaining.

"Any idea what that helicopter is?" she said. Vivian shook her head, her straight black hair rippling.

Ellen shrugged. Probably a military assignment, or some old kook out for a joyride.

Then she saw the second helicopter.

It was in the middle of the road, spanning the yellow line. She slammed on the brakes, screeching the F-150 to a halt, leaving a rubber streak in the road behind.

"What the hell?" Vivian whispered.

Two men stood in front of the helicopter.

They both wore cowboy hats and boots. They also wore carbines, slung casually over their shoulders. One unslung his gun, pointed it at the vehicle, and gestured for them to get out.

"Don't get out of the car," Vivian said, her voice rising in panic.

"Do we have a choice?" Ellen answered.

Ellen pushed open her door, stood up, felt the waves of heat rise from the road. The sweat trickled down her lower back and into her underwear. She had time to think this wasn't very feminine.

One of the men shouted something in Spanish at Ellen. She held up her hands. "Just look nonthreatening," she told herself. "It'll be over soon." She reminded herself that this wasn't the first time she'd been held at gunpoint. It probably wouldn't be the last, either. A brief thought of Brett flashed through her head.

"*Fuera, perra!*" the same man shouted. Ellen turned back to look at the car. Vivian was still inside, tears rolling down her cheeks, shaking her head.

"*FUERA, PERRA!*"

Still she didn't move.

Ellen had time for one thought—*Oh, shit*—before the Mexican pointed the carbine at the truck and fired a burst through the windshield.

The first bullet missed Vivian, but the second caught her directly in the face. Her head slammed back against the seat rest, the back of her head splattering. One moment, her pretty face was staring directly at Ellen. The next, there was no face, just a mess of tissue and tendon and bone and blood.

Ellen heard Vivian's body slump over against the car door.

Ellen didn't react. She went numb. This made *no sense*. Vivian was still alive. The helicopters weren't here. This was Texas, for God's sake, not the middle of drug cartel territory.

Except Vivian was dead. And the helicopter still sat right in the middle of the road. In Texas.

"*Pinche puta*," said the man with the gun. He spat a string of saliva into the dust. Then, to Ellen, in broken English: "Get on knees."

Ellen looked around quickly. There was nothing in any direction. Nobody.

She got on her knees.

The second man approached Ellen. Unlike his buddy, he wore a bandanna over his face; only his black eyes were visible. Ellen figured that this one made the decisions, the Boss—his buddy was a lackey.

"She worked for the governor?" the Boss asked. He had no trace of an accent.

Ellen nodded.

"You also work for the governor?"

Again, Ellen nodded. As she did, she felt the barrel of a gun against the back of her head. The shooter stood beside her, his carbine warm to the touch. Ellen closed her eyes, shut them tight.

"I'm not going to beg you," she said.

A pause.

Then the man in black spoke, slowly. In English. "Shoot her."

Ellen didn't have time to close her eyes before she heard the click of the trigger being pulled—and then the split-second click of the hammer hitting . . . nothing. The gun was unloaded. Ellen opened her eyes.

The shooter laughed. "*Se cagó encima*," he scoffed. Then he spit into the dust again.

"Get up," said the Boss. "Get in your car. And tell your boss to get his men the *fuck* off my border."

Ellen couldn't argue with him. She didn't have the strength or the presence of mind. She had gone numb; her brain had turned off the emotional spigot. She couldn't process what she was seeing. She could just get out of there. Now.

She pulled open the car door, and the iron smell of blood hit her hard. She studiously attempted not to look to the passenger's seat, where Vivian's body was already drawing buzzing black flies.

For a moment she couldn't move. Then, the icy feeling of anger began to creep up her spine. She slammed the car into gear and hit the gas, peeling off the road at a hard right angle. She gunned the engine, bringing the truck up to fifty mph. Sixty, seventy, eighty. She only knew one thing: she had to get as far away from these animals as she could, as fast as possible.

A few seconds later, in her rearview mirror, she saw the helicopters disappear into the distance.

She hit the brakes, skidded to a stop, the dust clouding around the truck, the engine growling. She looked down at her hands; her fingernails had bitten small, bloody half-moons into her palms.

She looked over at Vivian's corpse, the bloody mess of her head.

She closed her eyes.

Only then did she allow herself to scream.

BRETT

KABUL, AFGHANISTAN

IT WAS SHORTLY AFTER MIDNIGHT. The muddy puddle at his feet ran red with his blood. All he could think about was Ellen.

Ellen, living the rest of her life alone. Ellen, put through hell again. Ellen.

At night in Kabul, temperature dipped to below freezing. The good news was that the cold had helped stop the bleeding. The bad news was that he was in danger of going into hypothermia. He could barely keep himself conscious—he'd only been able to do so thus far by jabbing the butt of the M9 into his wound to feel that sharp pain. Now his arm was numb. If he fell asleep, he'd be a carcass by morning.

"Get up, pal," he said to himself, shaking off thoughts of his wife. "Time to go to work."

At night, the streets emptied completely. Even the Taliban fighters didn't want to be in the open—they'd be in nearby apartment buildings, no doubt huddled around their primitive fires.

Electricity had gone out in the city periodically over the last few weeks, with Taliban fighters bombing electrical substations. Every morning, allied forces were finding more and more freezing bodies in the streets, despite the pitiful hamlets they'd set up for the poor around the city. That was all bad news, but for Brett, it was convenient—there was nobody to spot him hobbling toward the Kabul airport.

The airport would still be in American hands, Brett knew. It was located just north of the city, about nine miles from the center of Kabul. If there was any place left in Afghanistan that would remain in American hands, that would be it. The American military essentially owned the northern portion of the airport. If he could make it that far.

Brett struggled to his feet.

He knew he'd have to stay quiet—with the Taliban presumably running the place, there would be a bounty out for US soldiers—but every time he brushed his shattered arm against a wall, swollen to twice its normal size, he gasped in pain. Then, reluctantly, he took the magazine out of the gun and bit down on it. Hard. Better to crack a few teeth than to be featured on CNN being dragged through the streets. And the empty gun wouldn't be of any use anyway.

The airport, he told himself.

The airport.

He'd seen the footage of the last helicopter taking off from Saigon, and he'd always groaned in horror at seeing it—it meant the end of a country. Now all he could think about was how the last soldier in that last helicopter must have felt.

Relieved.

By the time Brett spotted the airport, he couldn't feel his legs. The airfield was exposed, with plains surrounding it on every side to avoid the potential for snipers or antiaircraft attacks on the runways. *Thank God*, Brett thought, *it's a dark night.*

He stumbled forward toward the gates as he reached the empty field. The gates grew larger with every agonizing step.

Then, miraculously, the gate was before him. Brett grinned as it materialized in the darkness.

Except that the gate was open.

Blown wide open.

Then he saw it. To the northwest, something was burning. The acrid smoke of burning oil and flesh cut his nostrils. He wiped the sweat off his face and walked toward the helicopter. *My God*, he thought. *There is no last helicopter.*

He knew before he reached the helicopter what had happened. The smoke billowed in great black plumes against the blue-black night sky; the soft, angry flames spurted from the landing gear. The runway was clear except for the helicopter and the dozens of uniformed corpses lying nearby. Brett knew some of the corpses—they had been his men at the embassy. Many had been shot at point-blank range in the head.

Obviously, the Taliban had taken the airport, and they'd been ready and waiting when the ambassador's chopper arrived. A massive, coordinated assault. The Tet Offensive, except successful in every way.

The Taliban had waited for the helicopter to land, and then they'd shot it to pieces and executed the survivors.

"Son of a bitch," Brett muttered to himself.

Brett glanced at the horizon. The sun would be up soon, and the uniform would be a target. The field would soon be swarming with Taliban allies. He had to find a place to hole up and think.

The only place in sight was a nearby hangar, one of the military's famous steel made-to-order jobs. Brett didn't know whether it was occupied, but at this point, he didn't care—he felt a wild anger rising in him. He instinctively gripped his pistol tighter.

He made for the hangar. Even before he stepped inside, he could smell the death there. The horror when he did enter made him step outside again. The nausea felt hard and cold on his stomach. He shook it off, his head thickening.

Then he went in.

Blood covered the floor, the walls. It slicked the floor like oil at a transmission shop. The Taliban had used the hangar as an execution post, and there was a line of bodies lying on the floor, many of them wearing American uniforms. Those bodies had been mutilated obscenely, despicably. Limbs and organs were missing, flesh burned. They'd done it slowly. They'd enjoyed themselves. There couldn't be any other explanation.

"Animals," he said softly. "Fuck these animals."

One of the bodies looked familiar—the last body in line. It wore an expensive, carefully tailored suit. The face was unrecognizable. One of the hands was missing. Brett ripped the jacket off the corpse and looked at the inside lining. Embroidered on the inside of the jacket were three letters: *B.F.F.* Brett knew right away: it was Beauregard Frederick Feldkauf. The ambassador hadn't made it out after all.

For some reason, that small measure of justice made Brett feel just slightly better for a moment. Then he realized the enormity of the situation, the enormity of the loss.

It had all been for nothing. The staffer who had bled out on the roof. The servicemen and women who had died in the alleyways. The whole damn operation up in flames. And they hadn't even been able to successfully evacuate the ambassador.

He didn't have time to mourn—and he wouldn't have even if he did. Feldkauf, after all, was an asshole. His first order of business had to be setting his arm to prevent infection. Then he'd figure out what to do.

He looked around for materials to dress the wound, spotted a first aid kit still hanging on the wall. It would do for the gunshot wound. At least he'd live until morning.

But he still needed to set the arm. He didn't know how to do it. All he knew was that his arm was sticking out at a peculiar angle, and that he needed to fix that. As far as he could tell, there was no internal bleeding—the arm was swollen, but it wasn't bulging. But if he left the broken bone hanging around inside, it would cut an artery sooner or later.

Brett backed himself up until he was about two feet from one of the walls. Then he gripped his upper arm tightly, took a deep breath, and smashed his hand against the wall. The pain shot up his arm like a thunderbolt, making him gasp; involuntarily he screamed. Before he could think about it again, he smashed his hand into the wall again—this time, he heard the arm crack back into place. He lay back on the floor, his chest heaving, his stomach cold with sweat, tears of pain in his eyes.

Now, he thought, *let's stabilize this son of a bitch.*

He'd seen temporary splints before. All he needed was two straight sticks to place on either side of his arm and some cloth to tie them in place. The cloth wasn't hard to come by. The rods were.

Brett scooted around the floor on his butt, looking around for something that could serve the basic purpose. The Taliban had done a thorough job of cleaning the place out—they had made their living from scavenging for so long that they were sure to take everything of value. He'd been lucky just to find the first aid kit.

Half an hour later, he was still looking. He hadn't eaten or drunk in twelve hours, and he'd suffered a gunshot wound and a broken arm. His body was crying out for sleep, for reprieve, for any sort of relief.

Then he spotted it, gleaming dully in the dark structure.

Feldkauf's briefcase, still connected to his corpse. He clawed at the floor with both hands, the energy flowing through his veins. It was an old-school pop-top briefcase, a black leather piece with steel ringing the inside in strips. It had a combination lock on the front with three digits.

Brett tried the combination already in place. Nothing.

He sat for a moment, thinking. Then he tried the only thing he could think of: 266. B.F.F.

Miraculously, it popped open.

A Glock. A passport. Stacks of afghanis, stacks of dollars. A bag of a sticky, blackish substance—opium.

And a Xerox copy of a map, with two sets of coordinates. Longitude and latitude. 51.4231. 35.6961.

Iran.

41.440. 34.234.

Iraq.

Brett knew what it meant.

Brett had known of the CIA's discovery of weapons of mass destruction in Iraq for years. Everyone on the inside had known. The media had reported that the government had lied, that somehow, all the world's greatest intelligence agencies had been dead wrong. But that wasn't the case. Hussein had smuggled some of the weapons out of the country to Syria; others had been buried in the desert.

Beneath those coordinates.

And now they were in Iran.

Thanks to Ambassador Beauregard Frederick Feldkauf.

"Feldkauf, you son of a bitch," Brett muttered. "You sold us out."

Then he passed out.

PRESIDENT PRESCOTT

WASHINGTON, DC

"AT FIRST, THE NUMBERS DIDN'T make sense to me either, Mr. President," the young analyst explained. "The airlines have been doing well this year. This precipitous stock drop doesn't make sense. Yeah, some of their balance sheets could be a bit stronger, but there's nothing to indicate a recession coming."

Prescott looked at the nerd. He hated beating around the bush, and this guy with the knockoff suit from Joseph A. Bank and the pocket protector was doing just that. He seemed self-assured—self-assured as most cranks were. Prescott had never heard of him. But with General Bill Collier sitting right there, Prescott couldn't just blow this irritating asshole off. He had to at least *appear* interested.

Thankfully, that was his specialty.

"So," Prescott said, "what's your take?"

The analyst cleared his throat. "Let me start at the beginning. You remember 9/11?"

Prescott nodded amiably.

"Okay, so in the couple of months right before 9/11, there was a huge jump in currency in circulation. That probably means that somebody—somebody with an awful lot of money in domestic bank accounts, for example—cashed out in order to avoid blow-back after the attacks. See, they figured that if they were tied to the attack, their bank accounts would be frozen. So they preemptively grabbed their money and took it out of the bank.

"But that wasn't the end of the story." The analyst pushed his glasses up on his nose, his face reddening with his growing excitement. Prescott stifled a yawn. "Right before the attacks, somebody started shorting airline stocks."

Prescott's look of bewilderment was Tommy Bradley's cue to jump in—the chief of staff knew that Prescott would never admit to not understanding something. Part of his job involved taking that hit. "In English, please?" said Tommy.

"Shorting is where the price of, say, a share of McDonald's stock is now at $20. I tell you that I'm going to sell you stock in McDonald's next week for $10. Great deal for you, right? So here's my plan: I'll borrow a stock from the president. Then, I'll wait until next week, hope the stock is at $6, and sell the stock to you at $10. I'll buy a second stock and then go back to the president and give it back to him. I make $4. Now, the simple act of me selling you that option to buy for next week drives down the stock price, because I'm inventing a whole new supply of stock that doesn't even exist yet. So it's sort of a self-fulfilling prophecy.

"Well," continued the analyst, "that's what happened in the days before 9/11. There were a huge number of foreign reports about people seeking to borrow shares. The volatility in the airline shares jumped 30 percent between September 4 and September

7. Then, boom, September 11. The airlines get slammed. Stocks go through the floor. Somebody makes a bundle. Somebody who knew in advance."

Prescott leaned forward. "So what are you trying to say?"

"What he's trying to say," growled Collier, "is that we're about to get hit. Hard."

"And," said Prescott, turning to the analyst, "you think that this is going to happen soon?"

The analyst shrugged. "Could happen any time. I'm just picking up some signals."

Prescott thumbed his chin thoughtfully. "Seems to me," he said slowly, "that the 9/11 Commission report rejected all of that." Tommy found himself surprised. He didn't know Prescott had read the report.

"That report was flawed. Knew it at the time. Everybody did," said Collier.

"And just what are your credentials, again?" Prescott said to the analyst.

The analyst's eyes moved to the floor. "Well, you know," he mumbled, "I was an investment advisor."

Prescott's eyes flashed. "And this makes you an expert on economic terrorism?"

Collier broke in again. "Mr. President, this information should be fully analyzed, tracked down. Just for the sake of covering our bases."

"And just whom do you believe is moving this money around?"

"The money has been gathered in anonymous accounts. They're known as dark pools. We don't know who exactly holds the cash, but we have some guesses. The Iranians. The Chinese…"

"Guesses?" The president leaned forward. "You do understand that we have a very valuable trading relationship with China. If we move forward with a covert investigation, what are the chances the Chinese find out?"

Collier shrugged. "I'd say fifty-fifty."

Prescott spoke slowly. Like Collier was a third-grader. Which, in Prescott's mind, he essentially was. "Fifty-fifty. So you want me to risk our entire trade relationship with China—a country whose way of life is based on honor—based on a hunch from a random analyst with a background as an investment advisor?"

The general grunted. "All I'm saying is that we ought to check it out, sir. If only to cover our asses should something go wrong." Collier hoped Prescott would take the broad hint.

Prescott didn't. "Well, I disagree. This discussion is tabled." He stood up. "Gentlemen, thank you for your time."

The abruptness of the move startled the analyst, who jumped to his feet, stammering. "But Mr. President—this could mean …"

"I know what it could mean. But so could a thousand other things. Do you have any idea how many intelligence briefings cross my desk? I do appreciate your diligence. But I'll have to have my people look into your claims." He gripped the analyst's hand. Hard. "And I'll insist that you keep our meeting today under wraps. Can't be too careful, with the things the press will print." The Prescott smile emerged. Bill Collier felt his chest grip up with anger. But the meeting was over.

Fifteen minutes later, Prescott was on the phone with the Chinese premier, who quickly acquiesced to the request for a major bond buy by the Chinese government. Prescott thanked him profusely, promised him that the United States understood the position of the Chinese government with respect to military exercises in the South China Sea, but asked that the exercises take place sporadically rather than all at once, and then hung up. *And they say the Chinese are tough to deal with*, Prescott thought to himself.

Seconds later, his intercom buzzed.

"Mr. President?" said his secretary, a hot little handpicked blonde number named Marissa. "I've got the governor of Texas for you."

"Can we take a rain check?" Prescott felt too high to be brought down by the fat turd from the Lone Star State, that arrogant, bull-headed used car salesman. He hated Bubba Davis—who named their child Bubba, aside from dumb hicks from the South?—and didn't want to hear his drawl ruining his day.

"He says it's urgent, Mr. President."

Prescott groaned and picked up the headset. "Put him through."

The line beeped once. "Governor Davis, you are on with the president of the United States."

"Mr. President." Davis's voice was thick with anger.

"What can I do for you, Bubba?"

"You could send me some troops to the border, is what you could do. I'm sure you saw on the news about my staffer."

Prescott kicked off his shoes, put his feet on the desk. "Yes, sir, I sure did." He found himself accidentally blurring into a drawl of his own when he talked with the rednecks. "Tragic. Just tragic. Not sure what anybody could've done about it, though."

"*You* could have done something about it. You still can. It's an act of war."

"It's not an act of war, Governor, if it's not by a foreign government."

A pause. Then the storm. "Horseshit, Mr. President. You know as well as I do that the Mexican government is run by the cartels. And they killed one of my people. One of *your* people. Came right across the border in that helicopter and shot her right in front of my chief of staff. I got dead kids washing up on the Rio Grande and you're slammin' me in the press for tryin' to do some-thing about it. What in the Sam Hill is wrong with you?"

Now Prescott's ire was up. It was one thing to disagree with him. It was another to lecture him. Nobody got away with that shit. Nobody.

"You put troops on that border without my go-ahead, they're not going to have any power," he said. "You can give them the power to arrest, but as you know, anyone they arrest will then be processed by my Immigration and Customs Enforcement department. And we aren't interested in noncriminal undocumented immigrants." Prescott could almost hear Davis bristle at the euphemism. Good. He continued, "You can do what you want, but in the end, it's our choice anyway."

"But at least they won't be runnin' around the state in their helicopters. Power to arrest means power to fire on those who are a threat."

Prescott's voice went ice cold. "Let me be perfectly clear, Governor Davis. Your boys shoot anybody, and I'll have my DOJ dogs down there sniffing around you like you're a bitch in heat."

Another pause. "And then what?"

Prescott was thunderstruck. "And then what? And then I arrest your boys, shut down your operation, and bring charges against you for violation of federal law. That's what."

A long pause, this time. Softly. "And then what?"

"I don't have time for this bullshit, Bubba. You cross me, and I promise, you'll see the inside of a cell for a very, very long time."

Davis's voice came through solidly. "I read you loud and clear, Mr. President."

The phone clicked dead.

Prescott buzzed the intercom. "Marissa, get me Jazz." That was his nickname for Jasmine Jacks, the national security advisor, his longtime political mentor.

He could hear her sexy fingers manipulating the phone. "She's in the Situation Room, Mr. President. And she says you might want to get down there. Something about Brett Hawthorne."

ELLEN

AUSTIN, TEXAS

BRETT HAD LOST WEIGHT.

Funny that that would be the first thought to cross Ellen's mind when she saw him on television, but it was. He was always so self-conscious about the four or five pounds around his midsection he couldn't shake, what he liked to call the Famed Hawthorne Underbelly. That had to be gone. He looked gaunt. That jutting jawline she loved to kiss looked like skin stretched taut over bone. He looked like death. That was her first thought.

Her second thought was that this could not be happening.

Her man. The man she'd married and who had cared for her and who had provided her strength and to whom she'd given her entire life—a man she had never questioned about his honor, even when the front pages of every major newspaper in America smeared it—with a knife to his throat.

She was alone, watching him. He was alone, at the mercy of his enemies. This couldn't be real.

But there he was, his eyes staring out stolidly at the camera, wearing an orange jumpsuit, his face a mask of impassivity. Ellen knew one version of that look—the stubborn look that came into his eyes when they had an argument and he set his mind that he was in the right. When that look came over his face, the argument was over, even if he was dead wrong.

But the glassy stare that masked Brett's stubbornness—that she hadn't seen before. It had to be trained into you, she imagined. Nobody looked like that naturally.

Of course, it wasn't exactly natural to have a knife to your throat, either. And that's what the networks showed over and over, on a loop: Brett, on his knees, in that orange jumpsuit, with a man swathed totally in black, his face wreathed in material, a knife in his hand and at Brett's throat. He spoke with a British accent, although the facecloth made it impossible to know whether or not the voice came from him.

It all felt surreal. They'd released videos like this before. But never of Ellen's husband.

"The blood of innocents is on your hands, President Prescott," the masked figure stated in monotone laced with fanatical passion. "As you bomb our innocents, so we strike at the throats of your people. In the name of Allah, the most high, we will send you your general's head if you fail to withdraw your bombers within forty-eight hours."

The video cut to black.

Then, the face of the president, grim and obviously weary: "We will not bow before terrorists."

The media didn't take long to descend on Ellen's home outside of Austin, looking for comment. She obliged them, because she knew Brett would want her to. He had always told her that to run from the media was a waste of time—they'd print something anyway, true or false. So she told them that she wouldn't beg, and neither would her husband. While members of the administration urged her to issue a plea to the terrorists for mercy, she refused. She knew the look in her husband's eye well enough to know that pleading with terrorists was out of the question. And she knew it was useless anyway.

They would kill him.

She had seen the end of videos like this before. The first installment represented the threat; the second installment, invariably, represented the fruition of that threat. The jagged trunks of human beings, the sawed-off heads that looked too much like a horror movie and not enough like real life.

Her husband.

She reached out to the television, stroked his cheek. The cheek that had laid on her breast the first night they made love. The cheek that she had wet with tears the night of the miscarriage. His eyes blinked rapidly as she stroked the screen, almost as if he could feel her touch him across the world.

She felt tears well in her own eyes.

She couldn't cry. Not yet.

So she went to work as usual.

When she arrived at the capitol, she made straight for the governor's office. The halls were thronged with angry Texans—and angry Texans were anything but subtle. Some carried signs tacked to wooden planks: "CLOSE THE BORDER!" "ENOUGH IS ENOUGH!" "PROTECT YOUR PEOPLE!" She edged her way past one burly linebacker of a man, wearing a cowboy hat and a gun, which was perfectly legal in the state. That was reason enough for Ellen to love the Lone Star State. There wouldn't be any random shootings in this capitol building anytime soon, even if the media made it seem as though every civilian with a gun represented a threat to public safety. For every nut with a gun, she knew, there were ten willing to put him down.

She showed the guards her ID, and they waved her through. Two knocks on the door, and she stood across from onetime Republican presidential candidate and four-time governor Bubba Davis. After a stint in Vietnam back in the late 1960s, Davis—a big bear of a man, burly and fun loving—had come home without a job. He'd finally gotten one working on an oil rig. He loved the work, the feel of the equipment in his hands, and after a while, he felt good enough to go out on his own, with a bit of a bankroll from his dad-in-law. He lived frugally—and then struck it rich when he patented a new drilling technique that skyrocketed efficiency. Soon, Bubba Davis was one of the richest men in the state. So when his friends pushed him to run for state legislature, he hesitated—why give up the *Dynasty* life for backroom deals with cigar-smoking lawyers?

He hesitated until his local state assemblyman began calling for new environmental reviews of all drilling. The way Bubba figured it, he had no choice—his livelihood, and the livelihood of his workers, was at stake. He ran. He won. And he kept on winning. Turned out that his blunt nature and blustery personality worked great. His first campaign slogan: "Don't Let 'Em Hornswoggle You." In his opening campaign speech, he named the three top environmental officers in the state and read off how much they'd received from lobbyists for the environmentalists—and how much those environmental groups received from global competitors like the Saudi government.

Bubba Davis played politics like he played football: he pushed the line. The press called it "swagger." He just called it the Texas Way.

Now, though, the governor of Texas's face lit with rage. The man who had once picked up fellow soldiers and thrown them over his shoulder in distant rice paddies had turned to soft fat. Since Marge died, Bubba Davis drank too much, smoked too many cigars. And when he got angry, his face turned candy-apple red.

At the moment, his face looked closer to lobster crimson.

"Well, go fuck yourself then," he spluttered, slamming the phone down on his carefully crafted maple desk.

He looked up. "Oh, hey, Ellen. Glad you're back." He walked over and wrapped her in a bear hug. "Ain't nothin' to say 'bout Brett. Except that he's a tough, mean son of a bitch. If anybody can get his way out of that one, it's your old man."

Ellen nodded curtly, then sat down on the nearby settee. She didn't want to talk about Brett, even with Bubba. "Governor, what's the story here? My e-mail has been overflowing. I'm getting panic messages from the rest of the team."

Bubba planted himself heavily on the flowered couch across from her. "I'm putting more troops on the border."

"You know that's just for show."

"Not this time, it ain't."

Ellen felt an uncomfortable cringe rise in the middle of her stomach. "What do you mean, 'this time'?"

Bubba scratched at the back of his neck awkwardly. "You've seen the people outside. They've got a right to expect that they're safe in this state. That's why they elected me. It's why they keep electing me."

"And you *are* keeping them safe, Governor."

"The hell I am. Have you seen the crime statistics in El Paso? Used to be one of the safest cities in the state. Now it looks like goddamn Phoenix. I've got kidnappings. I've got killings. I've got local police in a tizzy, and I've got citizens pledging to go rogue if they don't get satisfaction from the government."

A shadow of a weary smile crossed Ellen's face. "So what else is new?"

"I'm not going to stand for it anymore."

"What can we do? You saw what they did to Vivian. And the feds hamstrung us."

"Not anymore."

The cringe became a pit. "What are you planning?"

"I'm going to give them the authority to shoot, Ellen," Davis said softly.

She couldn't stop herself before the words came out: "You must be out of your mind."

"I'm not. I've only been out of my mind to think anything would change. I talked to Prescott yesterday. He's stonewalling me. Threatened to send the feds against us, to arrest our boys, to arrest me, if I do a damn thing to stop this war. And it *is* a war. I knew Vivian, too, Ellen. I recruited her to the office. Knew her from when she was a little girl and took piano lessons with my wife. That funeral was the last one I'll be a party to."

"No, it won't," Ellen said. "Not if you do this. It'll just be one among many. Do you think Prescott is bluffing? It's just what he wants. He wants another Waco. And even better, a Waco created by one of his chief political opponents. Who do you think will stand with you? The media? They're in his pocket. Even your own allies will desert you. They'll call you a secessionist, a rebel. They'll string you up and you know it. Your allies are your allies right up until they're not."

"No," Bubba said slowly. "I don't think that's right."

"Oh, really? What's going to stop them? That little mob outside?"

"That little mob," the governor of Texas said, "isn't so little. I've got polls right here that say that seven out of ten of 'em think we ought to militarize the border."

"That doesn't mean they'll stand up to feds if Prescott gets mean. Polls don't mean a thing when the rubber hits the road.

Hell, polls were in favor of the Afghanistan War, until things got tough. And Brett found out how bad things can go when the public abandons you."

Bubba Davis stood up, began pacing, his boots thumping on the carpet. "What do you suggest I do, Ellen? We arrest border crossers, and the president just releases them. He just *doesn't give a damn* about us down here. We're political playthings for him, a convenient enemy so he can run his party-building scam, calling us racist rednecks."

"And you want to hand him that label on a silver platter?"

Bubba walked over to the windows at the back of his office, looked out at the hot Austin noon, the heat baking the grass beneath. The protesters screaming, sweating. He couldn't hear them, but he could see their mouths work, screaming at him to *do something*.

"Got any other options?" Bubba finally said.

Ellen went silent.

"Then it's settled. Draft me a statement. I'm gonna put these bastards on warning." He smiled. "Don't worry. They won't do shit. I know a coward when I see one, and Prescott's yellower than dehydrated dog piss."

"What if you're wrong, Bubba?" Ellen asked. "Are you ready for war with your own government?"

Bubba looked at her. Then his eyes seemed to focus far off. "They've been at war with us for a long time. I know. I went to war for them. I've been abandoned by my government once. I'm not going to be the one doing the abandoning this time."

SOLEDAD

CENTRAL VALLEY, CALIFORNIA

THE KNOCK ON THE DOOR came at nearly two o'clock in the morning.

It didn't wake Soledad—she barely slept these days, given the small city of SWAT team and surrounding militia members that had built up in two concentric circles around her home. It was tough to get exercise on the ranch now that she risked arrest if she strayed too far from her front door. Some of the militia members—now they called themselves Soledad's Soldiers—rode their motorcycles down the slight incline, kicking up dust in their wake, every few days and brought her groceries; one of them made sure that each time SWAT cut off her electricity, her generator got fixed.

But she'd basically been under house arrest for weeks, and she was damn sick of it. Too much time in one place made her anxious. Even the occasional big media spread didn't seem to lift her too much anymore—she felt like the whole game was rigged.

She was either hero or villain. She was always the story. Never Emilio and Juan. It was always Chris Matthews on the nightly news calling her a traitor or Michael Savage calling her a freedom fighter. It was always one or the other.

And it just didn't mean a damn thing. The state government went right back in and created an emergency dike to stop the river from flowing. Her farm went dry. The only difference between before and after the bombing was the military encampment around her house.

It just sat there.

Every day, the militia dwindled. Every day, a few more of the bikers peeled off, took their rifles and skedaddled. You couldn't expect them to stay indefinitely, after all. They had lives, families. And as the media attention waned, as the standoff lasted, more and more of them had to leave.

But SWAT remained.

Then, over the past two or three days, SWAT began to grow. She noticed a few more Humvees show up. Then some choppers. Their incessant flyovers kept her up at night, even when she was lucky enough to fall asleep.

But she was awake now. The knock startled her anyway. She had always figured that when the invasion came, it wouldn't come with a warning "shave and a haircut, two bits" thump on the door, but with a small battering ram through the door.

She opened it. A SWAT officer stood there, his gun down by his side. When she opened the screen door, he sidled in without permission, holding his right arm out, palm facing her, signaling for her to keep quiet. He shut the door stealthily behind him. Then, noticing her eyes fixed on his weapon, he placed it gently on the dining room table.

When he took off his helmet, she noticed his bright blue eyes. They stood out more because they were red-rimmed, whether from lack of sleep or from crying, she couldn't tell. The man stood no more than five foot ten, well built, Caucasian. A thatch of mussed brown hair stood nearly on end. He moved forward quickly and grabbed her by the arm. She could feel his powerful grip through her thick robe.

"You need to get out of here," he growled. "Now."

She pushed his hand off her arm, stood up to her full five two. "I'm not going anywhere," she said defiantly. "I know my rights."

"I don't think you're getting this, Miss Ramirez," he said. "They're coming for you. Tonight."

She felt the wave of nausea hit her so hard she almost stumbled. The possibility of this going bad had always lurked at the back of her mind. She steeled herself for it every day. But she always figured she would have warning.

Well, she thought to herself, *you do have warning at that.*

She looked at the SWAT member, puzzled. "Why are you helping me? My cookies can't be that good."

He laughed softly. "Maybe they are." A pause. "Or maybe I'm just sick of watching people get pushed around. Whatever it is, you need to get out of here tonight."

She gestured helplessly at her surroundings. "I'm a rancher. I'm not a paramilitary leader, no matter what *Time* says. Where am I supposed to go?"

"Won't matter when they come for you in the morning. Do you have a back door to this place?"

She nodded.

"Go get a suitcase ready."

"What's your name?"

"Aiden. Aiden Foster."

She smiled ruefully. "You ready to be a traitor, Aiden?"

He shrugged.

She walked over to one of the cabinets, opened it, took down a jar. "Well, we might as well split a cookie on that."

What do you take with you when your entire world is about to burn to the ground? She'd come to the Central Valley as a girl, grown up dirt poor, watched her father make his living in the dirt. But instead of running from the dirt, as he wanted her to do, she had saved up, bought a small property, built it up from nothing. A few horses. A few cows. She had grown it, hired men, brought families to live on the ranch. This ranch was her family. By the time she realized she was too old to have a family, she'd spent decades building up her patch of land. She'd picked every rock and plank on the place. She'd overseen every fixed wire fence, guarded every beef shipment from coyotes.

The ranch itself was her most valuable possession, her memories, her life's work. All of it.

After a few moments, she stuffed some clothes in a bag, grabbed a picture of the ranch as it was originally—an empty patch of land, her smiling from ear to ear, a young woman, her father standing next to her, a bemused smile on his face, his hand gripping her shoulder. Then she zipped it shut, threw on some jeans and heavy boots, and made her way back out to the living room.

That's all she could carry on her back.

Aiden waited, his gun ready, hand up to his lips.

"Foster?" The whisper wafted through one of the windows. "You in there, man?"

He didn't answer. Then he signaled for her to get on the ground.

A split second later, a smoke grenade came crashing through the window.

Foster rolled quickly to his right, picked it up, and threw it back out the window. "What the *fuck?!*" cried one of the attackers. "Foster, that you in there?"

"Fuck it," Foster muttered.

He leapt to his feet, began firing wildly through the shattered glass, too high to hit anyone. He heard at least two men curse and scatter. In the distance, he could see the lights of the choppers flash on. He dropped to the ground as a loudspeaker began blaring: "COME OUT, WITH YOUR HANDS UP! THIS IS YOUR FINAL WARNING!"

Then in the distance, a man yelling. One of Soledad's biker boys, she thought. "*Go to hell, you fascist assholes!*"

Gunfire. More gunfire in the distance. A few bikes, gunning their engines.

An explosion.

"Ma'am," said Aiden Foster, "I'd recommend we get out of here."

Soledad nodded, began to army crawl across the floor, dragging her bag behind her, as sniper bullets zinged through the windows, thunking into the sturdy oak walls. When they reached the bathroom, Soledad kicked the door shut behind Foster, began pulling everything out from underneath the sink. When she reached the bottom, she began pounding on it with her boot. Foster joined in.

The sound of the choppers whirring into life, angry wasps out for blood, washed into the house. Spotlights shined brightly in the crack beneath the bathroom door. Then the heavy-caliber 7.62mm rounds began crashing through the roof, bathing the bathroom in speckled light. As Soledad kicked out the last board and crawled beneath the home—as Foster followed, both of them belly-down in the dirt, covering their heads—the ceramic tiles Soledad had so carefully picked to match the décor shattered above them.

"Do you have a plan?" she yelled at Foster above the ear-splitting whine of the bullets.

"Hell, no," he said. "But I'll bet they do."

In the distance, the cavalry was coming. Soledad's Soldiers. At least a dozen bearded, gun-toting men on their steel horses, riding directly toward the SWAT lines. She could see it in the distance, Pickett's hog charge.

SWAT formed up, turned to face them, guns at the ready.

Which is when the chopper began to groan. It sputtered, crackled—and then dropped to the ground, right at the SWAT lines. It spiraled down, out of control, scattering the SWAT members as they tried to avoid the rotor blades. The air screamed with the dying whine of the chopper. Then it dropped and exploded into flame.

Soledad watched in horror as men, good men—men she had met, who were just trying to do their jobs—leapt out of the carnage, their entire bodies balls of flame. They screamed, rolled around on the ground, cried out for their mothers. Their comrades ran to them, tried to beat out the flames with the nearest available cloth, tried to kick dirt on them to put them out.

She looked at Foster, horror-stricken. His eyes were filled with tears.

"What the hell happened?" she whispered.

He looked away. "They didn't have to take this on," he said. "They could have said no. I did. Sometimes, you gotta make a choice."

He grabbed her by the arm and pointed toward the edge of the house, where four motorcycles skidded to a hard stop. Soledad pushed herself forward, trying desperately to block out the screaming. The gunfire continued near the helicopter site as a few of the bikers fired on those trying to help their wounded friends. "You've got to stop them," she told Foster. "Make it stop."

"I can't," Foster said. "It's too late for that. You know that."

Foster bodily picked her up and put her on a motorcycle behind one of the militiamen. She clung to his leather jacket as he twisted the throttle and peeled out, spinning his wheels before they caught hard ground, the bike leaping forward. Foster followed on his own motorcycle.

"Don't look back," Soledad whispered to herself. "Don't look back."

But she did, just long enough to see, in the distance, some of the flaming men go out, leaving nothing but smoking chars of flesh.

LEVON

DETROIT, MICHIGAN

LEVON FELT THE AIR AROUND him crackle with energy. It was something he had felt before, just before a fight—the switch that went off in the brain that notched the senses higher, made them more sensitive. The adrenaline flowing through the veins. The feeling that you'd burst from the inside out if the fight didn't commence, and right quick.

This felt like those fights multiplied exponentially.

That's because Levon knew that he wasn't alone this time. It wasn't him taking on some gang rival or him debating some white Republican Club sucker at the U. This was going to be flames and blood and struggle and power. This was going to be death and mayhem and hope and glory. This was going to be fucking big.

All Levon needed was the cue.

He'd discussed the cue ahead of time with the reverend. It would come on television, during a press conference Big Jim planned to hold with the mayor in the aftermath of the Kendrick

Malone killing. The killing of another young, innocent black man at the hands of the racist white establishment. The police targeting a kid—an unarmed kid, for God's sake!—just because he happened to be black and happened to be out at night at the wrong time.

That shooting had worked out precisely according to the plan.

Levon had one of his boys give little Kendrick a $20 bill to go and harass the cop. Kendrick, of course, thought it was just a piece of good, clean fun—messing with white cops was a rare joy, made you feel like more of a man. And with all the big boys telling him how he'd be a boss in the neighborhood if he baited the cop, he'd been enthusiastic. He probably looked forward to coming home and telling his buddies how he'd told that cracker ass pig to go to hell—stared right at him and cursed him to his face, made the pig back down. Kendrick knew he was supposed to go for his toy gun. They told him it would be a joke, that the cop wouldn't do anything, that the cop would pussy out.

Of course, Levon knew better. No cop could sit still when somebody went for the waistband. Police procedure dictated what happened next.

Levon made sure of one other thing, too: the only working camera at the gas station had the right angle. No sound. Stark spotlight on the two main characters. The blood, black in the black-and-white footage, seeping from the poor black boy. O'Sullivan sitting down, stunned. The other cameras, he'd had smashed or deactivated. One angle, one tape, one million replays on nightly news.

The headline writers couldn't help themselves. "8-YEAR-OLD UNARMED BLACK BOY SHOT DEAD BY WHITE COP," blared the *Free Press*. "MURDERER!" screamed the headline on the New York *Daily News*. CNN headlined the case the entire day, and the next one as well. Over on MSNBC, the talking heads could barely conceal their excitement. On Fox News, a few anchors urged caution while others talked of the legacy of racist policing across the country.

The president of the United States quickly sounded off on the case. He couldn't help himself; Mark Prescott hijacked his White House press secretary's gaggle, took to the podium, and told Americans that "the time has come for a great racial conversation in this country. Too many black boys have been murdered merely for the color of their skin. This must end." He announced that he would be sending his attorney general to Detroit to ensure that the local investigation proceeded according to law. "We'll ensure that justice is done for the family of Kendrick Malone. This is America, where there's justice enough for everybody, if we have the bravery to pursue it."

And now Levon waited.

He waited outside Coleman A. Young Municipal Center, named after the former mayor of the city—a man who'd been a racial pro in his own right. Fitting that old Coleman could make one more sacrifice in the name of racial justice. He'd be doing that tonight, if all went according to plan.

Before them stood an imposing wall, in front of which knelt a statue, the Spirit of Detroit—a twenty-five-foot-tall loincloth-clad man carrying a golden sphere with rays emanating from it in one hand, and a small family in the other hand. Levon had never known what the statue was supposed to mean; it just looked like a constipated Nordic Man to him. On the wall a large inscription from Corinthians read: "NOW THE LORD IS THAT SPIRIT; AND WHERE THE SPIRIT OF THE LORD IS HERE IS LIBERTY."

Horseshit, thought Levon.

Behind Levon stood a solid three thousand of his fellow Detroiters, mostly young black men. Levon had sent out his boys to round up the crowd, and they'd had an easy time of it after the media coverage. Facing the crowd, protecting the statue and a platform set up just before it, stood about a hundred cops.

Levon noticed a particular lack of weapons. He smiled to himself.

Media members surrounded the crowd, cameras at the ready, interviewing the odd protester here or there. He knew that a few media members would get hurt tonight—that's the way it had to be. A couple of reporters getting caught in the melee just showed that the mob was serious. If they were too well behaved, the media would dismiss them. A bit of blood got them hot under the collar. A bit of blood made the story hot. The way the media worked, the only way they'd pay attention was if somebody did something extreme—and then they'd defend the action, blame it on overriding anger at an unfair society. Levon knew a few of the journalists from U of M. They'd done the same thing back in their university days. Made them feel good about themselves, less ensconced in white privilege.

Levon had his men ringing the edges of the crowd, ready to prevent any non-approved persons from getting too close to the media members. No footage of fools, he'd promised the reverend.

And he intended to keep his word. Tonight, Levon intended to be the face on the news. Already, he'd done his best Malcolm X impression—early Malcolm, not that late-stage "Islam means peace" pussy shit—for the networks. "If we don't get what we want," he said, "if we don't get justice for Kendrick, this city is going to burn. We've been burning silently for too long. Our poverty burns beneath the surface. Our ignorance burns beneath the surface. We've been left for dead in this city, just like black boys have been left for dead all over this country. And this country must pay a price, if there is no justice."

The sexy blonde with the short skirt seemed turned on at that point. Breathily, she asked, "And what will justice look like?"

So he threw in a line just for good measure: "Justice will be done when people like you live in the mud you've made for us. Only then can we lift each other up."

Her eyelashes fluttered. That shit was magic, Levon knew. He'd learned it at the university, too. White coeds majoring in journalism were a cinch. Just drag them off their civilized perch and let them experience life outside their self-proclaimed white privilege, and they let you know that you'd be doing them a favor.

Levon glanced at his watch. 6:34. The mayor and the reverend were four minutes late. Good. Let the crowd get antsy. Let them get nervous and enraged. They'd need that energy. Bored crowds were the ones that turned the most violent when the gun sounded.

For now, they remained ominously silent. No banners. No signs. Just thousands of strong young black men and women—mostly men—ready to stand together against injustice. That's what the media would see—and the truth was that many of these young black men *were* ready to do that. All they knew was that they'd dealt with white asshole cops before, that their neighborhoods were full of crack and booze and poverty, and that somebody needed to fix things. And if nobody understood that, well, it was time to *make* them understand.

That time was now.

From behind the wall, the mayor emerged. Beside him stood Reverend Crawford, looking as solemn as Judgment Day. He spotted Levon in the crowd; Levon gave him an almost imperceptible nod. The reverend looked away.

The mayor was at the lectern now. Behind him sat Nordic Man, awaiting his words along with the rest of the world.

Mayor Jimmy Burns had a history with the city of Detroit. He'd grown up there, worked at one of the local law firms, become alderman, and then taken over for the last mayor after a corruption beef put him in prison for the duration of his term. He'd tried, with minor success, to push some reforms, most controversially staffing up the police department. That reform had failed when the DOJ consent decree came through. Crime had blasted through the roof under his administration, just as it had under his predecessors.

Now, he wiped his pasty white forehead with a handkerchief. He adjusted his glasses. He looked down at his notes.

"I..." his voice broke. "I have just met with area leaders as well as civil rights leaders across the country. And I can say to all of you that our investigation will be full and fair, and that justice will be done..."

"WHAT JUSTICE?" Levon shouted at the top of his lungs. The shout rang out like a gun report in the cold night air.

"Justice will be done," the mayor continued. "Officer Ricky O'Sullivan has been suspended from duty pending a full investigation. This deeply troubling incident has stirred the consciences of Americans from border to border. But I promise you, justice will not rest until the tragedy of Kendrick Malone..."

"WHAT JUSTICE? WHAT JUSTICE?" Levon was chanting now, at the top of his lungs. A few scattered voices joined in. Mayor Burns, momentarily flustered, clutched at the pages of his prepared remarks. The voices grew. Pounding. Angry. Steady. "WHAT JUSTICE? WHAT JUSTICE? WHAT JUSTICE?"

Trying to be heard over the chant, the mayor continued now. Reverend Crawford began nodding softly. "Until the tragedy of Kendrick Malone is answered with truth. We must uncover all the facts..."

Burns suddenly stumbled backwards as a rock struck him in the scalp. Almost in slow motion, his arms stretched for air, circling in a nearly comic pinwheel. He teetered on his heels for just a moment, hung in midair, then fell directly on his ample posterior.

A trickle of blood ran down his forehead, his shattered glasses draped over his nose. He looked as though he was about to cry.

A pause.

Now Levon nodded.

One bottle, trailing flame, soared through the air from the middle of the crowd. Glass, filled with an opaque brown liquid, a rag stuffed into its mouth, burning. Its flight path formed a graceful parabola, sailed over the mayor's head and, with pinpoint accuracy, smashed into the face of the Nordic Man, setting loose the gasoline within and setting the head of the statue into spontaneous flame.

Flames everywhere, flying toward the officers; canisters of tear gas; smoke filling the street; Levon screaming, his men ducking, throwing stones, charging toward the officers; random gunshots in the crowd; media members jabbering madly into their microphones, ducking, playing war correspondent; punches thrown, punches received, men lying on the ground, bleeding…

And then Reverend Jim Crawford, standing tall and proud in his immaculately tailored suit, at the mayor's podium. Shouting into the microphone: "STOP THIS! STOP THIS NOW! WE WILL HAVE JUSTICE! I PROMISE YOU! JUSTICE! JUSTICE!"

And the street gradually went quiet. The young men stopped rioting and screaming, and turned their heads to watch Reverend Jim Crawford.

The cameras focused in on Reverend Jim Crawford, friend to the street, community leader. Big Jim Crawford. The man who just saved Detroit.

Levon smiled.

MOHAMMED

TEHRAN, IRAN

"AMERICA HAS FALLEN. THE TRANSFORMATION from dar al-Harb to dar al-Islam has begun."

Mohammed watched, transfixed.

Ibrahim Ashammi's eyes glowed brightly, as they always did when he was excited. It was a peculiar quality that attracted many of his followers—they saw in that glow a fiery hope, warm and consuming. Hope for a new world. The Teacher, they said, brought hope.

"Today's attack has ensured that the crippled and weakened infidel giant that was the United States will never rise again. The emptiness and degradation of that perverse country has been wiped away, and the glorious reign of Allah has begun. Those that rejected Allah followed vanities, and Allah has destroyed them.

"Today, America has seen that those who reject Allah and hinder men from the path of Allah—their deeds will Allah render astray. Those who supported the Zionist entity have seen the consequences of their evil, and we will rain blow after blow upon them until they are utterly demolished."

A drop of sweat rolled down Ashammi's craggy face and embedded itself in his scraggly beard. Ashammi had lost weight in his three years in the mountains of Tora Bora, but he was finally putting it back on now that he was ensconced in his complex in Tehran. The government had granted it to him out of gratitude for his prior efforts against the Great Satan, with a yearly stipend that enabled him to live comfortably. In return, he had assured them that any efforts he put forth would be directed at non-Shia targets. It was a minor concession from him—his chief enemies resided in the West.

Ashammi wiped away the sweat. The flag behind him, green with white lines of Arabic, wafted gently to and fro as the rasp of the rusted electric fan pushed a breeze through its folds. Then his expression changed, just barely but noticeably—he was no longer the ardent zealot. Now he was the welcoming benefactor.

Mohammed was always amazed by Ashammi's total command of his emotions. Ashammi as benefactor—that persona had drawn Mohammed to him in the first place. He wasn't the only one; many of those who believed in him had come to him because of his outstretched hand. He looked into the camera and continued.

"But now I offer you the chance to meet your destiny under the one true religion by clinging fast to the word of the prophet Mohammed, peace be upon him. For those who believe and work deeds of righteousness and believe in the revelation sent down to Mohammed—for it is the truth from the Lord—He will remove from them their ills and improve their condition.

"Together we will dance in the gardens and rejoice in the fields. The word from merciful Allah is peace, and together, we must embrace peace."

Ashammi pointed at the camera. Mohammed, his youngest recruit—an attractive boy of seventeen, struggling to grow a scraggly beard—hit the stop button on the camera. Ashammi walked behind the camera, and Mohammed replayed the segment. After watching it again, Ashammi smiled. "Mohammed," he said, "it will be a great day. A glorious day. The weapons we got from the infidels in Iraq will be deployed."

Mohammed bit his lip. Ashammi saw it. "I see you are worried," he said. "Do not fear. Does not the Koran say, 'Those who have said, "Our Lord is Allah," and then remained on a right course—the angels will descend upon them, saying, "Do not fear and do not grieve but receive good tidings of Paradise" '?"

Ashammi walked to the window of the compound and threw it open. The sound of the afternoon *muezzin* wafted into the room. He took a deep breath. Then he pulled out a disposable cell phone and dialed.

A man's voice answered at the other end. He spoke with a thick Russian accent. "Yes?"

"Tomorrow," Ashammi said, then hung up abruptly. He turned to Mohammed. "Go, Mohammed," he said, "and Allah will go with you."

As Mohammed left, Ashammi knelt on his prayer rug.

When he got up, he turned to the door and smiled. There, standing before him, was a large American man in a military uniform. He wore a blindfold.

"Welcome, General Hawthorne," Ashammi said.

Mohammed glanced nervously around Café Naderi as he sipped his nana tea. It was a classy joint, and everyone wore a suit—it was a business café, located in the lower level of a hotel. It wasn't the kind of place that would kick up any sort of fuss in a Western city, but in Tehran, it was a rarity. In fact, it bragged that it was the last non-Islamic café in the city.

Which is why it was perfect for the meeting. It was crowded, so Mohammed wouldn't draw any suspicion; there were many non-Iranians, too, so Andrei would fit in. It also had the benefit of maintaining a solidly anti-regime reputation, so there would be no connections to any officials who had approved the operation. Intellectuals and writers hung out in packs and talked treason. For that reason, regime informers populated the place.

It was the last location the Western intelligence agencies would watch. After all, it was their home territory. If somebody was going to plan something, it wouldn't be at this café.

At least, that's what Ashammi was counting on. And Mohammed had complete faith in Ashammi. Ashammi was the man who had taught him the emptiness of secularism, the beauty of belief. He was a master strategist who had launched several substantial attacks on targets ranging from embassies to hotels to restaurants in America, Europe, and Israel. *He is with Allah, and I am with him*, Mohammed thought.

He just wished that Andrei would show up already. Even if this was a safe spot, he was getting sick of listening to the Western-style sinful music blaring over the speakers. *What*, he asked himself, *does it mean to "hit me baby, one more time"*?

Beneath the table where he sat was a small satchel. He had bought it at a local market along with a shaving kit so as not to draw suspicion. He tossed the shaving kit immediately, of course—it had taken him long enough to cultivate the beard—and kept the bag. This morning, Ashammi had crammed it full of euros (Iranian rials were far too inflated for this kind of payment) and handed it to Mohammed. "Good luck, my son," he said. "Stay for half an hour. No more. If he does not show up, leave." Then he stood up and hugged Mohammed tightly. "Take care, my son. You go on Allah's mission, and He will guide you. I promise you."

Mohammed looked down at his cheap Casio watch. Andrei was already twenty minutes late. Wild thoughts ran through Mohammed's head. Had Andrei been followed by the Americans? Had he been taken out of play by the Israelis? What if every minute he stayed here, the Zionists were drawing closer? He had heard the stories about the Jewish devils, about how they had blown the heads off of nuclear scientists with their headrest bombs, about how their computer specialists had stifled the Iranian nuclear program. If they knew what he was planning, the sons of pigs and monkeys would surely take him out of play.

Even as the panicked thoughts played with Mohammed's mind, a short, balding man in khaki pants and a white button-down shirt walked into the café. He was sweating profusely, and his shirt was stained through already. In his right hand, he rolled a small suitcase. He was struggling with its weight, cursing softly as he rolled it over his own feet.

A waiter approached him and asked if he wanted to store his bag. "No," the man said in fluent Persian. "I have just checked out of the hotel, and I wish to keep it with me. But I do have a bad back. Could you wheel it to my table?"

The waiter bowed, smiled, scraped—good tips were hard to come by. He ushered the man to Mohammed's table; the short man handed him a five-euro note and waved him away. He sat down across from Mohammed silently. Mohammed looked him up and down. "*You're* Andrei?"

The man nodded, amused. "You expected Dolph Lundgren, perhaps?"

A puzzled expression crossed Mohammed's face. "Who?"

The Russian guffawed, rolled his eyes. "But of course." He motioned for the waiter and ordered a few pieces of *gaz*. The waiter complied immediately.

"I love the service here," said Andrei. He scarfed down one of the pieces of white pastry. "Delicious."

Mohammed shifted in his seat uneasily. "Can we get this over with?"

"Nonsense," said the Russian. "It's not often I get to eat this well in this country. Besides, if we get up now, we'll only look rushed and suspicious. What's your hurry?"

Andrei took his time with the pastries, then ordered a cup of coffee. By the time he'd completed his meal, another twenty minutes were gone. Mohammed kept glancing at his watch. Finally, he'd had enough. "Sir," he said, his coal-bright eyes burning, "I wish to consummate our business."

Andrei sighed. "Ah, well. Speed is for the young. Let us walk outside."

Mohammed paid. Andrei thanked him, then got up. They walked outside, and Andrei hailed a taxi. After a few blocks, Andrei told the driver to pull over and let him out. He left the suitcase in the trunk.

As the taxi was about to drive away, the short Russian tapped on Mohammed's window. Mohammed rolled it down. "Good luck," he said in English. Mohammed nodded.

Mohammed watched him walk down a bright alleyway and lose himself in a local marketplace. Then he turned to the driver again.

"Take me to the airport," he said.

PART 2

COLLAPSE

BRETT

TEHRAN, IRAN

"Tomorrow."

The word hung in the air for a moment. Spoken in Arabic. Not meant for his ears. Brett was sure of that. He couldn't see a thing—the blindfold over his eyes prevented him from seeing the room. But the next words confirmed Brett's worst fears; he recognized the voice.

"Welcome, General Hawthorne," said Ibrahim Ashammi, in a clipped accent.

Brett's captors forced him to his knees. He felt them hit stone. Then he felt a sweaty hand remove the blindfold. Before him stood the world's most well-known terrorist since Osama bin Laden. Smiling.

"I hope you weren't too mistreated on your journey here," Ashammi said, turning his back to him. "We wouldn't want a famous war hero victimized by—how did you put it in your interviews—'barbarians'?"

Brett kept his mouth shut. He knew how this would go, and he knew that the taunting presaged something far more frightening. Instead of listening to Ashammi's monologue, Brett quietly scanned the room for tools, anything he could use. He almost didn't notice when Ashammi turned back around, thrust his face just inches from his own. Brett could smell his breath, the faint vestiges of *chelo khoresh* still on it. "General Hawthorne," Ashammi said, "I know you, and that you are a resourceful man. I also know that your country is a paper tiger, and that your president is a weakling. Weaklings watch as the world burns around them, thinking they are safe because they have a mirror, and they are lost in the reflection. That is why your country will lose."

Finally, Brett spoke. "America doesn't lose. We just convince ourselves not to win. You're the ones who will lose. We don't have to tape beheadings to frighten people into joining us."

Ashammi, to Brett's surprise, laughed uproariously, clapped his hands in delight. "Oh, you Americans, you don't understand at all. You're delightfully out of touch—I mean delightfully until you start dropping incendiaries on our children. You spend your lives fat and happy, eating at McDonald's, imagining yourselves superior because you have clean shopping malls and manicured front lawns. But while you sleep, while you watch your reality television, your children abandon you, no matter how many Patriot missiles you send against us, no matter how many American troops we have to bury in the sand.

"You see, we offer something you do not: a reason to die. We need not frighten anyone. *You* do the frightening. Because, you see, people are not frightened to die or to be killed, down deep. Down deep, they are afraid of dying without that death meaning anything. They are afraid that they will die and that a life of playing Xbox and watching your American movies and eating your American food and worshipping themselves will end with them in the ground, and their lives forgotten.

"And, of course, they are right. Their lives are meaningless."

Brett scoffed. "And yours, I suppose, are meaningful. Slaughtering women and children."

Ashammi grabbed Brett by his face, squeezing his jaw until it hurt. Brett clenched his teeth and stared into his eyes. "We will do anything for Allah. That is our strength, and your weakness."

Brett whispered, "There you're wrong. You don't know me, and you don't know my countrymen. We live for something. We live to kill bastards like you."

Ashammi laughed. "No, that I know, General Hawthorne. At least those of you left." He turned to his goons. "Take him to his cell."

The men seized him by his arms, pulled him to his feet. As they dragged him out of the room, he got a glimpse through a window, just a crack: the Azadi Tower, growing from the ground like a thick-rooted tree, culminating in a latticework tower. Brett suppressed a grin of satisfaction. He knew exactly where he was from the coordinates on Feldkauf's map. And he knew exactly what he had to do about it. And he'd heard Ashammi's one word: "Tomorrow."

He hoped his message would get to America in time.

They came for him in the middle of the night, the better to keep him off-balance. He'd been trained for such techniques, but too long ago to matter, and he'd awoken groggy, head pounding, nauseated by the casual beating handed out to him by one of Ashammi's lackeys. No marks to the face, of course—they wanted their victims looking clean and fresh before they sawed off their heads. But the big bearded kid had worked his torso over pretty well, and ground the bones of his arm against one another to boot. Yusuf, he'd heard one of the others call him. He wouldn't forget that anytime soon. Every time Yusuf had balled up his fist and driven it into his midsection, Brett had pictured cracking the lug across the head with a two-by-four.

They'd taken his uniform from him, forced him to dress in an orange jumpsuit, the uniform of their victims. When he'd gone to the bucket that served as a toilet, he'd noticed his urine had turned red. "Like Ali," he'd thought to himself, "after the Thrilla." But Ali had survived that.

This, Brett knew, he would not survive.

That wasn't his plan.

He'd formed the plan after seeing the Azadi Tower, gauging the distance from it, realizing that Feldkauf had given him the exact coordinates of the site. He needed them to release one of their typical terror tapes for it to work, but he thought they'd do that—they couldn't help themselves, couldn't stop from parading him on all the news networks. That was their triumph. They wouldn't win by fighting big battles, but by drawing recruits with the tapes.

He just hoped that the boys in intelligence picked up on the message he'd be sending. And he prayed that the film editor, or whatever cave dweller familiar with Windows Movie Maker they'd be using for this particular production, didn't chop up the film too badly.

Yusuf and one of his companions laughed and joked as they kicked him awake, grabbed him by the arms, pulled him down the dark hallway. He could see fluorescent lights shining through the cracks of the door before he got there; a ray of light caught the edge of Ibrahim's knife, which he carried on his belt. Yusuf looked down at him and, in his broken English, guffawed, "You be in movie now. Like movie star."

Brett muttered through gritted teeth, "Fuck you and your mother." Yusuf smiled. Brett smiled back. "Also, your goat," he added.

The door at the end of the hallway swung open. Waiting before a green flag sat Ashammi, his face bared. Normally in these videos, Brett knew, the terrorists liked to swath their faces in black scarves to prevent identification. For the jihad video of a major American general, Ashammi wanted to take personal credit. Yusuf and his buddy deposited Brett next to Ashammi, on his knees.

"General," said Ashammi, looking down at Brett, "I hope your accommodations were not too primitive. I must say, you look somewhat the worse for wear."

"No," said Brett, glancing at Yusuf. "Nothing I couldn't handle."

"Ah, ever the tough American. Well, the good news is that your suffering will not last much longer."

"Yours either, I'd bet," said Brett.

"But I will not suffer," Ashammi said placidly. "Remember, I serve Allah, and no matter what happens, he will be with me."

"I only hope he's with all the different pieces of you after we nail your ass with a Hellfire missile."

"Any plans I don't know about, General?" Ashammi smiled.

Brett smiled back. "Maybe. Maybe not. You'll find out soon enough."

Ashammi took a long ceremonial dagger from his robes. "General, I'm sorry to have to get down to business. I've enjoyed our conversations. But I will admit that I will enjoy killing you more, given how much Muslim blood you have on your hands. Now, I am afraid we don't have much time. Let me be perfectly clear. You will cooperate. If you say anything we do not wish you to say, I will personally cut off your testicles. If you do anything we do not wish you to do, I will cut off your testicles, and then I will slash your throat after letting you bleed."

Brett grunted. "You make a convincing argument."

"I have to admit, I am somewhat surprised at your reasonableness."

"I'm already going to get killed, I assume. No reason to lose my balls in the bargain."

"Very wise. All right, Hassan, record."

A young man, no more than seventeen, hit the record button on the digital Canon. The red light flashed. Ashammi began to speak.

When the taping was all over, Ashammi thanked Brett for his cooperativeness. Then he offered him a copy of the Koran. Brett turned it down and told Ashammi to stuff it up his ass. Ashammi smiled, then gestured to his henchmen to take Brett back to his cell.

Brett lay back against the stone wall on his thin mattress, thinking of Ellen. He tried to remember her face, the softness of her eyes; he tried to recall the feel of her body, every line of it silhouetted. He found himself crying. For himself, just a bit. Mostly for her. For the child they had never been able to have.

Then, slowly, he did something he had not done for years: he got down on his knees and he prayed.

"Dear Lord," he whispered to the darkness, thick with the stench of feces and urine, oppressive with the smell of sweat, "I know I haven't spoken with You for a while. But I need you now. I may never forgive You for what you did to my Ellen, why You took our baby from us. They say You have a logic all Your own, and I reckon that's the case, since I sure as hell can't understand You or the things You do. I know I've tried to do the right thing as I see it, and I haven't broken too many of the lessons I learned in Sunday school.

"And You know better than anybody that I've never been one for prayer. I always thought that some people treat You like a gumball machine, like if they pray just the right way and say just the right things, that You'll give them what they want, when this whole world is about something bigger than what any of us want.

It's about what You want, and I do hope that I've done at least a few things the way You want them.

"But now I'm not praying for myself. I'm praying for Ellen. Because after this, she's gonna be alone, Lord, and I just want her to be happy. You took her children away from her. Maybe I took myself away from her. But however it worked out, now she'll be on her own. Please let her find someone else. Please let her be happy for once in her life. Please let my sweetheart go on with her life, let her understand what I've done and why I've done it. Thank You, Lord, in advance. Amen."

Brett closed his eyes and dropped into an uneasy sleep.

PRESIDENT PRESCOTT

WASHINGTON, DC

PRESIDENT PRESCOTT ALWAYS FELT A surge of power through his body when he sat in the Situation Room. This is where they had all made their biggest decisions. It's where Kennedy read teletype during the Cuban Missile Crisis. It's where President Barack Obama had sat, watching SEAL Team 6 take out Osama bin Laden. And this is where, Prescott knew, he'd be sitting—at the head of the table—while American special operations troops dispatched Ibrahim Ashammi.

Intelligence had recognized General Hawthorne's signal within minutes of its first airing on the Ashammi hostage video. Hawthorne had spoken the prewritten message from Ashammi just as Ashammi had written it, prompting a national debate on whether Hawthorne should have complied with the propaganda requirements of the world's leading terrorist. But intelligence kept the fact that Hawthorne *hadn't* complied under their hat. While the rest of the world had watched Hawthorne's mouth, intelligence had watched his *eyes*.

Hawthorne had been blinking in Morse code. It was an old trick, one Hawthorne must have picked up from Jeremiah Denton, a Vietnam War–era POW. Denton, forced to tape interviews by his North Vietnamese captors, had blinked out the message "T-O-R-T-U-R-E" repeatedly in Morse code, giving the first evidence that America's enemies in Vietnam weren't the hippie-loving flower power communists the campus leftists preached about.

The trick must have escaped Ashammi, intelligence figured—how would he know Morse code in the age of text messages and cell phones?—and Ashammi had put out the propaganda tape too eagerly to fully vet it. Hawthorne's message had been brief but definitive: "AIRSTRIKE NOW. 51.4231. 35.6961."

The message prompted a full-scale debate inside the White House. It raised too many questions. First, was Hawthorne's location correct? How would he know where he was, given that prisoners were typically blindfolded and kept in windowless rooms before their executions? If Hawthorne was wrong about the location in a heavily populated area of Tehran, the United States could end up with the blood of dozens on its hands, and an international mess almost impossible to clean up. They could blame it all on Iranian nuclear weapons, but after Iraq, the public wouldn't be buying.

Second, even if Hawthorne was right, could American aircraft breach Iranian airspace to take out Ashammi? A strike in a populated area would require too much pinpoint accuracy for a missile; military aircraft would have to be utilized. Such an action would surely have grave ramifications for international politics, including ongoing nuclear negotiations with the Iranian regime. It was unlikely that Iran's military would be able to take out an American warcraft, but there was the real possibility that the Iranians could get lucky. If that happened, the Prescott administration would have to explain not only to the world but to the American people how a regime he'd called "borderline friendly" had killed Americans in order to protect a terrorist mastermind sheltered on their soil. Furthermore, the Israelis were sitting around *waiting* to strike Iran's nuclear facilities. With the Americans taking action on Iranian soil, they could take advantage of the situation to double up with a brief bombing campaign, sinking any possibility of a nuclear deal.

Third, what was the political upside? This third question was never spoken among the military brass, of course, but it was the question that drew the most attention from Prescott's inner circle. On the one hand, taking out Ashammi would be not only a great foreign policy triumph, but it would, in one shot, deflate accusations that Mark Prescott was too much of a coward to stand up to America's enemies. On the other hand, if Ashammi lived and the American public never found out about Hawthorne's encrypted message, he'd be seen as a bumbler, a Jimmy Carter on a mission to save hostages. They could still nail Ashammi later—he would just be shadowed until a more convenient time, perhaps when he traveled outside Iran. Then Prescott would give the order to kill him.

In fact, Prescott had been leaning in the direction of leaving things be, but two factors had decided him on action. First, Prescott wanted a taste of glory. He needed the domestic political support to ram through the Work Freedom Program. And it would be difficult for Congress to turn him down days after he had taken out the man responsible for the bombing of several American embassies. He already had his slogan written in his head: "Protecting America from Those Who Would Harm It, Abroad and at Home."

Second, some right-wing bloggers had caught onto Hawthorne's signal. Mostly, they were kooky survivalist types, the sorts of folks who posted conspiracy theories on message boards. But the CIA informed Prescott that such information, once it got out, could jeopardize any sort of attack. And if the information began to take hold, Prescott figured for himself, he'd be blamed for doing nothing. Already some of those nuts on Fox News had been making oblique references to the rumors.

But an airstrike was simply too risky.

And so he'd called on the CIA. It had now been four days since the tape; he knew it was possible that Ashammi had moved Hawthorne. He knew the operation would be near impossible. And unlike the bin Laden raid, this wouldn't be taking place at a quasi-remote estate. The operation would happen in the heart of Tehran, near one of its most prominent landmarks. It would have to be a perfect operation, with no unforeseen factors. His military advisors told him that the possibilities of success were far less than 25 percent.

He authorized it anyway. If they failed, he couldn't be blamed for trying, or if he could, he'd find a way to call it a well-intentioned mistake. If they succeeded, he'd have made the gutsiest call since Obama. Gutsier, even. What a hashtag that would make!

So now, he sat at the conference table in the Situation Room, surrounded by the members of his cabinet. The chairman of the Joint Chiefs, General Bill Collier, the only man in the room in uniform, bit his lip nervously. The rest of his cabinet leaned forward, watching the night-vision camerawork on the screen. The feed was choppy and slightly delayed, the audio rough and patchy.

On the screen, Prescott watched in fascination as the operatives approached the back door of a Tehran apartment building. They'd been flown over the border quietly, by helicopter; their journey through the desert had been followed every step of the way from the White House. After the initial group touched down, they'd separated, figuring that infiltration of the capital would be easier if they approached the city as individuals. The only hang-up had come when the truck carrying one of them had broken down on the road. That particular operative had been smuggled out of the country, his part of the operation scratched.

Now the CIA operatives, dressed in local garb, set a quick-burning charge on the outside of the ironwork door. It flared brightly, but in the alleyway, there was nobody to see it. One of the operatives gently nudged the door open with his foot. Before him spread a dark hallway.

"No lights," came an order.

"Check," whispered one of the men.

They crept down the hallway, visibility no greater than ten feet ahead. To the sides ran door after door. A light flashed on behind one of the doors; an old woman suddenly thrust it open. One of the operatives sprang forward, grabbing the handle and easing it shut. "Police," he bellowed in Farsi, hoping the rest of the apartment dwellers would hear him. "Stay in your home." She nodded, terrified, and let the lock click home. In Tehran, questioning the police would have been foolhardy.

The operative waved the team forward.

At the end of the hallway was another door, heavier than the normal apartment doors. The operatives placed another charge, let it burn through. When it finished, they nudged the door open with their weapons. Behind the door, a cement staircase led down, the angle steep, the stairs narrow. The men would have to move single file.

"Death trap," muttered the chairman of the Joint Chiefs.

"Shut up," shot back Prescott.

"No lights," the commander reiterated.

"Check," said the operative running point.

The men moved forward, slowly, taking the slimy steps carefully. Then, down the hall, they heard screaming. In English. Footsteps, charging directly at them. The operatives shouldered their weapons, aiming down into the darkness.

"What the fuck is this," one of the operatives swore softly.

Then he saw.

The cracked cement tore into the soles of Brett's feet, gashing them, but Brett hardly felt it—he hadn't moved this fast since high school football. "*GET THE FUCK OUT OF HERE!*" he screamed at the Americans standing twenty yards above him on the stairs. "*THEY KNOW YOU'RE HERE! GET OUT!*"

He heard the sound of a couple of safeties being switched off—and then he saw the guns pointed directly at him. "*RUN, YOU MORONS!*" he shouted. The operatives were blocking the stairs, standing there idiotically. Then again, he had time to think, he was covered with blood from head to toe.

He didn't have time to explain the blood, however. He didn't have time to explain the bodies of Yusuf and his fellow thug lying a hundred feet beneath them, several stories into the earth. He didn't have time to explain how he'd heard Ashammi walk down the hallway two days before—heard his cultivated Arabic recede along the hallway, fade in the distance, heard Ashammi inform Yusuf to guard the American pig general at all costs, not to let anyone in, that Allah would reward him for his good work.

He'd waited. He'd bided his time. For forty-eight hours, he had kept himself awake, waiting to hear any sign that Ashammi had stayed at the site. He'd cursed Prescott—the president had failed him again, ignored his request for an airstrike, let Ashammi escape thanks to dithering and gutlessness. Then, he'd begun banging on his door.

"Yusuf!" he yelled in Farsi. "Yusuf! Your pig mother whore is lying with the Zionists tonight. I shit on Mohammed's beard!"

When that tirade resulted in nothing more than some angry grunts from Yusuf, Brett turned it up a notch. His Farsi was limited, but as he knew that for every language, the first words to learn were the most colorful curse words available. Now he unleashed them over and over again.

Yusuf threw open the door, snarling.

And Brett hit him directly in the face with four days' worth of shit and piss. It hit him right in the eyes. Before he could wipe away the waste, Brett punched him in the belly with one hand, grasping for Yusuf's knife with the broken arm. The pain made him gasp.

Yusuf went crashing into the hallway, slamming his head on the stone wall. He bellowed in rage; his companion, the seventeen-year-old cameraman, came running down the hall, an aged Kalashnikov in his hands. Brett grabbed Yusuf with both hands, clenching his jaw, and spun him around like a tackling dummy. Yusuf spun, stumbled, regained his equilibrium, and then charged. Brett sidestepped him, deflected a clumsily thrown haymaker, and then stepped behind him and slit his throat.

Yusuf spluttered, his blood jetting from his neck in great bursts. Brett pulled his head back, opening the wound wider. As he did, the seventeen-year-old appeared in the doorway, shouting in Farsi. He opened fire just as Brett charged him, using Yusuf's still-upright body as a battering ram. He threw the giant Persian at the teenager, hearing the bullets thunk deep into Yusuf's flesh. Yusuf, clasping at his throat, tumbled forward, landing directly on his friend in the hallway. Before the boy could push Yusuf off, Brett jumped on top of Yusuf's corpse, pinning the boy to the ground.

Then, without hesitating, he stabbed the boy through the eye.

When he looked up, he saw the explosives packed along the ceiling.

Then he noticed a camera, operated by remote, in the corner of the hallway. It hadn't been there during his initial trip for the hostage videotaping. Now, however, it was, and it was moving.

Finally, he heard a voice from above, yelling in Farsi: "Police. Stay in your home." The Farsi had a slight American accent.

He pushed himself to his feet and sprinted, lungs screaming for air, down the hallway.

"*RUN, YOU MORONS!*" he shouted. When the operatives finally recognized General Brett Hawthorne, dressed in an orange jumpsuit and covered with blood, they turned and ran. They smashed their way down the hallway—no time for discretion now—as the basement exploded, rocking the ground beneath them. Two of the men fell; Brett vaulted them, yelling at them to get up, grabbing one by his bulletproof vest and virtually throwing him down the hallway with his good hand. Civilians' heads popped out into the hallway as the explosion registered; Brett looked over his shoulder to see them engulfed in the flame that poured down the hallway like water through a flooding pipeline. A blast of heat rocketed him through the door at the end of the hallway. The other operatives sprinted ahead of him; one man behind him screamed inhumanly as the fire caught him.

Brett turned back, pushed the man down into the dust, smelling his sizzling flesh as he tried to put out the flames. The man's screams finally stopped as he fell unconscious. One of the other operatives grabbed the burning man by one arm; Brett grabbed the other. Together, they ran down the alleyway into the darkness.

In the Situation Room, Mark Prescott sat back in satisfaction, wiping his forehead with a handkerchief, as the feed cut out.

Sparse clapping broke out in the room. The chairman of the Joint Chiefs turned to him, eyes wide. "They knew we were coming, Mr. President," he said. "They knew we were coming."

"What do you mean?" Prescott asked.

"The explosion. And then how do you think our guys got out of there so easily afterward? The Iranians must have known Ashammi was there. They've been housing him. They just didn't want to fight us directly, that's all. They were expecting Ashammi's thugs to take our guys out. When that didn't happen, they backed off."

"So the hell what?" Prescott replied.

"So that means that they're ahead of us. Way ahead of us."

"You worry too much, General. They failed." Prescott smiled the million-watt smile. "General, why don't you take the night off. We just rescued one of America's top generals with no casualties. We'll deal with all the rest tomorrow." He winked. "Except, of course, for the press conference. We'll do that just as soon as our boys are in Jordanian airspace."

ELLEN

AUSTIN, TEXAS

BRETT WAS ALIVE.

Brett was alive, and coming home to her. Ellen found the tears welling up in her eyes as she watched President Mark Prescott stare unwaveringly into the camera, announcing the rescue. He'd called her personally just a few minutes beforehand to let her know that Brett was safe. The conversation had been brief; he'd expected praise and thanks, and she dutifully gave it to him. She couldn't stand the man, of course, after what he'd done to Brett— elevating him, then betraying him, sending him thousands of miles into the teeth of danger to keep him away from the television anchors—but he'd made the right call.

Brett was coming home.

She repeated the thought in her head on a loop. Her stomach clutched tightly inside, a combination of joy and nervousness more profound than she'd felt on the day of her wedding. She realized that she hadn't seen her husband for a year. That she'd given up on ever seeing him again.

She turned up the volume on the television.

"...and we never leave our men and women behind," Prescott said confidently into camera. "General Brett Hawthorne has a heroic tale to tell, and he will tell it as soon as he arrives back in the United States and has time to recover with his beautiful wife, Ellen. But he, like our other heroes, deserved to come home."

The anxiety in Ellen's stomach turned to indignation. It wasn't enough for the president to make political hay off her husband's rescue after abandoning him in Afghanistan. Now he'd turn Brett's homecoming into a case for widespread troop withdrawals. She should have figured that would be the next shoe to drop.

And sure enough, Prescott jumped into that case with both feet. "I vowed on the day I became president that I would bring our troops home, that I would end wars of aggression we have fought halfway around the world," he said, using language stronger than he had ever used. Of course, he could afford to, after this public relations triumph. "And now, I will make good on that promise. Brett Hawthorne's rescue marks the beginning of the final phase of my plan to bring every American home from Afghanistan. Welcome home, General. And may God bless you and your wife and all the men and women of our armed forces serving in harm's way. And may God bless the United States of America."

Ellen angrily switched off the television. Then she leaned back on her couch and closed her eyes.

The phone rang. Ellen hastily checked her bedside clock—it read 7:56 a.m. She'd overslept; she'd taken a sleeping pill to calm herself down after the president's speech. Bubba had given her the morning off. "Hell, you deserve it," he'd said, "even if that husband of yours did get himself caught."

The determinedly cheery ring continued. She leaned over, picked up.

"Ellen Hawthorne," she said groggily into the phone.

"It's me, baby."

Involuntarily, tears sprang to her eyes. "Oh, God, you're all right. Brett…"

"We don't have time, baby. I'm here, I'm fine. I can't tell you where I am right now for security reasons—we're not in American airspace yet—but I need you to call Bill."

She immediately snapped to attention. Brett didn't need the loving wife right now—he needed the partner. She'd put on that hat so many times, it sprang to her without delay. "What's going on?"

"I need you to conference in Bill. He'll know."

"Why can't you call him directly?"

"I can't explain."

"I'm your only call? They're monitoring it?"

"You got it."

She scrolled through her cell phone until she came to the name: Bill Collier. She dialed. On the first ring, General Collier picked up. "This is Bill."

"Bill, this is Ellen. I've got Brett on the other line. I need to conference you in."

"Do it."

She put them on the party line. "Okay," she said, "we're all together."

"Thanks, babe," said Brett.

"Glad to hear you alive and kicking, kid," said Collier. "Thought you'd bitten it that time."

"Bill, I need you to get your boys on something. I need them to find a known associate of Ashammi's. Name's Mohammed."

"Well, why don't you give me something tougher to do? Like find a specific Mexican named Juan?"

"He's coming to the United States. He's about five foot nine, one forty. Skinny, maybe seventeen years old. Blue eyes, angular face, sharp, big nose. Get your boys on it. There's not much time."

"You got it, Brett." General Collier hung up.

"Are you okay, honey?" Ellen asked, after she knew Collier had clicked off the line.

She could hear him sigh audibly. "I don't know, sweetheart. I don't know what I'm doing here, why I'm doing it. What they did to my guys in Afghanistan . . ."

"I know, sweetheart, I know."

"Ellen, I wasn't supposed to live. That wasn't the message I gave. I blinked 'AIRSTRIKE.' Not tactical mission. Not rescue. Airstrike."

"But sweetheart, you're alive. You're coming home. I know you feel guilty. I know you never meant to leave your men behind. But you alive is better than you dead."

"Me alive isn't better than Ashammi dead. He was there, Ellen. He was *there*. I gave them the location; I knew they'd have time to take the shot. But Prescott, damn him, didn't have the balls. He just didn't. And now Ashammi's out there, planning. He's smart, Ellen, smart as hell, and he's steps ahead of us. We were lucky to get out of there alive. If it hadn't been for a stupid thug named Yusuf, we'd all be dead, and Prescott would have an international incident on his hands anyway, dead Americans and their body parts spread all over Tehran. Damn the man. *Damn him.*"

She found tears in her eyes again. Her man, her strong, unwavering man, so ready to die. "But you're coming home, sweetheart. You're coming home." On the other end of the phone, she could hear her husband exhale.

"You're right," he said slowly. "I'm coming home."

"Take a bullet for you, babe," she said.

"Take a bullet for you, sweetheart."

The line clicked dead.

One minute and twenty-nine seconds later, Bill Collier received a call from his wife, Jennifer. He let it go to voice mail. He was busy tracking down a man named Mohammed with ties to Ibrahim Ashammi.

The first phone call Ellen received came from Bubba. He told her to turn on the television. When she did, she saw the George Washington Bridge tilting in slow motion, cars falling into the Hudson. She saw the close-up helicopter footage of women and children screaming in their vehicles as the two-level bridge collapsed in on itself. She saw anchors weeping openly, real-time footage of relatives taping "HAVE YOU SEEN" posters to a makeshift bulletin board at the new World Trade Center. She saw President Prescott vow to track down the perpetrators of the attack, announce that America needed to pull together, despite its differences, announce that he would be mobilizing National Guard troops across the nation to travel to New York City for rescue and cleanup. She sat glued to the television for two hours.

Then she heard a knock at her door. When she opened it, Bubba was standing there. His face looked gaunt, ashen. She ushered him into the living room, where he settled his bulk onto her leather couch.

"I got a call from Prescott," he said. "He wants our boys out there ASAP."

"I know. I saw it on the news."

"I won't send them, Ellen."

She shuddered involuntarily. "You know by law that you have to. The National Guard can be mobilized by the president once a national emergency has been declared."

"Under Posse Comitatus, that isn't totally clear. But this ain't about law anymore, Ellen. It hasn't been for a long time. We pull our troops off that border, and I'll have more dead ranchers on my hands, more children floating up in that river. I don't have the stomach for that."

"There's another river with dead kids in it, Bubba," Ellen said.

He shot her a hard look. "You think I don't know that? I've seen the footage, too. And I'm damn sorry about it. But I'm not governor of New York. I'm governor of the Republic of Texas, and my first duty is to this state. We give up those troops, we might as well let Prescott open the border officially to the cartels and the smugglers. They're the only thing standing between us and a full-scale invasion."

"The invasion is slow motion. That situation in New York isn't."

He exhaled heavily. "I know that, too. But I just don't trust Prescott. Once he mobilizes the National Guard on behalf of the feds, he can put them wherever he wants—and he can put them where I can't order them to do a damn thing. Listen, Ellen, I'm not here to argue. I'm here to plan. And let me tell you, girl, that I'm doing this one way or another. If you can't commit to helping me, I'll find someone who will. There won't be any hard feelings." He paused. "But if you're with me, Ellen, if we can stand together, we can get through this."

She glanced at the television. The rescue crew was pulling another body from the water—a young girl wearing a Disneyland sweatshirt. It was footage, Ellen knew from 9/11, that they'd only show today, during live coverage—then the psychiatrists would explain to the network brass that showing such images was "triggering," and the pictures would disappear to spare the sensitivities of the American viewer. The scrolling chyron underneath the picture flashed quotes from Prescott's speech: "PRESIDENT:

WE WILL STAND TOGETHER...PRESIDENT CALLS UP NATIONAL GUARD...PRESIDENT TO REDEPLOY TROOPS TO NEW YORK AS THEY ARRIVE FROM WAR ZONES ABROAD...PRESIDENT VOWS TO 'TRACK DOWN THE PERPETRATORS'..."

Bubba said, "Ellen, it could get this bad for everyone down here, too. You've seen Prescott. You know him. That's why we have to protect ourselves."

"And what will Prescott do to us if we turn him down?"

"I know what he won't do," Bubba answered. Ellen lifted an eyebrow. "He won't send the National Guard."

Ellen shook her head. "I need to think about this, Bubba."

"Don't take too much time. I'm going to make this move, Ellen. You've stood with me the whole way, down the line. But if you can't be with me this time, I'll need your resignation on my desk this afternoon. There's just no time left."

SOLEDAD

MINOT, NORTH DAKOTA

THEY'D MADE THEIR WAY TO the farm gradually. At first, there were only a few—friends and family of the militia members, an agglomeration of survivalists and nuts. *I don't belong here*, Soledad thought. Then she realized that they were here because of her.

Minot, North Dakota, lay near the banks of the Souris River, a midsized town of forty thousand just south of the Canadian border. It was truly the middle of nowhere, Soledad thought. They'd moved north, then north, then north some more, out of the populated areas, out where it would take a lot of manpower to track them down. They'd nearly been tracked down in California; the authorities still thought they were there, having originally believed, mistakenly, that they'd been burned during the fire at the ranch. By the time investigators caught onto the fact that they were still alive, they were in Idaho. Every few days, they moved.

Until they reached Minot. In Minot, Aiden had allies and friends. His parents had come from there before moving south, and he still had a pack of relatives unafraid to lend him a covert helping hand. It wasn't like the FBI had a heavy presence in the area, and Aiden figured that everybody up here pretty much kept their mouth shut as much as possible. "Neighborly," Aiden had called it.

The only major employer in the area was the US Air Force base they'd all need to avoid, although since the attack, the base had been pretty much abandoned, with all the National Guard being called to New York for cleanup. The nearby turnoffs were all smaller towns, many of less than a thousand people. The land was relatively treeless, but Aiden had managed to find a more heavily wooded area for the group to hunker down; there had been an abandoned barn and a decent-sized cabin he'd rented in cash from a distant cousin under the table.

And there, the acolytes had begun to arrive. The first were men who had approached Aiden's family about finding help during the big call-up. They were mostly local boys, men who didn't want to be sent to New York for an indeterminate length of time, who had joined the National Guard mainly out of state pride and a feeling of local duty. Some were cowards; those, Aiden spotted and turned away. But some, he thought, could be useful.

Aiden had a few rules about the new recruits. No married men—they had too many ties that could be exploited by the government if their identities were uncovered. No cell phones— the government's surveillance programs were far too sophisticated to allow uncontrolled transmission. No Internet, for the same reason. And no leaving the base: a random spot check by a local cop could bring the entire weight of the federal government down on them, even if the feds were currently busy cleaning up the atrocity in New York. That meant that the group was immobile, in constant need of supplies.

Nonetheless, in days, the group had grown from the handful of original militiamen into a small force of nearly forty. Soledad had gotten to know each of them. She had a gift for connecting with people, the same gift that had made her a staple of the evening news coverage, and she was truly interested in all of them. It flattered most of them. And all of them were grateful for a place to go.

Aiden clapped his hands together, trying to warm them. Another freezing day in paradise.

They'd settled into a kind of routine. Every morning, Aiden would check the barn door, make sure that nobody had been snooping around, make sure that none of the vehicles had been moved. The early snow had been their ally: he could see by footprints who had been where. Next, he'd take the truck down to the road, see if he could spot any traffic coming or going, anybody snooping. He'd put together a little task force to walk the perimeter of the property and stand shifts during the day. Aiden wasn't taking chances.

After ensuring that the posse was alone, Aiden would take the truck into town. He'd pick up supplies with the cash the posse had brought with them. They were beginning to run short on money; Aiden figured that sooner or later, they'd have to begin sending in members to make withdrawals, a risky business at best. A disproportionate number of cash withdrawals would certainly raise red flags in the middle of nowhere. He'd been trying to come up with alternatives, but other than robbing banks, he couldn't think of a quick or easy solution.

After buying groceries for the forty or so men, he'd head over to the bar. Aiden wasn't a drinker, but he'd buy himself a beer and nurse it, sitting in back, watching the television screen hanging next to the deer's head over the liquor bottles. A week before, he'd arrived to find the bar closed up—an oddity on a weekday. At first he'd been suspicious that the authorities had found them, that someone would follow him from the bar back to the farm. But after driving a mile in the wrong direction, nobody in sight, he'd realized something else was going on. He'd flipped on the car radio and heard about New York. Aiden wasn't much of a praying man—he couldn't stand his Catholic school growing up, the nuns with their dull black shoes and brittle faces and yardsticks—but when he got back to the farm, he'd lit a candle. So had Soledad. Together with the men, they'd prayed.

Today, the bar was open. Aiden made his way inside, nodded to the bartender, and took his usual seat in the shadows, watching the television. More coverage of New York, of course, where authorities were still dredging the river for bodies. National Guard troops were pouring into New York and New Jersey, filling up all the available communities, straining capacity. The city had virtually shut down. The stock market had been closed ever since the attack. Curfew was still in place. The roads were heavily policed, travel heavily restricted.

The foreign policy experts were blaming Ibrahim Ashammi for the attack, but he'd stayed strangely silent. Normally, Ashammi couldn't wait to rush to a camera, and with an attack of this magnitude, most of the commentators had expected a big victory speech from the terrorist mastermind. Around the Muslim world, however, rallies sprang up celebrating the attacks: Palestinians in Gaza dancing and cheering, handing out candies; Muslim Brotherhood operatives in Egypt using the operation as a trigger for their own attacks on the US embassy; the Iranian mullahs leading vast crowds in chants of "Death to America," even as the president of Iran shed crocodile tears over American losses while simultaneously suggesting that America could not avoid terror if it continued to support the Zionist regime.

Aiden found himself enraged. These were the enemies. Not ranchers trying to make a living in California or pinstriped Wall Street muckety-mucks with private jets or Christian bakers who didn't want to bake a cake for a gay wedding. These monsters. These people who wanted to kill the decent and indecent alike, who didn't care what happened to the babies they were still finding washing up on the banks of the Hudson.

The bottle in Aiden's hand shattered. He'd been gripping it tightly in his fist without noticing it; a deep gash ran down the meat of his palm. He walked to the bar and asked the bartender for a towel, stanched the flow of blood with it. Then he motioned up at the screen. "Hey, buddy, is there anything else on? How about something a little less depressing." The bartender shrugged, tossed him the remote. Aiden began flipping channels.

When he hit MSNBC, he stopped. They weren't covering the cleanup at the Hudson or the investigation into the terror attack. Their cameras were focused on the streets of Detroit. Specifically, one of their reporters stood outside the Detroit detention center.

"This could get out of control," the reporter said, a hopeful gleam unmistakably shining in his eye. "This morning, a leader of the uprising, one Levon Williams, posted a list of demands on the website of the Fight Against Injustice and Racism movement, what they're calling the FAIR movement. Here's what we know about Levon Williams. He's a graduate of the University of Michigan with a degree in African-American Studies. No police record. Model citizen, by all accounts, owns a barbershop on Eight Mile Road. According to the public interviews he's done, he came back to the community in an effort to bring prosperity home.

"The shooting of Kendrick Malone prompted him to action, he says."

The footage cut to a shot of Levon on set with an MSNBC anchor, some carefully manicured white guy with 1950s-style black-rimmed glasses. "We have seen injustice stacked upon injustice," Levon said slowly. "Too many injustices to count. Kendrick Malone is just another victim in a long line of victims stretching back to the first black men and women stuffed into cargo holds to be sent to die on plantations in this country. We're not going to back down this time. We're not going to let this wave of brutality go unchallenged. We demand justice for Kendrick Malone and all the other Kendrick Malones who have died and all the other Kendrick Malones we want to keep from dying. Justice for Kendrick."

The anchor pondered this statement. "And what if Officer Ricky O'Sullivan is not prosecuted?"

Levon said, "The people demand justice. And the people will receive justice."

MSNBC cut back to its reporter on the ground. "Levon Williams, leader of the FAIR movement. Well, today, the FAIR movement listed its demands: immediate trial of Ricky O'Sullivan. A jury of his peers from the Detroit area—no transfer of trial to a more sympathetic venue. More equity in the economic system of Detroit and surrounding areas. A complete makeover of the police force, including the firing of the police chief, with officers drawn from the local community, and an end to what they call the 'occupation' directed against people of color."

Now another anchor, female, appeared from the MSNBC studios on split-screen with the reporter. "Gil, have they said what they will do if their demands are not met?"

The reporter gestured to a sign in the crowd: "RICKY O'SULLIVAN, DEAD OR ALIVE." Then he said, "If the feeling I'm getting from the crowd is any indicator, it could get very ugly very quickly."

Soledad sat on the porch of the cabin, watching the snow fall. She had a blanket wrapped around her; she thought she probably looked like her ancestors had, without any modern conveniences, garbed in an old quilt, breathing steam into the air. In her hands, she held a cup of tea, sipping it every so often, reading yesterday's newspaper. She was mildly relieved to see that she'd been knocked completely out of the newspaper for the first time since the conflagration in California.

The door to the cabin opened behind her. She turned to see Ezekiel Pope—grizzled, older than the other recruits. He was black, came from Los Angeles. Their California background had been their point of connection. He'd joined up with the air force decades ago, and he'd been just about ready to quit thanks to the military cutbacks: he'd never rise higher than lieutenant colonel. He'd been called into his superior's office just after the New York attack, told to round up his men and get ready to ship out to New York.

For some reason, he'd come to Soledad instead.

Aiden said he hadn't given a reason for deserting. But he said that Ezekiel was trustworthy. Soledad had no option but to trust Aiden's judgment.

Ezekiel looked over the snow falling silently into itself. He wore heavy work gloves on his hands, and an M4 slung over his shoulder, a maroon scarf around his neck. Soledad gestured at the gun. "What's that for?"

"We're gearing up."

"Gearing up for what?"

Ezekiel laughed. "Well, you tell us. After all, you're the Terrorist Mama. That's what they're calling you now, you know. Ever since the escape."

She felt sick to her stomach. She'd wanted to feed her workers, water her animals. That was it. Opening up the waterway had just been necessity. She hadn't wanted anyone hurt or killed. "I'm no terrorist," she said.

Ezekiel spat into the snow. It steamed, hissed out. "Last time I checked, didn't matter much what you had to say about it. They'll drone you just the same. I know. I worked for them." He stood, turned to walk into the house. Then he turned back to her. "Listen, Soledad. You can either hide out and hole up and wait for them to turn you into a pile of guts, or you can figure out what comes next."

"Sounds like you have some ideas about what *should* come next."

He laughed. "I always do. That's why they never made me bird colonel."

"What's your plan?"

"I always say the best defense is a good offense. So does Clausewitz. When your force is small, concentrate it and hit them where they're weak."

"Who are 'they'?"

"The same people who shut down your farm. The same people who attacked you."

"Those people are Americans."

"It isn't American to do those things. America means more than being born here. It means believing certain things."

"So we should shoot those who disagree?"

"Only if they shoot first."

"I don't want more blood," she said.

"Then you went into the wrong business, woman. Blood's about all that's guaranteed from here on in. And you can't stay here forever. You've got to keep moving. Move or die." The screen door whispered closed behind him.

LEVON

DETROIT, MICHIGAN

LEVON COULDN'T BELIEVE WHAT HE was hearing.

Reverend Jim Crawford sat there, in the conference room of the MGM Grand—the room had already been scanned for bugs and been found clean—in his expensive suit, explaining why he thought Levon should get his people off the street. Now.

Levon had seen Big Jim's press conference with the mayor the previous week. The mayor, still sporting a bandage over his gashed forehead, had thanked Big Jim profusely for stopping the violence, for cutting short the possibility of a riot. Big Jim grinned the high-wattage grin, and told the mayor that he did so knowing that the two of them could work together to fix the deeper problems plaguing the city. Problems of inequity, he said. Problems of racial justice. Mayor Burns nodded along, knowing that he had no choice—he could use the photo op with the civil rights icon in his reelection campaign.

Newsweek put Big Jim on its cover. The headline: "THE PEACEMAKER." The photo framed his head with a halo. In the piece, Big Jim said that Detroit would have to pursue a complete makeover of its obviously racist police department. That meant community policing in the truest sense: drawing police officers from the community itself. That didn't mean hiring officers from outside, the way they'd hired Ricky O'Sullivan. It didn't even mean hiring black cops from outside the city and forcing them to live in the city to get to know the people they protected. It meant hiring longtime residents of the city, even people with backgrounds. "America," said Big Jim, "is the land of second chances. You want to know why our community doesn't trust the police? They don't trust the police because to them, the police are strangers, and the other way around. And it takes more than living in the community a few months to earn trust.

"I'll tell you what," he told the *Newsweek* reporter. "It takes more than even being a good policeman. It means having *been through* what these folks have *been through*. It means knowing that just because somebody got sent up to prison for some stupid drug crime that wouldn't have gotten a white boy six months in the can, that doesn't mean their life should be over. It means understanding that there is a legacy of racism in this country, and that the police have historically been the arm of the racist establishment. That's stuff you can only know if you've lived it."

The reporter asked, "Are you saying that everybody on the force must be black?"

"No," replied Big Jim. "I'm saying that everybody has to have the right kind of *experience*. And if that means being black, that means being black."

The interview had caused an uproar. They'd even quoted Levon in it, asking him what he thought of Big Jim's leadership. Levon told them that without Big Jim, the whole street would have gone up in flames. "Big Jim," he told them, "is standing up for us. So long as he does, and so long as we get justice, we can make this city whole again."

Now, however, Levon regretted he'd ever laid eyes on Big Jim. He'd been foolish to have trusted the man; he'd figured he could always outplay him. Everybody thought Big Jim was past his prime, that he'd run his course. After a youth of rabble-rousing and race-baiting, he'd entered the mainstream. He'd been invited to the White House. He'd appear from time to time outside some big chain store, accusing them of institutional racism, then pick up a large donation for his action group and disappear again. Jim Crawford, Levon had thought, could be handled.

Clearly not.

"Listen, Levon," Big Jim said, leaning back in his leather chair. "We've done a lot of good here. Justice Department will come in, force the PD to engage in some systemic change. The DA will probably indict O'Sullivan. You've got the mayor on the run—just keep on top of him, and he'll do most of what you ask for. You're gonna be big in this city. One day you'll be able to get what you want out of these people, you play the cards right."

Levon just stared at him. "So that's it?"

"Yeah, that's it."

"And what was I? The sucker?"

"No. You were the bad cop. And I was the good cop. That's how the game is played. You're too young to remember Marion Barry. Now *that* was a professional. Played the game to perfection, man. He told the Black Panthers that they ought to make a little trouble in town. Then he played the moderate, told the white folks that he could calm them down if they just signed a few checks. One time he told me, 'I know for a fact that white people get scared of the Panthers, and they might give money to somebody a little more moderate.' You, Levon, are the new Panthers. And I'm the moderate."

"So what did you get out of the deal? A big donation to the action fund?"

The reverend grimaced. "What's so wrong with that? Every dollar in is a dollar we can use to fight the system. And don't worry. Everybody has to play bad cop sometimes. I did it back in the day. Now it's your turn."

Levon hesitated. Then he slowly clenched his fist. "And what if there's no room for good cop? What if the time for the good cop is over?"

Big Jim actually laughed. "You think you're the first one ever to feel that way, don't you? Boy, you don't know shit. This ain't slavery. This ain't Jim Crow. This is just the ghetto. I've seen 'em all over, and I'll tell you what: burning the ghetto down doesn't do anything but make room for people like me to clean up. You'll know that some day."

Levon went quiet. Then, after a long pause, he spoke. "Reverend, opportunities like this come along once in a lifetime."

"No, boy, they come along once every three weeks or so. I know. I've mapped it out." He stood, then put his heavy hand on Levon's shoulder. "Now, Levon, if you think I'm gonna leave you hanging like this, that's where you're wrong. See, I've got a proposition. Here's what I'm gonna propose. The mayor needs a community group to give him the green light for his activities, lend him political cover. I'm not going to be in town long enough to carry that forward. But you can. You'll be a big man in this city, Levon. Go mainstream."

Levon stood up, peered down at Big Jim. "There's only one issue, Reverend. You said that the white cop *might* be indicted. What if he isn't?"

Big Jim looked straight at Levon. "Well, that's why we've got a system, right? Get your boys off the street. They're making us look bad."

Levon shook his head. "System. Sorry, Reverend. Even if I wanted to, I couldn't get my boys off the street. And I'm sorry if they're making *you* look bad. See, it turns out, I have some bad cops, too."

Big Jim grit his teeth. "Fast learner, kid. Fast learner." He looked at his watch. "I've got a meeting with the mayor."

"I'll come along."

He shook his head. "No, kid, you won't. You'll do what you're told. Remember, you were nobody before I got here. And I can put you right back there with just a snap. After all, I'm the man who saved Detroit. You said so yourself. But don't worry. You've got spunk. I'll keep you in the loop, give you a call when we're done."

But he didn't.

As the hours passed, Levon began pacing the hotel conference room. Then he called one of his deputies, took the elevator down to the parking lot, got in his car, and headed back to the barbershop.

It was already packed when he pulled up. In the shop sat a slightly overweight black woman. Regina Malone clutched a handkerchief to her face; her heavy makeup was streaked with tears. She looked like she hadn't stopped crying since she found out about her son, Kendrick, and the truth was, she hadn't. Kendrick had been her youngest boy, a good boy, she told the media, shot to death because of police racism. The president had called her, offered his condolences, told her he'd stop at nothing to get to the bottom of the case.

The Wayne County prosecutor hadn't been as forthcoming. She'd been elected through a fluke—the entire government in Wayne County sprang from the Democratic Party, but Kim Donahue had lucked into her job, running at the same time that the Democratic candidate stumbled into jail over a sex and corruption scandal. She'd effectively been appointed to office with no opposition. A graduate of the University of Michigan Law School, Donahue had thrown her hat into the ring almost as a lark—there was no other reason for a white Republican to run for county prosecutor in a 52 percent black district, where Democrats outnumbered Republicans by near-Cuban-election margins. When she found herself in office, she'd been faced with a massive backlog of unresolved cases, including murder and rape cases. She'd quickly developed a close relationship with the beleaguered police department.

Now the prosecution of Ricky O'Sullivan lay in Kim Donahue's hands.

Regina Malone, standing next to Big Jim, had called a press conference at which she asked Donahue to recuse herself, given her ties to the police department. Donahue had refused, stating that she would ensure that justice was served, and that if anyone implied her skin color meant she couldn't be objective, they were racist. The line made national headlines, turned Kim Donahue into one of the most polarizing political figures in America.

Levon got out of his car, and Regina Malone clutched at his arm like a drowning woman clutching at a life jacket. "Levon, you gotta see this." She dragged him, her grip iron, into the barbershop, where the crowd had gathered around the lone flat-screen television in the place.

There, on the television, stood Kim Donahue. The chyron read: "DA ANNOUNCES NO CHARGES AGAINST POLICE OFFICER RICKY O'SULLIVAN." She looked directly into the camera, her blonde hair shining softly in the sun. Levon thought he detected a hint of a smirk on her face. "No matter what the media may think, no matter the pressures brought to bear, I have only one agenda: the people's agenda. And that agenda is not the agenda of the mob. It is the agenda of justice under our state and federal constitutions. Ricky O'Sullivan was entitled to due process. The evidence does not support manslaughter; it does not support murder in the first or second degree. We all grieve with the Malone family. But we must not pile a miscarriage of justice on top of a terrible tragedy."

Levon grabbed the remote off the counter, hurled it at the screen. The screen cracked. "Bullshit. This is bullshit."

Through the cracked glass of the television, the picture shifted. Now, the mayor stood next to Big Jim. Mayor Burns spoke first. "We may not all agree with the decision of Prosecutor Donahue," he said. "I promise you that the Justice Department will engage in its own investigation. But we ask that everyone please remain calm, allow justice to take its course." Big Jim stood next to him, nodding at every word. Then Big Jim stepped to the microphone. "We will not stop here to ensure that justice is done. Rioting, looting, violence will not help anything. We heard your call, 'No justice, no peace,' and I join that call—let us have peace so that we may have justice."

The black female news anchor appeared in studio, well-coiffed and manicured, tears in her eyes: "Officer Ricky O'Sullivan is due to be released today from prison; the time and location of his release have not yet been given, due to safety concerns." Then, unable to hold herself back, she muttered, "Awful, just awful."

Levon turned off the television and turned to face the crowd in his barbershop. For the first time, he noticed the news cameras all around him. And he realized that, suddenly, he had the advantage: Big Jim was standing next to the mayor of the most racist city in America, and he was standing next to the black mother of a black child who had just been shot by a white cop—and that white cop had just been allowed to walk by a white DA.

The camera zoomed in on Levon. He forced himself to cry, just a tear; he looked up at the browning tiles of the ceiling. Then, he exhaled slowly and looked directly into the camera. "Enough dead children. It stops today." And he silently led the crowd from his barbershop, walking the long miles toward the criminal justice center, picking up stragglers, then groups, then dozens, then hundreds along the way, a sea of faces, a sea of enraged faces, all of them with the pain of centuries written on them, each burning with an ember that Levon fully intended to stoke into an open fire.

BRETT

NEW YORK CITY

BRETT SURVEYED THE DAMAGE FROM the top of a nearby parking lot. It stretched before him like a diorama: unreal, in miniature, too dramatic for life. Since the attacks, all commercial air travel had been shut down, thanks to warnings from the Department of Homeland Security. The terror chatter had actually elevated after the attack. DHS thought the airlines could be targeted again, given the focus on the destruction of the bridge.

Brett's homecoming hadn't been much of one. By the time he landed, his rescue, if you could call it that, had been blown off the front pages by the terror attack. His flight back to Texas had been canceled, and he'd been stashed at a local hotel, with guards on him at nearly all times—the president was obviously worried he'd talk to the media without handlers nearby. Ellen had hinted via phone that some big move was imminent in Texas from the governor, but he hadn't had time to focus on that: he'd been more focused on helping out Bill Collier. Collier's wife, Jennifer, had been on the bridge. They still hadn't dredged up her body.

The day after his arrival, Bill had met Brett at his hotel. He'd dismissed the security for a few minutes. Brett could see that his friend had aged a century in a day—his face looked craggy, his eyes sunken. Bill had been married to Jennifer for a long time. He'd also lost his daughter in the attack, an eight-year-old he'd called his Little Trooper.

But Bill Collier would have no time to grieve until the cleanup was handled. Bill told him that National Guard units from across the country had been activated, ordered to New York to assist with the national crisis. He told him that the president would use the opportunity to call for a massive spending package on infrastructure, urge further cuts to the military to "build up on the home front."

Then he told Brett that he'd be personally ordering him to New York City.

"The president won't like that," Brett had said.

"Tough. My patience for bullshit goes out the window after I watch them search on television for my daughter's body," said the chairman of the Joint Chiefs of Staff. "I'll make whatever excuses I have to make. I want to know who is responsible for this. And right now, you're my best lead. You're the only person who's seen this Mohammed. I think Ashammi's behind it. So does intelligence. He hasn't taken credit yet, but I want you to track down whoever it is you think you saw."

"You said it yourself: it's a needle in a haystack."

"We might have a lead. But I need your eyes on it. I'm sending you to New York on the next military flight. I'll make excuses to the president. But I'll need your word that you stay away from the media. That's the only thing Prescott cares about."

Brett nodded. Then, slowly, he said, "I'm sorry about your family, Bill."

Collier grimaced. "Yeah, me too," he said. "Me too. Now go get the pieces of shit who did this so I can bomb them back into the sixth century."

The next morning, Brett had flown to New York.

Now, looking at the damage, Brett punished himself for not having been able to warn intelligence sooner. If only he'd used the Morse code to tell them something was coming from Ashammi. If only he'd blinked the name Mohammed. In his heart, he knew it wouldn't have helped. America had blinded itself in the name of peace—and Brett knew that hope wouldn't buy peace anyway.

He turned his back on the Hudson, where the sunken bridge still lay slumbering under acres of water, the calm of the surface masking the graves of thousands of Americans. The American public had called the Iraq War too bloody, the Afghanistan War too costly; combined, America had lost fewer than seven thousand people. Now, on one day, they'd lost far more than that.

His cell phone rang. It was Collier. "Get over to JFK," he said. "They'll be waiting for you."

The airport felt like a mausoleum, completely empty, completely deserted, utterly quiet. The planes sat at their terminals like sleeping grasshoppers. Abandoned vehicles dotted the tarmac. Brett sat in a secure room, flanked by two members of the Port Authority security team. Before him, on a cheap plastic table, sat a laptop, spreadsheets of flight manifests open. Brett quickly narrowed down the location of the flights—there were obviously no direct flights from the Islamic Republic to New York. Most stopped in Frankfurt or Munich or Dubai. There was no guarantee Mohammed had flown into New York, either—he could have flown into Newark, or even Boston Logan or any nearby area airport.

After realizing that there were simply too many combinations of flights to check every itinerary and every manifest, Brett finally dispensed with the politically correct pleasantries. "Jim," he'd said to one of the officials, "I want access to the customs files."

"If you don't mind me asking, sir," murmured the official, "is there somebody we're looking for particularly?"

Brett said, "Yes. An Arabic-looking young man."

The official hemmed and hawed. "I'm uncomfortable with that, sir. That's racial profiling."

"You're not doing the profiling. I am."

"Well, now I'm a party to it."

Brett stared into his face. "I. Don't. Care. Just do it."

"Sir, it's against regulations, though."

"Look," Brett burst out, losing his patience, "I don't give a rat's ass at this point whether it's racial profiling or not. Maybe you're right. Maybe Mohammed is a light-skinned Norwegian woman or a Cherokee elder. Or maybe he's a Persian or Arabic-looking son of a bitch who hangs out with other Persian or Arabic-looking sons of bitches who look like Ibrahim Ashammi. If I end up being wrong, and he looks like Helen Mirren, feel free to tell *The New York Times* editorial board about it."

The official scurried out of the room. Brett turned back to the manifests. There would be hundreds, maybe thousands of possible leads, men who had flown from the Middle East through some midpoint in the days between Brett's capture and the bridge attack. With just a name, Mohammed, he wouldn't have enough.

He picked up his cell phone, tapped it against his wrist. Then he scrolled through his contacts. When he reached the name "Hassan Abdul," he dialed.

The café was virtually empty. That would have been odd on a normal day, but with the entire city under virtual military occupation, it somehow felt normal. Brett had been in war zones before, and this felt like a war zone. The smell of ash still hung over the city days later. Every so often, a military convoy would pass down Fifth Avenue, or the occasional ambulance, siren blaring. Brett had seen the real-time coverage of the September 11 attacks. This felt bigger in every way.

The man across the table from Brett had grown since high school. He wore a short-cropped beard now, as well as a *taquiyah*. He'd also taken to wearing a pair of rimless round glasses, which he wore perched on the tip of his nose. Behind those glasses, though, it was still Derek, smiling eyes, the kid who'd once sung "Ebony and Ivory" to get him out of a confrontation with a mammoth named Yard. Brett and Derek had kept in touch after high school; Derek had gone on to the University of Illinois. There, he'd become enamored of Islam, in particular the later teachings of Malcolm X—the ones, Derek said, that Elijah Muhammad and Louis Farrakhan ignored. "They didn't shoot Malcolm for being a racial radical, or for yelling about the white man," Derek said. "They shot him because he taught true Islam. The Islam of peace. They didn't kill him until he changed his name to el-Hajj Malik el-Shabazz and started talking about how Islam taught tolerance for religious plurality and political differences and racial diversity." Derek's own brand of Christianity, he'd told Brett, had seemed washed out and pale next to this broader religion; his mother had taken him to church once in a while and given him a whupping if he'd been caught skipping Sunday school, but he didn't know much about Jesus other than the pictures of the white man on the wall. He'd found his peace in Islam, changed his name to Hassan Abdul—"Beautiful Servant" in Arabic.

Hassan had gotten active at his local mosque, gone on *hajj*, experienced the magic Malcolm X had talked about. He'd also experienced something else: the perversion of what he believed his religion to be. In Saudi Arabia, he'd seen corporal punishment taking place. He'd seen the repression of the regime, and he'd heard the complaints of citizens whispering about the corruption of the monarchy, the loose talk about religiously purer heroes, men like Osama bin Laden. Upon his return to the United States, he'd moved to Virginia for work, attended mosque at the Dar Al-Hijrah Islamic Center near Washington, DC.

There, he'd met Anwar al-Awlaki. Charismatic, scholarly, soft-spoken, brilliant, al-Awlaki quickly built a following in the mosque. His classes were deeply conspiratorial, charismatically magnetic. The Zionist entity, he said, was responsible for Muslim suffering the world over, an outpost of Western colonialism and racism; groups like Hamas, Hezbollah, and al-Qaeda were fighting for a stronger Islam. Hassan Abdul said nothing. He did nothing. He thought perhaps this was just another strain of Islam. After all, Malcolm X had spoken in favor of ideological diversity.

Then, on September 11, he'd seen al-Awlaki's impact. The government linked al-Awlaki to two of the hijackers. And the Saudi government had backed the mosque because so long as outrage was focused without rather than within, it served their purposes.

After September 11, Hassan spoke to Brett, and Brett set up a covert meeting with the Federal Bureau of Investigation. Hassan Abdul became a mole. His jobs changed over the years, as did his location. His responsibility under the Bush administration had been to provide leads on possible terror suspects attending mosques in prominent urban areas. For the past several years, he had been stationed in New York City. At the mosque, he posed as a borderline radical—he spoke regularly about the injustices of the wars in Iraq and Afghanistan—but during his off-hours, he spoke frequently with a connection at the FBI. When al-Awlaki made contact with the treasurer of a local mosque via e-mail, the FBI found out, because that treasurer was Hassan Abdul.

With the election of Mark Prescott, however, the FBI had undergone certain changes. The monitoring of mosques had largely been shut down, deemed offensive and inefficient by the new administration. Hassan still received occasional contacts from the FBI, but the lack of regularity made it difficult to track secondary suspects, or to continue long-term monitoring of those who left the area. Over time, Hassan cut off contact altogether, frustrated with the lack of investigative follow-up.

Then he received a call from Brett.

Hassan adjusted his glasses. "I don't know who's behind the bridge attack, Brett. I'm sorry."

"I didn't expect you would."

"Then why are you here?"

"I don't think it's over. And I need you to help me find someone." Brett laid out what he knew about Mohammed: the name, the fact that he'd heard Ashammi specifically address him in Tehran.

"It's not a lot to go on. How do you even know he's coming to New York, as opposed to some other city? How do you know he wasn't involved in the original attack? Has the government even locked down the bastards who planted the bombs?"

"I don't know, Hassan. All I know is that there's something more to this. And I know that he is religious. The way that Ashammi spoke to him. If he's here, the only way to find him will be through the mosques."

Hassan laughed. "You could try the strip clubs, too. The 9/11 hijackers weren't Islamic enough to avoid seeing some unclad Western women before their flights."

"I've thought of that, too, but all the strip clubs are closed. Seriously, Hassan, please dig around. See if you can spot any new faces. I think he's here."

Hassan got up, stood over his old friend. "I put myself at risk to help preserve the truth of my religion once. Your boss cut me off. Why would he not do so again?"

Brett stood up, towering over Hassan. "Because this time, my boss doesn't know anything about it. Derek—Hassan—I know you're angry. You should be. So am I. But if there's anything we can do, now's the time to do it."

"You don't need to convince me, white boy. I just want you to know why I'm doing this. And it isn't for your president."

"Believe me," nodded Brett, "neither am I."

Hassan nodded. "I'll be in touch when I've got something for you." He turned toward the door, then turned back. "There's good and bad in everyone," he crooned, a smile suddenly creasing his lips. "We learn to live, we learn to give."

Brett laughed., "Each other what we need to survive. Together alive."

Hassan gave him a quick thumbs-up. Then he was gone.

PRESIDENT PRESCOTT

NEW YORK CITY

ICONIC MOMENTS.

These were the moments that Mark Prescott had always wanted. FDR standing before Congress, declaring war on Japan. John F. Kennedy in Berlin. Reagan at the Berlin Wall. George W. Bush in the wreckage of the World Trade Center.

And now, Prescott, standing on the precipice of the Hudson River, with the Coast Guard still dredging the waters, with the wreckage of one of America's greatest public works projects mangled behind him. No iconic moment could take place without tragedy lurking in the background.

An American flag flapped in the breeze behind him, forlorn against the bright blue sky. Prescott had his best men work on the speech. He'd given it a personal touch, too—he'd rehearsed it down to the last inflection. If there was one thing Mark Prescott knew how to do, it was hit the emotional high notes. And there would be little need to press emotional buttons after an event that had already become known by its date, like December 7 and September 11.

Prescott didn't wear a suit for the speech. Instead, he wore a Windbreaker, allowed the media to join him for a ride-along with the Coast Guard through the scene. As he looked over the waters, tears came to his eyes—genuine tears, not manufactured ones. This was *his* country, and these were *his* people, and if not for the tragedies of the past, they would be driving through the city today, living their lives. The cameras clacked loudly in the background as those thoughts crossed his mind, and he briefly hid his face from them. Of course, that would make the front pages of the newspapers, too.

The cameras broadcast him to hundreds of millions the world over; he stared above the camera line so that he appeared to be looking into the distance, into the future. He had positioned himself so that the light hit him squarely in the face. He spoke without notes, without a teleprompter—no niggling critics would be able to call this staged. His moment had arrived.

"My fellow Americans," he said, "we have experienced the greatest single attack on American soil in our history. Two days ago, we lost thousands of American lives: men, women, children.

"But let our enemies hear this: we remain strong. We remain unbowed. We remain unbroken, unwavering, unshaken. We stand together, and our unity is our power. Today, our enemies rejoice in our tragedy. Tomorrow, they will see us rebuild from these ashes, restore what once was, rebuild our America: better, stronger than it was before. They hoped that their destruction would cause us to question ourselves, question our course. They hoped that we would surrender our philosophy, our way of life.

"They were wrong. And so today, I speak to those who attacked us. We will never surrender. We will never give up. You think you are strong and we are weak for our freedoms. It is you who are weak, and we who are strong."

He paused, let the words echo over the crowd before him. Then, he inhaled, preparing to continue. This would be the moment when his soaring rhetoric would pull the crowd together, give them hope. This would be the moment when adversity turned to power. This would be…

A voice cried out from the back of the crowd. "YOU DID THIS!"

Prescott was momentarily startled. Then he began: "In times of grief, we do not walk alone. We walk together, yes, but we walk together holding the hand of a higher power, a power that believes in a higher justice…"

The voice again: "YOU DID THIS, MR. PRESIDENT!"

A murmur carried through the crowd. The voice continued, and suddenly a few of the cameras swung around from facing Prescott toward the lone protester. It was a woman, overweight, wearing faded jeans and a T-shirt with holes in it, her hair chopped short. "YOU DID THIS, MR. PRESIDENT! MY HUSBAND IS AT THE BOTTOM OF THIS RIVER BECAUSE OF YOU, MR. PRESIDENT!"

Prescott tried to seize back the moment, kept speaking into the sky: "A power that believes in America just as we believe in Him, and who will guide us through difficult times that try us…"

"MR. PRESIDENT, YOU OWE US ALL ANSWERS!"

Now all the cameras were turning to face this woman. Members of the Secret Service closed in around her, seeing her as a potential threat. Prescott could already see how it would play out on the evening news: crying victim hustled away as the president of the United States looked on.

It wouldn't go down that way. That was no iconic moment. This woman was about to undermine the nation's unity in order to place blame, not on the terrorists who had committed the atrocity, but on the government that tried to stop it. Prescott could feel his stomach clench in anger. Instead, he stopped, looked directly at the woman, and then held up his hands to the Secret Service. "Stop," he said. "Let her speak. We are all grieving."

One of the Secret Service men had his hand on the woman's upper arm by this point. She shook it off roughly. Then she started pushing her way to the front of the crowd, shoving members of the press aside. Prescott waited for her, seething quietly. When she got to the front, she climbed up onto the makeshift stage. Prescott could see the hatred in her eyes, could feel the rage. Her hands were shaking. In one of them was a photo. She held it up: a picture of her husband, gray mustache, heavyset, sixties. The microphones picked up her words. "Have you seen my husband, Mr. President?"

He shook his head dumbly.

"I didn't think so. He drives that bridge every single day to get to his job. I'm sure he was on it when it collapsed. You promised, Mr. President, to keep us safe. I know, because I voted for you. You promised that bringing our troops home would change everything, that ending those wars would make us safer here at home. And now I'm asking," she choked back tears, "if we're really safe. How can we be really safe after this? My husband won't ever come home again, probably, because you didn't keep us safe. He served his country in Vietnam, and he came back to this country, and all he asked was that our country honor his service. How can you keep us safe?" She stared at him, eyes glowing.

And he suddenly saw a way forward. He leaned forward, let a tear roll down his cheek, and hugged her. She tried to pull away, initially; he held her tighter. Finally, he felt her sob against his chest, the tension go out of her body. The cameras flashed around him.

The moment.

Time stood still. This was the image he'd been seeking ever since his election: Compassionate. Caring. Strong.

Now he waved for a couple of Secret Service agents to come forward and usher her from the stage. They moved quickly; within moments, he was onstage alone again, the sun reflecting brightly off the river.

He spoke slowly, deliberately.

The moment.

"We have made mistakes," he said, gesturing to the woman. "I have made mistakes. Those mistakes were made out of a desire for revenge against others, out of a desire to strike back against those who hurt us. We go to war to protect ourselves, but we end up weakening ourselves. Vengeance is God's, we know. Our job is to build.

"And build we will. Safety does not lie in aggression. It does not lie in defensiveness. It lies in our continual demonstration to the world that we will build, no matter what comes. Together, we will raise this bridge again, greater than it ever was before. Together, we will rekindle our relationship with each other, frayed and fractured thanks to the exigencies of war.

"We will not be hampered by the past. Our swords will be beaten into plowshares." He motioned out over the thousands of American troops now working along the shoreline. "Our bravest and finest men and women will be put to work rebuilding; no more nation-building abroad. Thousands upon thousands of those men and women are coming to New York, to rebuild, to revitalize. It's time to build ourselves up here at home.

"Now, some will ask whether such actions bring safety. And here is what I say: Safety does not come through the fear of the gun or the height of our walls. Safety comes from love. Yes," he continued, "love. Love for each other. Care for each other. Sacrifice for each other. And that's what I'm going to ask of all Americans now. Not anger, not lashing out, not blame or knee-jerk reactions. Love. Love your neighbor. Love your country. Stand together. And together we will rise. For in times like this, in times of tragedy and horror, it is love we most need."

He paused for one moment more, looking out at the New York skyline. The cameras clicked.

The moment.

The president relaxed in his hotel room after the speech, flipping through the channels. The coverage was nearly universally ecstatic, though one guest commentator on Fox News had the gall to ask whether the president had any leads on the perpetrators. The host, uncomfortable with politicizing the moment, moved the guest quickly off the point. The chyron read: "PRESIDENT: A TIME FOR LOVE." Over and over, channel after channel, the footage of the hug played as if on a continuous loop.

The knock at the door disturbed Prescott's reverie. Tommy Bradley peeked his head in. "Come in, Tommy," said the president magnanimously, muting the television. "Have you seen this fucking coverage?"

Bradley grinned weakly. "It's phenomenal, Mr. President. Just phenomenal."

"Let's see them try to stop the Work Freedom Program after this, eh?"

"Mr. President…"

"What is it? Spit it out."

"Did you know that Brett Hawthorne is in New York?"

"No, but why the hell should I care where he is? He's a free man, isn't he?"

Tommy bit his lip. "Well, you see, it's what he's *doing* here that could be problematic. I just got word from my guy at JFK that he's digging around flight manifests, and that he's asked to see pictures of Arabs first."

"Jesus Christ. Racial profiling? Right after the 'love' speech?"

"And they say that the media probably will figure it out pretty soon. I mean, these things have a way of leaking."

"Je. Sus. Christ. Who the hell gave him authority for this?"

"My guy didn't know the answer to that."

"Well, track down the general. Should have left that pain in the ass in Iran. Jesus." And he turned up the volume to hear himself speak once again, his voice blaring through the hard-wooded presidential suite: "*Vengeance is God's, we know. Our job is to build.*"

ELLEN

EL PASO, TEXAS

GOVERNOR DAVIS'S REFUSAL TO SEND the National Guard to New York sparked a firestorm across the nation. He cited precedent—hadn't the governor of California refused a federal request to place National Guard troops on the border?—but in the aftermath of the bridge attack, he didn't get much sympathy. "Everyone knows that Texas thinks of itself as its own little country," shouted one MSNBC commentator into the camera, "but this time, their hick governor has shown himself to be deeply unpatriotic. You don't get to be a star on the flag of the United States and then go AWOL when your country needs you. John F. Kennedy said, 'Ask not what your country can do for you, ask what you can do for your country.' In Texas, Bubba Davis says, 'Ask not what you can do for your country, ask how you can leave them hanging in their time of need.'"

Davis stood fast, though. He refused the requests for the National Guard, redeployed them to the border. He told the media that the crime rate across the state had dropped dramatically. He pointed at the rapidly dropping illegal border crossings, explained that the drug trafficking had been cut dead.

It didn't help. Day after day, the media ran with the story: a president calling for love and unity, and a southern secessionist governor looking like George Wallace. Never mind that Davis had stood with the marchers of the civil rights era: he now stood on the side of the Old South, the media proclaimed.

Before long, Davis turned to Ellen to be the face of his defiance. She refused.

The president of the United States, she told Davis, had brought her husband home in one piece. He'd made mistakes, she knew. He'd exiled her husband based on lies, separated them for years, slashed the military, undermined the mission, she thought. But in the end, he'd brought Brett home. And that was all that mattered to her.

"Okay," Bubba had said, "then I need you on the border. Somebody has to head up this outfit, and if I go down there, they'll accuse me of outright insurrection. You're competent, your husband is a well-known military figure, and well, damn it, you're a woman. And those sexists in the press won't label a woman an insurrectionist."

So now she was back in El Paso.

She had to admit that the border felt different. It felt safe, for the first time ever. Military vehicles patrolled the Texas side of the river, with checkpoints set up to funnel visitors and workers through after checking identification. Soldiers, many speaking Spanish, spoke with the locals, helping to direct them to the local ranches. She'd been there for a week, and there hadn't been any dead kids in the river. Every so often, a black helicopter would buzz the troops on the American side of the border; Ellen thought it might be members of the same drug cartel that had killed Vivian.

She even thought she'd seen one of the men wearing a bandanna over his face.

She told the generals of the Guard that she didn't want to see any fire at the helicopters unless fired upon; things were bad enough without starting a war. In the last few days, the helicopters had buzzed closer and closer, probing, prodding American response. The Americans merely observed. The Guard had no intelligence capacities; the feds hadn't been particularly responsive since Davis's big announcement. But Ellen had some private investigators do some digging. What they found shocked her.

Ciudad Juarez, they said, was run by the Juarez Cartel, one of the most dangerous criminal enterprises on the planet. Its leadership had been passed down through the Carrillo Fuentes brothers, who had turned it into a massive regional player, competing openly with powerhouses like the violent Sinaloa Cartel and spending a large chunk of their earnings on bribery of Mexican police officials. Operating across more than a score of Mexican states, the Juarez Cartel had engaged in bloody wars with the Sinaloa Cartel across the country, including in Ciudad Juarez.

Perhaps its most famous product, aside from drugs, was creative methods of dealing death: in 2006, a reporter for the UK *Guardian* detailed the horrors of what came to be called the House of Death, where US informants had been implicated in complicity with multiple murder. The House of Death had been discovered and put out of business years before, but the cartel still operated in force. The city of Ciudad Juarez became the center of a renewed turf battle between the Juarez and Sinaloa cartels for control of the drug trafficking routes into Texas.

Only now, the violence in Juarez had stopped. The presence of American troops on the border meant that drug shipments slowed to a virtual standstill. Ellen's investigators told her that the truce could mean only one thing: a plan to stir things up along the border. If the cartels could draw national attention to Texas's militarization of the border, the media, they figured, would react by calling on Texas to step down. After all, the president of the United States had already labeled Texas treasonous for its failure to send help to New York. Any incident along the border that could be dumped at Davis's feet would benefit the cartel; there simply was no national will to stand up to aggression along the southern border, not when the country was already recovering from the greatest terror attack in its history.

And so Ellen's job had become to prevent violence. That job, she knew, would be a lot tougher than merely walking some troops back and forth along the Rio Grande or even flying patrols over the border. For three weeks, she'd kept the peace. She'd have to do better, she knew. One incident gone wrong could end Davis's dreams of a safe Texas.

Ellen's cell phone rang. New York number. She picked up.

"Hey, sweetheart." Brett's rich baritone rumbled through the phone.

"Hey, babe," she said.

"Miss you." His voice sounded thick over the phone, almost tearful. Just a few days ago, they'd been so close to reuniting. Now, with commercial air travel shut down and the crisis in New York, it could be weeks, they both knew. But this was something new, too: Brett never talked like this. Since the rescue from Iran, Brett hadn't been himself. She could imagine why, and she could imagine his face. She longed to reach out and touch it.

"Miss you too. How's Bill?"

"He's hanging in there." Another pause. "Are you okay?"

"Yes."

"That's a no." He laughed. So did she. "Davis made a mistake not sending the troops, you know."

"I know," she answered. "And I have a feeling something's coming here. Something bad."

"I'm getting the same feeling."

"It's not over, is it?"

A long pause. "No, I don't think it is."

Someone knocked at the door to Ellen's office. "I've gotta run, babe," she said. "Take a bullet for you."

"Take a bullet for you, sweetheart."

She hung up.

"Come in," she called.

At the door stood a sergeant in the Guard. He held out a piece of paper. "Ma'am," he said, "this came from HQ."

She took the slip from his hand. She read it quickly. Then she dropped it and ran for the elevators.

The command headquarters was no more than a set of mobile homes set up along the border, within sight of the Rio Grande. Normally, Ellen operated out of the US Air National Guard military base at Biggs. By the time she arrived at the mobile home, a small crowd of journalists had formed outside. As she stepped out of her car, the cameras clacked away. The focus of the nation was certainly on New York, she thought, but that didn't make the regional journalists any less hungry to get their footage on the national broadcast.

She saw the box as she stepped inside the empty room, sitting on a makeshift desk, a table somebody had culled from the local rec center. The box was cardboard, wet at the bottom. A wet plastic bag sat beside it. The box had been carved open at the top. She crept up on it, the pressure in her chest screaming at her not to look inside.

She did anyway.

A head. The head, more specifically, of one Lieutenant Jeff Jefferds. Jefferds, a member of the Texas National Guard, had been imprisoned in Mexico for months, held by the authorities there. Aside from a small group of activists, Jefferds had been all but abandoned after his imprisonment; the Mexican government claimed he'd driven across the border loaded down with weapons. He claimed it was all a big misunderstanding, that he'd been going hunting and made a wrong turn. His history of mental illness didn't help him much on that score.

Now the holes in his head that used to hold eyes stared through Ellen. Written on his forehead in blue ink was one word: "TERRORISTA." She held back the urge to vomit.

She turned away, thinking. It was a genius move, she concluded: so offensive that there would have to be *some* response from the Texas government, a crime directed not at the national government but at an individual claimed by the Mexican government to be a criminal. It played directly to Davis's soft spot: abandonment. He'd want to retaliate. He'd want to push across the border into Ciudad Juarez. And Prescott would want no part of it, not while he was still trying to woo the president of Mexico to endorse his job creation plan, and not while he had the entire world unifying around him.

Her cell phone rang.

The name flashed across the screen: Bubba.

She picked up.

"I heard about it, Ellen."

"I'm looking at it right now, Governor."

"Then you know what we have to do."

"No, Governor, I don't," she said.

"This is America, dammit, not Afghanistan. This shit can't happen along my border."

"It's America's border, Bubba."

"But America won't do shit to protect it. They failed. Now it's my turn."

She took a deep breath.

"Governor," she said, "you do this, and you could be looking at open conflict with Prescott this time. No more playacting. No more excuses."

"You think he's going to send his boys down here to shoot at our boys over us killing some drug dealers?"

"I don't know," she answered. "But neither do you."

"Everybody on earth has called the president's bluff," said Davis. "Everybody. He's caved every time. What would make this time different?"

"You," she answered. "He hates you."

"That won't make his *cojones* any bigger, girl." He laughed. "This has been coming for a long time. I'm looking forward to seeing some dead criminals for a change."

The line went dead.

Ellen closed the box softly, walked outside, and looked at the river. "*Alea iacta esta*," she whispered. "Damn, damn, damn."

SOLEDAD

MINOT, NORTH DAKOTA

AIDEN BURST THROUGH THE FRONT door of the cabin, sweating. Soledad stood. As she did, the men inhabiting the cabin stood up, readied for danger. Ezekiel picked up his M4.

"We need to talk," Aiden said.

Soledad nodded. The men filed out of the living room, into the outdoors. Ezekiel nodded at her. "You need anything, holler. I'll be outside," he said.

Aiden collapsed into a broken-down sofa, breathing hard. Then he leaned forward, staring at Soledad.

"We need to go to Detroit," he said.

"Detroit?" she laughed. "I thought we were staying off the grid, holing up. This is the first time in weeks they haven't been looking for us. And you want me to take all these men into the heart of the firestorm?"

"I wouldn't ask it, but Ricky needs my help."

"You mean that cop? The one who shot the black kid? I heard they just let him off on the radio. They'll get him out of town."

Aiden shook his head. "No. They won't. Those pieces of shit just took over the detention center."

"They'll let him out. Probably just shake somebody down."

"I don't think so." He reached forward, picked up her portable radio. They sat, listening to the commercials for carpet cleaner and gold. Then the news came back on. A newscaster, speaking in somber tones, his voice cut by static interference. "The protesters—*SHSHSHS*—gathered outside the detention center—*SHSHSHS*—chanting that they want their own trial." Aiden switched the radio off. "It's an old-fashioned lynch mob," he said. "They're not going home without a head on a pike."

"Why do you care? Bad shit goes down in this country every day."

His eyes shifted to the ground. When he looked back at her, his eyes were watery. "We're friends. He saved my life once."

"So now you want to return the favor."

He nodded.

"But this isn't just about you anymore," she said. "I've got forty guys out there who abandoned everything they had to come out here and try to be left alone. You want me to put them into the middle of a shitstorm."

"The storm is coming to you."

"They're distracted. They'll leave us alone."

"For how long?" Aiden grimaced. "I'll bet Ricky thought they'd leave him alone. That he was doing the right thing. Damn idiot." Aiden looked at her, his eyes begging. "I don't know what to tell you, Sole. All I can say is I'm going. If you can help, I'd be grateful. If not . . . all I can say is thank you for helping me find something I'd been missing."

"What's that?"

"A reason to do what I do. To fight."

It stirred something in her. The same feeling that had once forced her to get up at 3:00 a.m. on her ranch. The same feeling that had forced her to build from the dust up, and had forced her to hire criminals to bomb a government installation. A feeling of helplessness in the face of something larger. All she could do, she finally figured, was to chip away at that feeling, bit by bit.

"Maybe I'm a damn idiot, too. But I'll talk to them all. We'll head out at nightfall."

DETROIT, MICHIGAN

They arrived in the evening, a chain of cars and motorcycles taking refuge in the abandoned Michigan Central Station, the old rail depot for the city. Aiden guided them through the dark—the electric lights in this part of the city went out long ago, and the city didn't normally send workers to fix them, fearing crime—and the caravan pulled into the empty grass field in front of the building. It stood above them, glorious and decayed, an image from a science fiction film, backlit against the waning twilight. Soledad shook her head. So much promise. All of it wasted.

They made shelter in the building itself, a Beaux-Arts masterpiece tagged and chipped by years of vagrants and hoodlums. A few elderly homeless drunks still lay around the place; Aiden left them where they were. Together, the group of thirty climbed up the stairs to the tower, an unused set of floors crumbling from disuse. At least, Soledad thought, nobody would bother them here.

Aiden whispered information about the building as they climbed, his voice resonating in the ill-lit halls. For years, the city had tried to rehabilitate the building; it had been bought, rebought, bought again. They'd considered bonds, taxpayer subsidies, anything to get the building restored. Nobody had bothered.

Detroit was a disaster area; investing money in the city would be a massive waste.

Aiden had grown up in Detroit, he said. He knew the city well. His grandfather worked for General Motors, had a union job that was supposed to keep him employed all his life. Then foreign cars began flooding the American market, and the auto union contracts meant that American car companies couldn't compete. Jobs started fleeing. As they did, the government of the city decided to raise taxes dramatically on the people who still held jobs, on the companies that still decided to stay in town. They left, too. Mayor after mayor took office promising to bring business back, then pandered by crushing businesses that remained. The tax base disappeared.

The place became a wasteland. White families moved out into the suburbs. Black families couldn't afford to follow. The city self-segregated.

Aiden thought he was the only white kid left in the city. Then he met Ricky O'Sullivan. The two became fast friends, joined at the hip. Their parents went to church together; they fought back bullies together. Ricky was the straight arrow, Aiden the budding juvenile delinquent eager and ready to do anything to make friends. They grew distant as Aiden hooked up with new friends, missed school.

One day, Aiden's mother saw Ricky in church, asked him if he'd seen Aiden. Ricky lied to cover for him; Aiden, he said, was probably at the library. Then, hands gripped into fists, still wearing his Sunday suit, he went looking for Aiden. He found him in a rundown tract house, surrounded by a couple of dropouts, high on weed and drunk off his ass.

"Aiden," Ricky said, "your mom's looking for you. She missed you at church."

One of the losers laughed. "Yeah, mama's boy, your mama's looking for you."

"Shut up," Aiden slurred to him. "Yeah? Well, tell her I'm out here."

"I'm not going to do that. I said I'd come and get you."

Aiden laughed, a high-pitched whine that eventually tapered off into a snort. "Well, you tried, Boy Scout. Now get back home to your mama."

Ricky grabbed him by the scruff of his T-shirt. "Get your ass home, Aiden."

"Or what?" Aiden sneered.

"Or this." Ricky punched him in the face. Aiden went down like a load of bricks, laying on his back in the dirt. "You're a loser, Aiden, and if you're not careful, you'll end up like these ones." Aiden started to push himself to his feet, his lower lip bleeding onto his chin. Ricky hit him again, clipping him right on the point of the chin. Aiden wobbled, fell.

Ricky picked him up, took him home, cleaned him up, and got him home to his mother. That was the last time Aiden got high.

After high school, they went their separate ways. Aiden joined up with federal law enforcement; Ricky went to school, then joined the police academy. They chatted on Facebook from time to time, but their friendship fell into acquaintance, and finally into complete disuse.

Until now.

Aiden went silent. The small fire in the center of the tiled conference room reflected light off the mildewed walls.

Soledad turned to Ezekiel. He stepped forward, warming his hands on the fire. Then he made a circle with his hands.

"Imagine the detention center in the center of our map. My hands are the crowd. Now, they're rowdy, and they're waiting for

O'Sullivan's release. That's why the cops have him locked down tight. But the protesters know that eventually the cops will crack, release him, put him out there on his own. They just have to find the right button to push. And they're going to move fast now to push it.

"So here's the plan. We have to wait for the right time. We're not interested in taking on the police. They're armed, and they're scared, and armed and scared cops are just as likely to shoot us as anybody else. Instead, we need chaos for the cover. Every riot is led by a few key characters. Everybody there may look like they're ready for war, but most are there to show their friends that they're brave. The authorities know that, so their chief task is to arrest the rabble-rousers and let the rest sort of fade away.

"If that happens, we'll never get Officer O'Sullivan out of there. I guarantee you that whoever is leading this thing is smart and capable. This is not amateur hour."

One of the men in the back piped up. "Why don't we just grab him off the street when he's released?"

Ezekiel guffawed. "Have you seen us? We stick out like a KKK rally in Harlem. No chance they don't find us and at least neutralize us. No, here's what we're gonna do."

Aiden took out a garbage bag, pulled from it four uniforms. These he tossed to Soledad and three other men, who stepped forward to put them on. "Now, for the rest of you guys, I've got something really special."

He opened a duffel bag. In it were T-shirts. When the rest of the men saw them, a few jaws dropped. Soledad chuckled. "Well," she said, "you've gotta die sometime."

LEVON

DETROIT, MICHIGAN

FOR TWO DAYS, LEVON STOOD in the cold. He had his men bring him food and clothing. He slept on the sidewalk. Next to him slept the mother of Kendrick Malone. With them slept hundreds of others. Every day, local businesses shipped out supplies for the group, eager to be seen as caring for the plight of the righteous protesters.

And still, they didn't release Ricky O'Sullivan.

Perhaps they thought that the crowd would dissipate. Perhaps they were waiting for federal intervention—intervention that wouldn't come. The president had already declared that this was a local matter, and the resources of the state had already been redirected to the disaster area in New York City. There would be no cavalry.

And so they waited. Each day, members of the media crowded around Levon to hear his words. But each day, the number of media dwindled. The attention span of the nation ran shorter and shorter these days. With the cleanup in New York, the investigation underway to identify the culprits for the attacks, and the situation on the border, the media had a full lineup without having to go back to the same pictures of the same people lying on the same street.

The time had come, Levon knew, for action.

But action required provocation. So far, the authorities had been smart: they had holed up, put nobody on the street, waited for the ire to burn itself out. They hadn't made any statements other than to praise the peacefulness of the protesters and suggest their sympathies for the protesters' cause. The city of Detroit didn't run well anyway—what was a few days of crowded streets and delayed services?

Meanwhile, Levon itched. Big Jim had already told him he could negotiate a way out of the stalemate—he said that Levon could become a player by accepting the verdict, demanding change from the feds, and being granted an informal say in the appointment of officials up to and including police officers. He said that Levon should just let O'Sullivan go, show that he was the bigger man. Already, Big Jim had gone on national television urging the president to send more federal officials to talk about the future. The nation's eyes had been riveted on Detroit, but with Big Jim's imprimatur of legitimacy, the Detroit-federal solution was gradually drawing the steam out of the kettle. Levon knew he couldn't hold out much longer, and that he might be forced to take Big Jim's deal.

And then they arrived.

Like a blessing from the skies, they came. There weren't many of them, but there were enough: white men, riding motorcycles, planting themselves in the midst of the newly minted tent city. And they wore T-shirts: "FIGHT THE THUGS."

That got the media's attention. But oddly enough, few of the men wanted to talk to the media. One, in particular, bowed his head anytime the cameras came near. Levon denounced them for the cameras—"Who are these white supremacists, coming into a city white racism has ruined, and accusing us of racism for standing up for our human rights?"— but secretly thanked God for bringing them. It kept the fight alive, at least for another day.

Big Jim Crawford lounged in the marble shower of the luxury suite at the MGM, enjoying the feeling of the dual rain heads slapping him with their steady stream. He'd been penning an op-ed for *The Wall Street Journal*, and the steam of the shower cleared his senses, helped him think. He'd get what he wanted, he knew.

He always did.

The game had become almost too easy. Big Jim didn't think of himself as a con artist or a shakedown expert. He thought of himself as a leader in need of resources to bring change. If that meant skimping on taxes, what of it? Who hadn't cheated in the United States? Who had clean hands? So long as he spent his days fighting for social justice, why shouldn't he enjoy the benefits of a nice house, the ministrations of a young mistress? Martin Luther King Jr. had been sainted for his civil rights work, and nobody looked twice at his various financial and personal improprieties. The cause cleansed him, as it should have. History eventually deemed everyone either a saint or a sinner, no in-between.

The next step in Detroit, Big Jim knew, would be to give Levon an option for withdrawal with some grace. He'd already pressed Levon, and he knew Levon was waiting, hoping for something big to happen, but that seemed unlikely with the nation's attention riveted elsewhere.

Big Jim climbed out of the shower, reached for his towel, wrapped it around his bulk, and gazed at himself in the mirror.

He needed to lose some weight, and he sucked in his gut. When he got back to New York, he told himself, he'd start the diet.

Suddenly, he felt out of breath.

He plunged forward, grabbing the sink with both hands, but he could feel the strength in those hands weakening. He tried to push his fingertips into the marble, but they wouldn't grip; for some reason, a desperate need to hold himself up rushed over him, and as he felt his bulk dragged toward the cool floor, away from the fogged-up mirror, he had the odd thought that the floor was red.

Then he realized it was. It was red and slippery with his blood.

He lost his grip, and his face hit the oozing puddle hard.

He never saw the man who fired the second round into his head.

Levon had his men watching Soledad's men for any concerted movement. The T-shirted motorcycle gang seemed too professional for Levon's taste; he'd originally thought them a group of overwrought, racist kooks, but they always seemed to encamp at the inflection points in the crowd—bottlenecks, thin spaces. They met up at night in one of the tents, but kept a guard stationed outside, armed.

Now, Levon's men told him, the T-shirt gang was on the move.

There were eight of them, all told. Four had their hogs planted in the corners of the street, ready to move off at the first sign of trouble. Three of the other four planted themselves near the front of the crowd, near the steps to the detention center.

The lone remaining man, a white-bearded, big-bellied bear in his mid-sixties, stood near the center of the crowd. A group of young protesters screamed obscenities at him; he stood his ground placidly.

A buzz built at the back of the crowd.

More white men, all wearing the same T-shirts, pulling up on motorcycles. Silent. Saying nothing. The crowd of protesters moved up on them, expecting a confrontation.

That's when Levon's phone rang.

He picked up, heard the crying. He hung up without saying a word. His gut churned. Then he set his teeth.

He raised his right arm, his fist clenched.

"THEY KILLED BIG JIM!" he screamed. Then, again, this time for the cameras, which he knew would be zooming in on him: "THEY KILLED BIG JIM! TEAR IT ALL DOWN! TEAR DOWN THIS CORRUPT SYSTEM!"

Wailing and screaming broke out on the street. Women sobbed. Young men shouted, tore at their clothes. "THEY KILLED BIG JIM! THEY KILLED BIG JIM!" Media members, most of them white, stepped back a few feet from the seething crowd. A few lone police officers at the front of the crowd—Levon hadn't even noticed police officers on the street at all—stepped backward quickly, moving into the detention center for protection as their compatriots opened the doors for them.

One of Levon's men, a teenager carrying a tire iron, sprinted through the crowd until he was right in the face of the big-bellied white man. He grabbed him by the beard, twisted it until the man fell to the ground. Then he screamed, raised the tire iron, and brought it down with a sickening *thunk* into the man's belly. Levon's men pushed forward against the glass doors of the detention center; Levon could see the cops cowering inside.

"GIVE US O'SULLIVAN!" Levon screamed as he climbed the steps to the detention center. "GIVE US THE CHILD MURDERER!" A member of his entourage handed him a brick as he made his way forward.

He strode up the steps, the cameras catching him from behind, his huge back framed against the lights inside the detention center.

Then he reared back and hurled the brick, spiderwebbing the plexiglass door.

Behind Levon, the street exploded into chaos, protesters and rioters merging into one throng. The bearded white bear had disappeared into the center of the crowd, his body trampled, kicked, stomped, spit on. Hundreds of people gathered in a circle to watch, to participate.

On the outskirts of the riot, the motorcyclists revved their engines, fending off rocks and bottles. One motorcyclist pulled out a handgun and fired it into the air, scattering the crowd near him, but drawing a fusillade of debris from all quarters. The street broke up into a series of running battles, bikers leveling their weapons, avoiding firing into the crowd directly. One biker revved his engine and then plunged it directly into the center of the crowd, screaming, trying to reach his bearded comrade, who by now was lying motionless, blood streaming from his ear.

Someone handed Levon a crowbar, and he raised his powerfully muscled arms, then brought the crowbar down with brute force against the windows. After a few blows, they shattered, and he made his way inside.

The room was empty.

"Find O'Sullivan," he growled as six of his men sprinted down the halls.

The detention officer unlocked the cell holding Ricky O'Sullivan, and it creaked back on its hinges. O'Sullivan backed up quickly into the corner, his bulk filling it.

"You leave me alone," he said to the masked woman in the police uniform. She wore a bandanna over her face, and her gun was pointed directly at the head of the detention officer.

"Follow me," Soledad said, the mask muffling her consonants. "We don't have time to argue. You either come now, or you come later in a body bag. Can you hear that upstairs?" She motioned toward the ceiling, where the pounding thumps of running feet were clearly audible. "They're coming for you. Aren't they, kid?" The detention officer nodded. "And I don't think they want to play patty-cake. Jim Crawford's dead."

For the first time, panic came over O'Sullivan's face. "Who killed him?" he asked.

"Do you want to play twenty questions, or do you want to leave this building alive? Get your ass in gear."

Soledad lowered her weapon. "No threats. Aiden said you don't respond to threats. Silly me."

At Aiden's name, Ricky brightened. "Okay," he said, "let's go."

Soledad forced the detention officer into the cell. "Hide under the bunk," she said. "Hopefully they won't have a key."

Then she and Ricky took off down the hall.

"Do you have any idea where you're going?" O'Sullivan asked.

"Motor pool," she said. "We're gonna get ourselves a vehicle."

Behind them, at the other end of the hall, Soledad could hear the pounding footsteps nearing, the shouting, then a gunshot and more running feet, nearing. She and O'Sullivan crashed through the door to the stairs, sprinting, lungs burning, toward the basement.

Aiden was waiting for them in the covered garage, behind the steering wheel of a SWAT van. The back doors to the van were open, only about thirty feet from the stairwell. Soledad and O'Sullivan jumped in, slammed the doors closed, just as four young black men burst into the garage behind them. Two ran at the van; two more ran for motorcycles, searching for the keys.

Soledad pounded on the barrier to the van's driver's compartment. "Go!" she screamed. "Go! Let's get the hell out of here!"

"Not without Ezekiel," Aiden replied.

"What? He's not here?!"

"He'll be here any moment."

Now two of Levon's men had reached the van; one began slamming on Aiden's window, while the other tried to pry open the back of the van. "Hold on!" Aiden shouted, throwing the van into reverse. The man at the back of the van shrieked as his head banged against the iron of the door; Soledad felt sick to her stomach at the bump as the wheels hit him. But Aiden kept backing up until there were just a few inches of room between the rear doors and the elevator next to the stairwell.

"Ezekiel's coming," Aiden said. "Any second."

Now the man at the driver's side window started pounding at the glass again, cracking it. Aiden calmly pulled out a .22 handgun, rolled down the window slightly, and fired. The bullet hit the man in the shoulder, knocking him to the ground. "Stay down," Aiden said quietly. "You'll be fine."

The elevator doors pinged, opened. Inside, Ezekiel sat on the floor, his mouth open, breathing hard—blood ran down the side of his police uniform. Soledad leapt out of the back doors, grabbed him by the arm. "Stay with me, Ezekiel," she said. "We're almost out. Almost free." He grunted, threw his arm over her shoulder; O'Sullivan grabbed him by the collar and hoisted him into the van.

In front of the van, the two would-be motorcyclists had found keys somehow and swerved their motorcycles to block the exit. To get out, Aiden would have to go right through them. And they held handguns.

"Damn it," said Aiden. Then he sighed. "No use for it, I suppose."

He gunned the engine, rammed his foot to the floorboard. "Fill your hands, you son of a bitch," he muttered. The motor-cyclists gunned their own engines, zooming right at the front of the truck. They didn't have much control over their aim, but they fired anyway; the glass cracked as a few shots landed square on the windshield.

Aiden saw their plan before it materialized. They would separate, come around the back of the van, and follow; they would then pick up more and more of their crew, and the whole thing would turn into a running gun battle.

As they began to split, Aiden braked hard, turning the wheel 90 degrees. The van swung around, doughnutting—he heard a satisfying smash as the side of the van swung into one of the motorcyclists. The other motorcyclist was now directly in front of him. He got off the bike and ran as Aiden drove the SWAT vehicle directly over the cycle, crushing it beneath the wheels.

Aiden turned again and drove up the ramp into the night.

In the back of the van, Soledad looked at Ezekiel. "You gonna be all right?"

"I'll be okay," he grimaced.

She smiled ruefully. "You did guarantee blood. You weren't lying."

He laughed, coughed blood into his mouth, and spat it out. "Didn't think it would be my own."

"You never do," Ricky O'Sullivan said into the dark warmth of the night. "You never do."

They told Levon about O'Sullivan's escape about an hour later. By then, the street fights had died down—the motorcyclists were gone. The police had fled the detention center. Now Levon stood on the steps, overlooking the smoking street. A few bodies lay out there, bleeding. It looked like a war zone.

He turned to face the reporter, the camera directly in his face. She'd asked him a question before he found out O'Sullivan was gone; he'd completely forgotten it. "What did you ask again?" he murmured.

"What comes next?" she asked. "The mayor is vowing to keep order."

Levon looked out over his burning city. *His* burning city. "We don't need the mayor to keep order," Levon said. "He's just as corrupt as the rest. We're in a war now. You saw them out here, on their motorcycles, with their racist T-shirts. White supremacists killed Reverend Jim Crawford tonight. No pretty words are going to bring him back.

"So here's what America needs to know: Detroit is now in our hands. We will have justice. And it starts with the mayor. But that's not where it ends. We want to work with the police officers who will serve justice. If they won't, we will have our own forces of justice. Brothers will not burn down brothers' businesses. There will be no looting. No violence. That's not what Big Jim would have wanted.

"We're going to build something new in this city. Something better on these ashes. Wherever Ricky O'Sullivan is, we will bring him back to justice, too. This is the beginning of a new era."

Levon gestured at the street. "The blood you see here tonight, that will be repaid in freedom. So tonight, I call for the people of my city to join me. It is time to rise up and claim our freedom."

In the distance, the sun began to rise.

PART 3

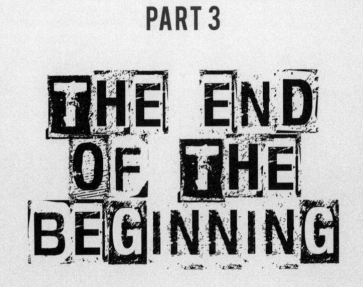

THE END
OF THE
BEGINNING

BRETT

NEW YORK CITY

THE CALL FROM HASSAN CAME in the middle of the night.

"I think I have something," Hassan said. Brett could hear the fear in his voice. "It could be nothing, or it could be something."

"What is it? What's wrong?"

"Rumors, I thought. But they're not rumors. How fast can you get over here?"

"Fast."

Hassan gave Brett his address. Brett threw on his clothes, picked up his service weapon, and slid it in the small of his back. Hassan had sounded worried enough for that.

Closing the door to the hotel room, he glanced down the hall stealthily. Nobody who wasn't drunk or having an affair would be coming down the hall at 2:00 a.m., he figured, but better to be paranoid than blithe.

Sure enough, a buzz-cut man in a black suit waited at the elevator. *Federal*, thought Brett. There was only one reason for him to be waiting: the president wanted to see General Brett Hawthorne. And there was only one reason the president would want to see General Brett Hawthorne: to stop his investigation. The meet-up at the airport had been too high profile. He'd been too cavalier with his agenda, and the president had other priorities. The last thing Mark Prescott wanted, Brett figured, was bad publicity right after a terror attack. "Islamophobia in the Top Ranks." That's how the headlines in the *Nation* would read. And Prescott read the *Nation*.

The man in the black suit locked eyes with Brett, began walking toward him.

After years of riding the bureaucratic bull, Brett had one key rule: better to ask forgiveness than to seek permission. Which is why he was relieved to see a door to the stairs on the other end of the hallway. And fortunately, he was on the second floor.

He turned his back on the suit and walked toward the door. He heard the padding steps behind him, opened the door, closed it, and then took the stairs half a flight at a time, his knees throbbing. Behind him, he heard the door slam open, and then the man's voice: "He's running. We'll grab him in the lobby."

Brett had no such intention.

Instead of exiting at the lobby level, he continued sprinting down into the basement area. He'd planned for this eventuality ever since he arrived at the hotel; in Afghanistan he'd acquired the useful habit of locating exits and scoping out his location. He knew the maze of hallways and doors in the hotel basement, and he quickly navigated them, waiting long enough to ensure he'd lost his pursuers. When he emerged onto the street, he found himself alone.

Nice try, suckers, Brett thought with a grim smile.

Hassan lived in the Washington Heights area of New York—the area nobody wanted to walk at night. He'd taken a small second-floor flat near the 168th Street subway station, an old building refurbished with cheap appliances and cheaper flooring. He'd furnished the apartment sparingly, except for a pair of floor-to-ceiling bookcases filled with religious tomes. When Brett arrived, sweating, Hassan nodded silently, then ushered him to a beat-up leather couch.

"Tea?"

"No, thank you," Brett replied.

Hassan walked over to the bookcases, slid aside some of the volumes. Then he pushed one of the panels on the rear wall of the bookcase. It opened quietly. Hassan slid out a thumb drive, loaded it into his laptop, sat the machine on the coffee table before Brett.

"Do you know this man?"

A video file popped open. It showed a young, slim Muslim man, wearing jeans and a long-sleeved shirt, shaking hands with another *thawb*-wearing man at the mosque. Hassan hit pause.

"Do you recognize him?"

Brett nodded. It was Mohammed. "How did you find him?"

"You weren't followed, of course?"

"Of course."

He hesitated. "I have backdoor access to most of the security cameras in the New York mosques. It has taken me years."

"How much of that is legal?"

"Under this president? Don't ask if you don't want to know."

Brett sighed. "So tell me when that footage was taken."

"It was taken four days ago." Hassan anticipated Brett's disappointment. "I know. Too long. But finding a man named Mohammed in a mosque in New York is like finding a Jew named Goldstein in a synagogue here. You're bound to find some false positives. But this one stood out. That imam he is talking to— Anjem Omari—is trouble. He's been under FBI surveillance on and off for years. Right now, off."

"So what do you know about my man Mohammed?"

"Not much. I know that he has a close relationship with Omari."

"Where does Omari live?"

Hassan laughed. "You can't be serious. You want me to go over there and talk with him? It puts my entire operation at risk."

"No," said Brett slowly. "*I* want to go and talk with him."

Hassan laughed even harder. Finally, he began coughing, pounded his chest until it subsided. "White boy, you're out of your mind. You don't know the first thing about him. Did you know he's tight with Prescott? That he's given opening prayers at the New York Stock Exchange? He's high profile. And you think you're just going to waltz over there and ask him some questions, and that he'll answer you?"

Brett nodded. "Something like that."

"Now why would he go and do something like that?"

"You leave that to me. What's his address?"

It took Brett a bit over an hour to reach the imam's home outside the I-287 loop. The imam actually lived on a rural compound off the road. In the dark, Brett missed the turnoff twice. The gravel clanked off the underside of the cheap Toyota Hassan had borrowed from a friend. The woods showed black against the early glimmers of rising sun. In the distance, Brett could see that the light was already on in the home—*fajr* prayers, the earliest prayers. By the time he drove up, the front door was already open. A thick oak of a man stood in the doorway, bearded, wearing a *taquiyeh*.

Brett stopped the car in a cloud of dust.

"Hello," he said. "I'm here to see the imam."

"It's early," said the man. "The imam's office opens at 9:00 a.m."

"Tell him the Teacher sent me."

The mention of Ashammi's nickname caught the oak man up short. He took a step forward. "We know nobody of that name."

A hand crept up on the guard's shoulder. Then the soft voice of the imam. "It's all right, Mahmoud. I know this man." The guard moved aside, revealing a white-bearded, fiftyish, willowy man. His deep-set eyes gazed out at Brett, seemingly looking beyond him. Brett found it slightly unsettling. "Come in," said the imam.

Anjem Omari, Hassan had told Brett before Brett left for Jersey, was no one to be trifled with. He'd been rumored to have deep connections to various Middle East–based charities with their own connections to various terror groups. He fronted for a variety of Islamic human rights organizations dedicated to fighting Islamophobia, and it was in that guise that he'd become a go-to face for Prescott. The Prescott tenure had seen several small, lone-wolf attacks; each time, Prescott had cited Omari as evidence that the moderate Muslim community was alive and well in the United States. Omari spoke frequently about *jihad* as an internal struggle; he denounced terrorism, but evenhandedly decried American occupation of the Middle East and Israeli actions against Palestinians. His frequent appearances on network news made him a well-established media personality.

Now he ushered Brett into his richly decorated library, mahogany and grand, pictures of himself with Prescott and past presidents lining the walls. He sent his oak man for some tea. This time, Brett accepted. When the guard was gone, Omari turned his distant gaze to Brett—and the distance suddenly disappeared. *Hassan*, Brett thought, *wasn't lying.*

"So," said the imam, "what can I do for you, General Hawthorne? I am so glad you made it back to us in one piece. Allah must have protected you from harm."

"Indeed, he must have," said Brett. "I come here seeking your advice and help."

"And yet you mentioned the Teacher. Why would you think I know such a monster?"

"No reason," Brett said carefully. "But I am looking for a man, and I think that, given your prominence, he might approach you."

"I'm approached by many Muslims. I am blessed by Allah in having a wide following and a grand platform. How would I know the man you seek?"

"His name is Mohammed," Brett explained. "I know exactly who he is. He is perhaps seventeen years old. His beard is not yet fully grown. And I know that if he came to you, you would surely turn away his advances, thanks to his relationship with the Teacher. But you might also hope to convince him over time to join you in your cause, and leave his radicalism behind. After all, you are an influential voice."

The corner of Omari's mouth turned upward in a humorless grin. "Perhaps, General," he murmured. Then, louder. "But I know of no such man. Or rather, I know of too many such men."

"I think you do."

"Are you implying that I'm lying to you?"

"No," said Brett. "I'm flat-out telling you you're lying. I know you know such a man. So either you can continue spouting this line of bullshit and I can have you detained and questioned, or you can tell me the truth."

Omari laughed out loud. "No, I don't think you have that sort of pull, General. You may be a hotshot with a particular segment of the population, but, as you say, I am somewhat well connected. Gentlemen, please come in."

The door behind Brett opened. In came the federal agent from the hotel, his face impassive. Another black suit–clad fed stood next to him. Brett pushed himself to his feet. "Imam, I believe we'll be talking again."

Omari stood as well, looked Brett in the eye. "No, I don't believe we will."

PRESIDENT PRESCOTT

NEW YORK CITY

"You have got to be kidding me with this," Mark Prescott said. His eyes bulged. His face had turned beet red. "I'm trying to hold the country together, and you're out there fucking *supporting* the enemy by targeting Muslims? How am I supposed to counter the accusations?"

Brett sat on the couch, watching the president rage at him. On the way to the hotel, the Secret Service agents had been utterly silent; they refused to answer any of his questions, give him any information at all. But Brett figured that they must have picked up Hassan as well—how else could they have found him at Omari's?

Prescott continued to yell. "I elevated you. I *made* you. I *saved* you. And this is how you reward me?"

Brett could feel the anger building. He flexed his fist, then let it go, an old trick Ellen had taught him to take his mind off his temper. It wasn't working.

"Tell me. I expect an answer. What were you thinking? I gave you back your life."

"No," Brett said softly, dangerously. "I *signaled* you. I told you to hit the building."

Prescott scoffed, disbelieving. "You can't be serious. You wanted me to start a war with Iran? After Iraq? After Afghanistan? We just finished pulling the troops *out*, for God's sake. We got you out, didn't we?"

"That wasn't the goddamn point!" Brett never cursed, but now the filter was gone—he couldn't hold it back any longer. "The point was that I had intelligence that said Ashammi was there. My life for his. That was my trade to make. I just needed you to do your damn part. And you chickened out. As usual."

"I could toss you out of the military for this, General." Prescott's eyes were steely blue dots in a puffy red field. "You've gone too far this time."

"Go ahead. I'd love to tell the press just why you did. Because you couldn't keep this country safe. You weren't willing to make the tough choices."

Prescott went quiet for a moment. Then, oddly, he smiled. "Well, I'll make this tough choice, General. At least for you. You can either walk out of here and stop this nonsense, or you can keep going. If you keep going, I'll instruct my attorney general to draw up federal charges against you for violation of Imam Omari's civil rights. And this time, there won't be any sending you to Afghanistan."

"Mr. President, I would think not. You lost that country, so there wouldn't be much to send me *to*, would there? I just want you to think about this, Mr. President: all those people out there would be alive today if you'd just followed my advice. I'll tell that to every camera I can find."

Prescott reached down to the coffee table and picked up the remote control. He flipped the channel to CNN, where the anchors continued to gush over Prescott's big speech. "General," he said, "I can afford a few public relations hits right now. Rally 'round the flag effect, and all that. You'll be seen as an ungrateful rube looking to hit back at the man who saved you.

"Your time is over, General," he concluded. "Now get out of my sight."

Brett looked back at him as he headed toward the door. "I understand our enemies better now, Mr. President. You're not a very credible bluffer." He turned his back and slammed the door behind him.

Prescott woke from his nap an hour later to Tommy Bradley's face. Written across it was panic.

"Jesus," he grumbled, "what now?"

"Mr. President," said Bradley, "I think you'd better come see this."

When he stumbled his way into the living room, the footage from the television made him stop in his tracks. "REVEREND JIM CRAWFORD ASSASSINATED," the chyron read. "WHITE SUPREMACIST GROUP WITH TIES TO 'TERRORIST MAMA' IMPLICATED." Above the chyron ran the footage of continuing riots in the streets of Detroit. Then the anchors cut to some strong-jawed young black man named Levon Williams. They billed him as "Protest Leader."

"I call for the people of my city to join me. It is time to rise up and claim our freedom," he said.

The CNN anchor looked worried. "Levon Williams, the man you just saw there, was a close associate of the Reverend Jim Crawford. Jim Crawford, dead at fifty-four years of age, gunned down, we are told, in the bathroom of his hotel room. Crawford was in Detroit to calm tensions after the killing of eight-year-old Kendrick Malone.

"Law enforcement sources tell us that Soledad Ramirez, the fugitive wanted in connection with the bombing of government offices in Sacramento, California, earlier this year, was spotted during the chaos in the aftermath of the Crawford assassination, entering the police station. Sergeant Ricky O'Sullivan, who had just been cleared in Malone's killing, is missing as well."

The footage flashed to riots in Cleveland, Washington, DC, Los Angeles.

"The cities are burning," said the anchor. "The death of Big Jim Crawford has opened wounds Americans hoped had healed long ago. We still await comment from the president of the United States on this."

The moment had to end sometime, Prescott knew. But for it to end this quickly—for things to fall apart this quickly—felt like a blow to the stomach. He plopped back heavily onto the sofa. "Well, Tommy, what do you suggest?"

Bradley scratched his head. "Seems to me you've got two choices. One is to allocate resources from New York to these various cities. We've got governors beginning to call, asking for help from the feds; they want some of the Guard members we've brought here back in their states."

President Prescott shook his head. "No. Bad imagery. You remember Ferguson. You put guns on the street, you might as well tell the media you're a racist looking for street warfare. Next option?"

"We parlay."

"With whom?"

Bradley pointed at the TV, where CNN flashed footage of Levon again. "Him."

"What do we know about him?"

"Well educated. Popular. Some criminal connections. FBI has had an eye on him for a while. They say he runs a shakedown racket."

Prescott guffawed. "So did Big Jim, and that didn't stop anybody from sainting the bastard. Can you talk to him?"

"Will do."

Levon had set up his headquarters inside the now-abandoned detention center. Overnight, Levon had become de facto mayor of the city.

Without the force of the National Guard to back them, the local police had fallen into a standoff position with the protesters, but Mayor Burns refused to authorize action to push Levon and his men out of the building, believing that such action would be too provocative. Levon had quickly set up a system of runners among various positions in the city—he knew enough about surveillance practices that he didn't trust electronic communications.

The city had gone silent and cold; many residents wanted to flee, but feared that they couldn't get out of the city limits without being brutalized by roving bands of street gangs. The gangs had even set up roadblocks on the major traffic arteries. They were confiscating property from those who tried to leave, telling them that everyone had to be searched in order to ensure that there was no connection to the white supremacist group that had murdered Jim Crawford.

Levon didn't know the extent of his power yet, of course. Mayor Burns said that eventually things would be put back under control; he'd put in a request to the governor, and the governor had put in a request to the feds. But soon enough, things would calm down. In the meantime, he urged patience and restraint.

Levon, on the other hand, called for action. He humored every reporter, gave a quote to every journalist. He trotted out Kendrick Malone's mother as often as possible, making his own case for authority bulletproof on the back of her grief. Levon's long-term plan, he told the media, was "justice." He didn't define it, and they didn't have to know that he meant to run for office on the back of his organized resistance. It had worked for Marion Barry, Big Jim had said. It would work for Levon Williams.

All that changed at 8:34 a.m.

The phone rang on Levon's desk. When he picked it up, a female voice answered. "Mr. Williams?"

"Yes?"

"Please hold for the chief of staff to the president of the United States."

This has got to be some sort of fucking prank, or some sort of media hit, Levon thought. But when he heard the voice on the other end of the line, he knew it was neither.

"Mr. Williams? This is Tommy Bradley."

Levon leaned back in his chair, kicked his feet up onto the desk. "Mr. Bradley, it's good to speak with you. I voted for your boss, you know."

"Why, thanks, Levon."

In New York, Bradley paced the hotel room nervously. "Levon, I just want to express the president's *true admiration* for your move-ment. We want to thank you for trying to tamp down the violence, to keep things under control under very difficult circumstances."

Levon grinned ear to ear. He'd heard men beg him before. To have the surrogate for the most powerful man on earth preparing to do it was something entirely different. "Mr. Bradley, I really appreciate that sentiment. What can I do for you?"

"Well, Levon, it's like this. We couldn't admire your stand on social justice more, particularly in the wake of this tragedy with Jim Crawford. I know you and he were close friends. The presi-dent wants to ask you for a favor. Please keep your followers from committing acts of violence."

"Well," said Levon, "I'm doing the best I can. I can't hold everybody back. It's a passionate time…"

"Yes, yes, of course we understand that. But if you could do your best."

"Listen…In order for me to keep my credibility with my people, they're going to need the president to say something in solidarity. They're going to need to know that he endorses our movement for justice. They turned out for him at the polls, and they know he's with them, but they need some sort of sign. They're going to need him to pledge to stop police brutality against our people, and they're going to need his promise to reopen the Ricky O'Sullivan case."

Bradley coughed. "We can do most of that, Levon. But that last one, that's out of our hands. We don't control the DOJ."

"Well then we might just have a conflict here. I've got a lot of very angry people, and they're very angry for a reason."

There was a silence on the other end of the line. Levon heard some murmuring—he thought he heard Prescott's voice. Then Bradley was back. "Levon, as it so happens, I do have another idea that might serve both our interests. You're going to have to trust us."

"For how long?"

"Not too long. You'll see something on the news."

"What?"

Bradley sighed. "I said you'll have to trust us. Can you hold off for forty-eight hours? I promise, it'll be worth your while."

Levon paused for dramatic effect—he wanted Bradley to remember he was in control. Then he answered, "Sure, Mr. Bradley. Sure. Anything for the president. Love that man."

"Thank you, Levon, and he sends his regards." The line clicked dead.

And Levon smiled.

ELLEN

EL PASO, TEXAS

THE TROOP MOVEMENT ACROSS THE Mexican border began early in the morning with helicopter incursions into Mexican territory. The intel provided by captured border-crossers proved accurate based on the aerial photographs taken by state-owned drones, redirected across the border. The Apache attack helicopters veered low over Ciudad Juarez and fired directed rockets at a small duplex on the outskirts of the city. It went up in flames; Governor Davis watched the real-time broadcast, yelping as the duplex disappeared in a puff of smoke and dust.

"There goes one of the bastards," he smiled. That bastard was one of the leaders of the Juarez Cartel.

That was just the first attack of the morning. Over the next two hours, Texas National Guard attack helicopters would raze several buildings and strafe a small convoy of vehicles attempting to escape. The concentration of troops on the border made it nearly impossible for the cartels to try any cross-border action, and Ellen had ensured antiaircraft ordinance availability should any unforeseen black helicopters attempt to land on the American side of the border again.

That night was quiet—the quietest it had been for months.

The next day, though, residents of El Paso woke to a terrifying sight: a National Guardsman hanging dead from a billboard in the center of town. Painted in broad block letters were the words "PLATA O PLOMO"— silver or lead. In other words, pay us, or die.

Governor Davis wasn't in the mood to pay.

He ordered an immediate full-scale investigation, and he put Ellen in charge. She knew that nobody had crossed the border after the Texas National Guard incursions. That meant that the cartel had agents on the American side of the border.

For years, there had been rumors of significant drug cartel inroads into the city. Not just the civilian infrastructure—the city government. Just a few months earlier, nine former law enforcement officers were convicted on federal drug charges. The attorney general had said, "This creeping corruption resembles third-world country practices that erode the social fabric of our communities."

Drugs, money, corruption. The triangle couldn't be broken. And so the cartels had honeycombed their way through the force, using people with access to the border to work across the border.

Ellen acted swiftly, placing National Guard troops in the local police centers, increasing security along the border. Within hours, the Border Patrol had caught two men attempting to flee into Mexico. After questioning, Ellen had them detained indefinitely pending further investigation into their activities the night of the hanging. And she redoubled deployments to the border to stop any further infiltrations and deter any attempts by collaborators to escape into Mexico.

All of it was good policy. None of it made for good pictures on front pages around the country. And Ellen was stunned by the magnitude of the coverage.

The media coverage exploded with a protest on the other side of the Rio Grande: nothing but women and children. As the sun came up, at least a hundred women stood, carrying toddlers and babies, waving their hands and screaming for the National Guard to let them cross. The National Guardsmen stood their ground. They didn't point their weapons—Ellen and Davis had agreed there would be no such activity, for both moral and media reasons—but they looked threatening enough in their uniforms, young, strong, square-jawed. The cameras zoomed in on their impassive faces, contrasting them with the tear-stained faces of young children standing in the heat of the day.

It wasn't hard to gather who had tipped off the cameras: one of the biggest magnates in Mexico owned several major media outlets in the United States. Ellen wasn't surprised at the number of cameras showing up—obviously, this was a big story. Still, she resented the intrusion: there had been zero cameras for the murdered National Guardsman, but get a few dozen crying women on the border with their kids, and the media had a field day.

The cameras eventually found their way to Ellen for comment. "We will maintain the security of the people of Texas," she said. "Our immigration services have not screened any of the people out there. We're sure most of them are wonderful people who want to come here and work and build a life without taxpayer help, but we simply don't know who they are, and without screening them, we're not going to open our borders to anyone who wants to cross. We have the body of a National Guardsman hanging from a billboard that tells the story of what we get when we don't check those who cross the border."

The headlines hit almost immediately: "Texas Governor's Top Aide Says Immigrant Women, Children Pose Security Threat." Ellen could have slapped herself—she should have known better than to give them any material they could misuse. Then again, what material *wouldn't* they have misused? She vowed to ignore any calls coming from a media number.

Still, the news from Texas remained tertiary. And that meant that the operation to clean out drug cartel operatives in Ciudad Juarez continued to operate on the quiet. The Mexican military knew enough to avoid a significant confrontation with the National Guard; there were still honest members among its ranks who wanted the area cleaned of cartel influence. Each day, small groups of National Guardsmen raided Ciudad Juarez, usually by motor vehicle convoys across the border. The cartel members had picked up on the nature of the offensive action and had inserted themselves into heavily civilian areas, cutting down on the ability of Texas forces to strike without facing the prospect of urban warfare. Now, more dangerous search and destroy missions had been authorized.

The American side of the border remained silent.

Until it wasn't.

The first news of the massacre hit the airwaves three days after the Ciudad Juarez raids began. According to early reports, six people, women and children, had been found dead on the Mexican side of the border. They were protesters, and their bodies had been riddled with bullets. Over the course of the morning, the number increased: six, then twelve, then finally twenty-six people, all women and children, found shot to death on the banks of the Rio Grande. Everyone figured it for a drug cartel hit.

Then the footage came out.

Ellen saw it on the evening news, as the network anchor intoned, "What you are about to watch is very graphic. Younger viewers are advised not to watch." She then cut to grainy, close-range video of a man in a National Guard uniform, from behind, walking up to a group of tents. "Get out of thar," the National Guardsman said in a thick Texas accent. "Get out of thar, you little wetbacks."

A few children, rubbing their eyes, came scurrying out of their tents, their mothers following. Seeing the barrel of a gun, they raised their hands. The screen went white with the fired shots: flash after flash, again and again. When the night vision calmed, the smoking bodies of two dozen innocents lay on the ground.

The screen cut back to the anchor. "Our sources on the ground tell us that this tape has not yet been verified," she said. "No one has yet claimed credit for this horrific attack. Calls for comment to Ellen Hawthorne, chief of staff to Governor Bubba Davis, have gone unreturned."

Ellen quickly took out her phone—and sure enough, there in her messages were two voice mails from a 212 area code. *Son of a bitch*, she thought.

Now the phone rang again.

"Ellen," said Bubba, "get your ass back to Austin tonight."

"I want some answers on this, Ellen," Davis said, pacing back and forth, his thick body tense with energy. "I've got the president of the United States calling me every five minutes, and I'm putting him off for as long as I can."

Ellen gripped her fists. "I didn't ask for this, Bubba. I did it as a favor to you."

"Some favor," he said. "I've got two dozen dead kids and their mamas and a boy in a National Guard uniform responsible for all of it. A boy I kept here in Texas instead of sending him to New

York like Prescott wanted me to do. Do we know who the little bastard was?"

"Yes," she answered. "We do." Before leaving for Austin, Ellen had spent the night questioning all of the command-level National Guard officers she could get her hands on. A consensus seemed to be emerging on the name and nature of the culprit. And it wasn't pretty.

"His name," she said, "seems to be James Eastin McLawrence. Buck sergeant."

"Don't they all have three names," Davis muttered.

She passed him a photo of a young man in National Guard uniform. His eyes were open a shade too far, bright blue and off-putting. His mouth was slack. "McLawrence joined the Guard after dropping out of high school and getting his GED. Not a stellar candidate for higher rank. Barely at the bottom rung. He's full active duty. His parents live over near Lubbock. No friends in the Guard, at least none that wanted to speak with us."

"What set him off?"

"We don't have any hard info on that yet, Governor. But there are at least a couple of rumors. One says that he had it out for illegal immigrants ever since his dad lost his job at a manufacturing plant that moved south of the border. Another says he was short on cash and paid by the cartels. The third says he's just crazy. Simple as that."

'That doesn't make things simple for me. Who's the cameraman?"

"Your guess is as good as mine."

Davis leaned back against his desk. "Ellen, I need you to go to New York."

"Why New York?"

"Prescott wants me there. And I don't want to go. I can't go. I've shown him up in front of the entire country, and now he wants me there to humiliate me in front of the entire country for this massacre. Hell, he could have a local DA down here draw up charges against me so that they're frog-walking me when I get off the plane. It's a setup."

Ellen shook her head. "I still don't understand."

"They won't touch you because of Brett."

That actually drew a laugh from her.

"What's so funny?" asked the governor.

"You just don't know Prescott. He hates Brett. He's always hated Brett."

"But that doesn't matter, Ellen. Your husband's a national hero. You go to New York, the story isn't gonna be some dead Mexicans south of the border. It's going to be the reunification of the soldier and his wife. Prescott won't see it coming. He'll want me to negotiate with him, and instead, I'll be giving him the V-J Day nurse picture. Your husband's still got his admirers."

Ellen had to admit that the idea appealed to her. She hadn't seen Brett in nearly a year now; she'd missed him awfully. Every time they flashed his face across the television, her chest ached from missing him so much.

"And what do I say to Prescott?" she said.

"You tell that son of a bitch that we're not going to back down off the border, not for him or anybody. And if he asks you about McLawrence, you tell him that we're investigating. Turn down any federal offers for help. We don't need the feds down here mucking up our operation."

"That won't be easy. Cross-border murder falls under federal jurisdiction."

"He's busy. He won't mind. And it'll allow him to save face, to put me up for public scourging. I'll be the bad guy southern hick who won't let the sweet-faced Yankee down here to fix things. That's what the media's looking for anyway, right?" He sighed.

"And what's your endgame?" she said.

"Endgame? Darlin', this thing here's been going on since the Alamo. There's no endgame. Just a game that won't end any way except us holding our ground or cutting and running. But don't worry—you just play him for time. We'll find our Private McLawrence. And we'll string him up by the balls. You say that to the cameras. How soon can you be ready to fly?"

Her heart beat heavily in her chest. *Brett*, she thought. *Brett*.

"I can be ready tonight."

Her phone rang as she sat in the National Guard terminal, waiting for her flight to gas up. It wasn't a number she recognized. It came up as a 212 area code; this time, she figured, she'd best pick up to at least hear what the media had prepared. At worst, she could give a "no comment."

But when she picked up, it was Brett.

"Honey, don't come to New York." He sounded winded, hoarse.

"Brett, what's going on?"

"I can't say for certain yet. Just *don't come to New York*. Something bad is going down."

"How do you know that?"

"No time to explain…"

The line went dead.

SOLEDAD

NASHVILLE, TENNESSEE

THEY CAMPED OUTSIDE THE CITY. No fires. No lights.

They'd separated after Detroit, split up to avoid being followed. They set the rendezvous for Nashville three days later. Soledad recommended that they wend their way through several states to throw any would-be trackers off the scent. She took Ezekiel west, then south. Aiden took Ricky east, then doubled back through Kentucky.

Nearly all the men made it. A few apparently decided they'd had enough after Detroit, after seeing their faces on television, labeled white supremacists. They took off for the hills; Soledad told them to ditch all their electronic gear, to make for the northern border if they could.

The ones who were left looked like they'd been through a war.

Eddie was the worst. Fatso, as they all called him, had taken a tire iron to the gut, then gotten stomped at the center of the crowd. He'd been in and out of consciousness ever since, his fever spiking radically. Just before hitting camp, Ezekiel told Soledad, he'd started twitching, then gone quiet.

When Aiden and Ricky drove in, Soledad motioned them over. They put down their kickstands, turned off the hogs. Aiden's eyes were shining. Ricky still looked stunned. Aiden strode over to Soledad and picked her up in a bear hug. She waited until he put her down, then gestured at Fatso.

Aiden knelt down beside him. "Do we have anybody who knows anything about medicine?"

She shook her head. "We need to get him to a hospital."

"It leaves too much of a trail."

"We don't, he'll die."

Aiden stood up. "Doesn't look like he has much of a chance anyway."

Soledad felt anger well up in her. "Aiden, we did this your way. And Fatso knew what he was in for, or at least he thought he did. But we're not leaving anybody out here to die. Your friend here seems very nice and all, but it wasn't part of the plan to trade Fatso—Eddie—for him."

Aiden scratched his stubble. "He knew the stakes, didn't he?"

"Nobody really knows the stakes until their number hits. Come on, Aiden, I need your help."

Aiden made no move for his motorcycle.

Soledad stared at him, uncomprehending. *After all this way*, she thought, *he's still a soldier, and I'm still the amateur.* Then she shuddered. *No*, she thought again. *I'm the one who makes the call.*

"Colonel."

Ezekiel stepped forward.

"Give me a hand with this man." She leaned over the body, felt the heat emanating from the burning skin. She gripped him around the biceps, put her back into it—and moved him nowhere.

Embarrassed, she gripped him tighter, pulled again. When she looked up, Ricky O'Sullivan stood next to her.

"I didn't ask anybody to do this for me," he said, eyes far off. "But no one is going to die because of me ever again." He looked up at Aiden. "Get your ass in here and give us a hand, shithead."

Aiden spat on the cold ground. Then he leaned in, wrapped his large hands around Fatso's ankle. "I swear, Ramirez, this isn't going to end well."

She actually laughed. "Which part of running from the feds, then invading a heavily armed police station and grabbing the highest-profile cop in America sounded like it was going to end well?"

Suddenly, Ricky broke into a smile. A genuine smile. Soledad could see why Aiden liked him, felt so loyal to him. "She's got you there, Aiden," he said.

"Shut up," Aiden grumbled, pulling Fatso toward the van.

They dropped Eddie off at the emergency room of a local clinic. Ezekiel stayed with him—as the only person without a national face in the group, he seemed like the safest bet. "Keep your electronics off," he told them. "If you need to get in touch, find a pay phone along the highway." He gave a handshake to Aiden, one to Ricky. "See you fellas on the flip side," he said.

Then he wrapped Soledad in a bear hug. "I'll meet you at the rendezvous. If I don't show up in two days, I'm not coming. Just move on along."

"Why don't you come along now, Ezekiel?"

"Fatso here'll need some looking after. He has a family. Just want to let them know where he is. Maybe they can come pick him up before anybody comes looking for him. Maybe."

"Okay."

She, Aiden, and Ricky turned to head for the exit. Then she turned back. "Ezekiel," she said. "Thank you for everything."

He smiled. "You bet, ma'am. It's been an honor. See you in a couple days. You keep safe out there." Then he reached into his backpack, came up with his maroon scarf. He handed it to her. "It'll be cold. You'd best take this."

She smiled, nodded, and wrapped it around her own neck. They headed for the door.

As soon as they left the room, he picked up a phone from the nurse's station. He stared at it for a solid several seconds. Then he dialed a number.

"You let my girl go now," he said. "That was the deal."

"Okay, Colonel," said the voice at the other end. "A deal's a deal."

The headlights from the hogs carved a three-pronged gash into the darkness. To one side of Soledad, Ricky rode; to the other, Aiden. The night was silent except for the rumbling of the engines. The murky smell of the trees washed over Soledad—for a second, she felt herself smiling. Smiling, truly, for the first time since the drought. She felt free. She was safe; she led a group of good men, men unwilling to bow to a system that hurt people callously, that condemned them to an unled life as the price of living in a civilized society. She knew they called her a barbarian in the press. With the humid air of the Tennessee forests surrounding her, she couldn't care less. Somewhere, Emilio knew what she was doing, and why she was doing it. That's all that mattered, that someone remembered.

She glanced over at Aiden, then Ricky. At least a few people remembered. It had cost lives, but at least some people would remember.

"Aiden, I'm sorry I dragged you into this," she yelled at last.

"Sorry?" he grinned. "I've been waiting for this all my life. Something to fight for."

She glanced over at Ricky. His mouth was set in a tight line, his gaze focused on the dark horizon. "Nothing left to fight for," said Ricky. "You guys know what you're up against?"

Soledad felt a churning in her stomach. "Yes, I think we do. After what happened at the ranch. After what happened to you."

"They won't let us go, you know," Ricky said. "They say we killed Jim Crawford. They say we're white supremacists."

Soledad said, "Do I look like a white supremacist?"

"'White supremacy comes in many forms.' Direct quote, MSNBC today."

"They're nuts."

"Nuts, but effective."

Aiden shook his head. "Ricky, you worry too much. They want you gone. They want you disappeared. We took care of that for them."

"Oh really? And what about the Terrorist Mama here?"

Aiden growled, "You mean the woman who saved your life? Without her, you're waiting for that mob to burn you down."

Ricky shook his head again. "You think they won't? Man, you don't have a clue."

Soledad said, "So we keep moving. They're short on manpower and supplies. They have better things to do."

"No," said Ricky. "They don't. We *matter*. Don't you see? The headlines matter. For you and me, we look at the country and we say, 'Hey, look, big problems to solve.' They look and they see people to exploit. You. Me. Aiden, once he pulled his head out of his ass."

Aiden laughed. "Pretty cynical. So what do you suggest?"

"We scatter."

They went silent, the sound of the motors whirring on open road permeating the night.

"No," said Soledad finally. "We stick together. That's how they've kept us under their thumb all this time. No more. If they track us down, they track us down. But we'll stand together, or we'll fall separately. If it's good enough for Benjamin Franklin, it's good enough for me."

"You do realize," Ricky said wryly, "Franklin took off for some French whoring for most of the Revolutionary War."

It thundered overhead, and the clouds opened up.

"Shit," she heard Aiden say. "Just what we need."

A bolt of lightning flashed across the sky, temporarily blinding Soledad just enough that she swerved. Then she straightened out, following the other two. In the distance, thunder sounded. *A bit of rain like this*, she thought, *and we'd never have had to bomb that damn building to make our point.*

Another flash of lightning.

In the distance, she spotted a dark dot against the lightning. Not a cloud. Something solid.

Aiden spotted it, too. He hit the brakes, hard. So did Ricky. She skidded to a halt beside them.

"Turn off your lights! Get off the road!" Aiden grunted.

The three of them accelerated into a graded irrigation ditch by the side of the road. "That's a military drone," Aiden said. "Too small to be anything else."

"They could be looking for someone else," Ricky said.

"Like hell," Aiden shot back.

The drone glided low through the sky; it couldn't be more than ten thousand feet from the ground. It flew over them, and they crouched down as it did. "Did it see us?" Soledad asked.

"Not yet," said Aiden. "But I've never seen anything like that over here. Last time I saw something like that was Afghanistan. We used to call them in sometimes. What the hell is a Predator doing all the way out in the middle of Tennessee?"

"I don't know, bud," said Ricky, "but I think we ought to get out of here."

Aiden gunned his engine, drove directly for the tree line. Soledad and Ricky hit the gas and swerved to follow, carving a mud swath into the weeds behind them. She leaned forward over the handlebars, trying to will the machine forward. "Don't look back!" Aiden yelled. He was forty yards ahead of them now, picking up speed, almost at the tree line.

Soledad looked up anyway. The drone was almost above them now, and dropping closer for a better look. "Peel off!" Soledad shouted to Ricky, who nodded and began veering off to the right, back toward the road. She stopped her bike dead, then flipped it around and drove to the left.

The drone stayed on Aiden.

Soledad didn't see the drone fire the Hellfire missile—she wouldn't have had time for that. The explosion at the tree line blew her completely off the motorcycle. She covered her head, hit the ground feet first, then tumbled into the irrigation ditch.

She peeked over the edge.

The first twenty feet of trees had been completely obliterated. The embers of the splintered, burning trees floated through the air. On the ground, its rear wheel spinning, Soledad could make out the twisted metal of Aiden's bike. Near it, she could see what looked like a white lump of flesh. A mangled arm. A torn fragment of a maroon scarf she'd handed him to wipe off his handlebars.

She felt an arm on her shoulder. "Get to your damn bike!" Ricky shouted into her ear. "They're coming back around!" She tried to get to her feet, but her left leg wouldn't respond. Looking down, she could see the black ooze of blood creeping through her pants.

Ricky swung her roughly onto his back, then pushed himself onto the cycle. He cranked the throttle. "Aiden," she moaned. "Son of a bitch." Behind them, the drone dropped to attack altitude.

DETROIT, MICHIGAN

"GOOD NEWS, MR. WILLIAMS," SAID Tommy Bradley. "Things have been taken care of."

Levon smiled. "Thank you, sir."

"What's better," said Bradley, "we got the Terrorist Mama as well, plus a deserter from the SWAT team designated to take her down. So this will play really well in the press. We'd like you to thank the administration to the media, if you would."

"Absolutely, sir."

"Just so you know, Levon, the president is very proud of what you've done there. You've kept people under control in a bad situation. It won't be forgotten."

"About that, sir." Levon coughed. "I can only keep them tamped down for so long. My people are agitated about that attack, still. O'Sullivan being dead, that helps. But they still think the mayor is a shill for white privilege."

Bradley went quiet on the other end of the line. The other shoe was about to drop, and he knew it. He didn't expect Levon's boot. "I don't know how long I can keep these people under control," Levon continued. "I'm going to need some authority to reconstitute the police force."

"I can tell you the president isn't going to use federal forces, Mr. Williams."

"I'm not asking for that. I'm asking for you to swing some weight with the mayor. He had a deal with Big Jim. He told him he'd be remaking the police department to better reflect the community. You were going to send the attorney general to oversee the situation. There's no need for that now, but a word from you and the mayor will get out of the way. Just tell him to appoint me to a civilian oversight board, and let me bring some good people into the force."

Levon could hear Bradley hesitate. He pushed harder: "Your man has a reelection campaign coming up. Pardon me for saying so, but it seems to me that in the aftermath of what just happened, and with your big jobs program coming up, you're going to need every minority vote you can get. Every black vote. Michigan's a swing state."

"So what are you proposing?"

"I'm just saying that there will be an awful lot of grateful people here if they knew President Mark Prescott stood with the community in reshaping its racist police department. You let me reconstruct the police department, I can guarantee voter turnout will be extremely high anywhere we tread our feet."

"Anywhere you tread your feet?"

"Mr. Bradley, have you ever been to Eight Mile? On one side, there's garbage. On the other side, there's money. That money's there because they lived off that garbage. Did you really think my people were going to sit still and let them sneer at us over their ivy gates?"

Bradley blurted uncomfortably, "If that's a threat of violence, Mr. Williams, we can't countenance that."

"It isn't. It's a warning. We're going to need to keep the peace. Only one way to do that. We need more badges, and people who trust those badges. Call it a pilot program. Better, have the mayor do it. Maybe he'll do it to save his job. One call. That's all it will take."

"Why do you need us to intervene at all?"

"Because if I make the same…offer to the mayor, he'll call the governor, and the governor will call the president, asking for help. You really want that?"

"Mr. Williams, you make a convincing case," said Bradley. "I'll be back in touch later today. Oh, and Mr. Williams? Let's keep this between us."

"Wouldn't have it any other way," said Levon, grinning.

Within days, the applications began piling up on Levon's desk. He'd moved over to the mayor's office, taken up virtual residence there, along with his secret political weapon, Regina Malone.

His first meeting, with the head of the police union, Lieutenant Billy Baron, had gone poorly: the man was old school blue and didn't want to hear about changes to the department. He pointed out that they all had contracts. Levon, enjoying his newfound power, let the man stew for a few minutes. Then he told him he had every intention of honoring the contracts—there just might be a few more cops riding desks. The new boys, he said, would take over the streets. No more Ricky O'Sullivans.

Now things were running smoothly, though. Levon slotted personal interviews with each of the possible new officers. Each was slotted for ten minutes. Meanwhile, Levon worked with a committee, appointed by Mayor Burns but confirmed by Levon, to rewrite the use-of-force policies within the department. The mayor insisted that his civilian commission was blue ribbon, and that its recommendations be adopted.

Levon carefully crafted the new language. "The community expects," the manual now read, "and the Detroit Police Department requires that officers use *only* the force necessary to perform all duties, and that multiple areas of consideration be assessed before any force is used. When force is used, it must be proportional. Such areas of consideration include, but are not limited to: medical condition, mental illness, physical limitation, drug use, emotional instability, and race."

Under the "race" definition, Levon wrote, "Racial and cultural stereotypes have been utilized to dangerous effect in the past by members of this department. Racial profiling has led to disproportionate stops of those of African-American descent, and to disproportionate arrests and use of force against those of African-American descent. To that end, officers must take into account the prevailing cultural norms of any area they police, and respond to the cultural sensitivities of both suspects and the more general community."

When told of the new strictures, dozens of officers quit right away. "Good riddance," Levon told the mayor. "Less pensions for you to pay." When Billy Barton walked into Levon's new office and slapped down a list of four hundred officers willing to quit over the new standards, Levon looked him dead in the eye. "Well," he said, "I supposed it can't be helped. Change has casualties."

The media embraced Levon's new standards as groundbreaking. Racial sensitivity, they said, had never been used as an actual policing criterion, but nowhere was that criterion more necessary than Detroit. "Had Ricky O'Sullivan been taught and held accountable under these standards," Levon said, Regina standing beside him, "perhaps Kendrick would still be alive today.

Showing attitude to police officers is something a Detroit cop should have understood, had he been properly trained. Don't call our kids thugs just because you don't understand the experiences they've had growing up. They've seen cops pull over their dads, drag them off to jail. We have an entire generation of missing men in our community. Sensitivity is the key."

More officers dropped out.

And Levon began to build his force. He began with those nearest to him. At first, he thought to use only men and women with no criminal record. That would prevent anyone from claiming that he wanted to undermine the nature of the force. But he soon realized that too many young black men had spent time behind bars. He quickly changed the rules, with the mayor's approval: now anyone who had been convicted of a nonviolent felony—most of these were drug crimes—could be considered for employment.

"Policing only works," Levon told CNN, "if the police reflect the community. It just isn't effective to say that our law enforcement ought to be clean as the driven snow. Given the amount of racism against our community, and the disproportionate imprisonment of young black men, we cannot insist that everyone have a clean record. It's just not realistic. We've ensured that nobody with a violent criminal past can join the force, but as our country becomes more tolerant of marijuana, and as we reexamine the legacy of the failed war on drugs that has robbed so many black sons and daughters of their fathers, we see this program as a way of both rehabilitating young black men and strengthening law enforcement. Think of it as converting people from criminality to standard-bearers for a new, more tolerant America."

More plaudits. More resignations.

The final blow to the police enrollment standards came in the area of education. The standard for the department had always been a high school degree or an equivalent. Now, with the applications pouring in, Levon had to face the fact that not enough applicants had graduated from high school—many had dropped out. Again, he cited racial disparities in changing the policy, explaining that every trainee would be given remedial education necessary to do the job. "How can you expect people to work their way up the ladder if we don't give them the chance to get on the first rung?" he asked.

Within a week of the new policies going into effect, the constituency of the police academy had turned over by 40 percent. The old department had been more than 60 percent black; now it was nearly 90 percent black. It had also grown younger by approximately ten years on average. It would take a few months to siphon in the new recruits, but the force would change dramatically.

When Levon made the cover of *Time*, his picture emblazoned over the headline "THE NEW FACE OF LAW ENFORCE-MENT," he knew the time had come to make the next move.

That move came against Detroit Energy, which supplied most of the power to the entire southeastern Michigan area. For years, thousands of Detroit customers had failed to pay their bills. They simply assumed that the city would pick up the tab—which, for years, the city did. But as the tax base shrunk, DTE took it on the nose, and began enforcing its own rules, cutting off the power to some 25,000 customers per month, many of them in the Detroit metropolitan area.

The mayor understood his new role now. Levon knew that. The mayor knew that. He had become a rubber stamp, content to receive media paeans for pushing Levon's prescriptions into law. When Levon told the mayor that the next step would have to come in the form of energy fairness, with winter approaching, the mayor acquiesced.

Mayor Burns held a press conference, Levon at his side. "Detroit Energy," the mayor said, "has been defrauding its customers for years. Leaving them at nature's whim instead of working with them to help them through tough times. For years, the people of Detroit have paid their taxes and their bills, and the money has made its way north of Eight Mile, outside the Detroit city limits. We've got thousands of kids here getting ready to bunk down in freezing homes, just because a hard-working single mother can't afford the bills this month. Who are we as a society? Are we going to give each other a hand up? Or are we going to give way to our baser natures, our greed?"

That bright and sunny Tuesday morning, the CEO of Detroit Energy, Gerald Montefiore, found himself accosted by dozens of cameras. Montefiore was an overweight, well-tailored, shorter, elderly gentleman with a Monopoly-man mustache. Glaring into the cameras, he told the mayor and the city of Detroit, "No one has the right to steal, even if they vote to steal. And the mayor's new paramilitary force, his new police force, they can't violate the law just because they have the guns."

Levon responded on behalf of the mayor's office. "Our new police force represents the community of Detroit," he said solemnly. "And we can't be bought by any corporation. The city of Detroit is not for sale. America is all about the fair shake, all about caring for the least of us. Every citizen has a right to running water, clean air, and electricity. If Detroit Energy refuses to make its product available to everyone, we will be forced to take measures to enforce the rights of the people of Detroit."

Montefiore refused to attend a meeting with Levon and Mayor Burns. Instead, he sent his lawyers. Levon refused bluntly to even get in a room with them. "Eels," he told Burns. "You just let me take care of this."

The mayor had no choice but to comply.

That night, electric lines all over the city went down. Actually, that wasn't precise enough: electric lines just *outside* the city went down. The suburbs surrounding Detroit were plunged into blackness. Grosse Pointe, Dearborn, Ferndale, Oak Park—they all went dark at approximately 8:00 p.m., right in the middle of dinner. The calls to Detroit Energy began flooding the company; calls to the police force skyrocketed as criminals took advantage of the cover to begin looting.

Levon's police were conveniently busy elsewhere.

Within forty-eight hours, Detroit Energy had turned back on the power throughout Detroit. "We have seen the error of our ways," Montefiore told the media. "Crime springs from despair; despair springs from poverty. The only way to combat poverty is to allow young people, students, hard-working parents to keep receiving their electricity. Electricity makes a better life."

He didn't mention the billion-dollar check the city of Detroit signed, based on borrowing against junk bonds. Neither did Levon. Neither, of course, did the headlines.

BRETT

NEW YORK CITY

BRETT COULDN'T STOP SWEATING.

It wasn't that Prescott's threats scared him. Not after the public scandal with Dianna Kelly, bullshit though it was. Not after Afghanistan. Not after Iran. Not after spending years apart from Ellen. Prescott would be better off burying the whole situation politically, avoiding the backlash, making some payoff to Omari. This would blow over.

Brett wasn't sweating for himself. He was sweating for Hassan.

He'd been a fool. He knew that now. He'd been a fool far too often: trusting Prescott, serving in his administration, and then telling Omari that he knew about Mohammed's association with him. Omari could backtrack the story.

He'd been vague enough about where he'd obtained the information, he reminded himself. But there could only be a certain number of possibilities. Doubtless, Omari was tracking down every single one.

Then Brett thought of Prescott, and started sweating even more. How had the Secret Service found him at Omari's home, unless they'd tracked him? And if they'd tracked him, wouldn't they have tracked him to Hassan's house? He'd thought he'd lost them, but where had they reacquired his trail?

He sat in his hotel room, itching to do something. His hands clenched closed, open and closed. But now he feared using the phones—they'd surely be tapped by this point. He wouldn't be able to get free of the guards again. Somehow, he had to warn Hassan what was coming. He didn't trust Prescott not to pass on Hassan's information to Omari somehow. If that happened, Hassan would be as good as dead.

He had no choice.

He picked up his phone and dialed Hassan's number. Hassan picked up on the first ring. "General Hawthorne," he said. Brett picked up on the cue right away—Hassan knew they were listening.

"Hassan Abdul, I've heard so much about you. A mutual friend of ours referred me to you. He said you could answer some questions about Koranic philosophy for an article I'm writing about my experiences in Afghanistan and Iran."

"I think I might be able to contribute."

"Can you come over to speak in person?"

"Absolutely. What is your address?"

Brett gave him the address, then turned up the volume on the television. He knew they'd hear the conversation he was about to have with Hassan—their surveillance tools weren't going to be thwarted by Joy Behar braying the background—but he figured the noise might mask their movements somewhat.

Fifteen minutes later, Hassan knocked at the door.

"Mr. Abdul, so good of you to come," Brett said. He took out a pad of paper and wrote hastily as he spoke. "I was wondering if you could fill me in on the definition of jihad in non-Islamist jargon."

He wrote, "Followed to Omari's by Secret Service. They contact u?"

Hassan shook his head. Then, as he answered the question verbally with a long, meandering commentary on Koranic philosophy, he wrote, "Tapes hidden but not secure."

After another twenty minutes of phony discussion about the Koran, Brett said, "Thank you so much. I may have some more questions later, but that's enough to go on for now. Thanks for coming down. Perhaps you can stop by for dinner, so I can show my appreciation?"

"Why don't you pick me up at my place?" Hassan answered.

"That sounds fine, Mr. Abdul," said Brett. "See you tonight."

When he arrived at Hassan's apartment that night, Brett could feel the eyes of the federal agents on him. He'd spotted them right off the bat—hell, they hadn't even bothered to try to be subtle. They picked him up from the moment he left the apartment, through the subway system, and all the way to Hassan's apartment. When Hassan let him in, he immediately held up a piece of paper to his chest. "They stopped here today," it said. "The tapes are gone."

Brett's face went white. So they'd known all along. And then they'd waited for Hassan to leave the apartment to ransack it. "Son of a bitch," he whispered to himself.

Then he read the rest of what Hassan had written. "Found your Mohammed," it read. "Flatbush." Below it, an address.

Brett nodded slowly. Then, as they made small talk, he wrote, "Sorry. Will pull strings for u. U should b safe here. They r watching."

He said loudly, "I'll be ready to go in just a moment, Mr. Abdul. May I use your restroom?"

"Of course."

"Thank you." He gripped Hassan by the shoulder. "Thank you."

Brett made for the small washroom at the end of Hassan's hallway. Hassan lived on the second floor; Brett stuck his head out the window, took a look. The bathroom backed up to an apartment complex, a small alleyway. He knew he wouldn't lose his tails for long—they'd catch up with him. But if he could stay one step ahead for just a few more hours, he might have a shot at this Mohammed. He leaned his shoulder against the window frame, rammed it upward. He felt the jolt through his still-healing arm, but he shook off the pain and gradually pushed his feet through the window. Then, hanging by his fingertips, he dropped.

He landed softly, his athletic background taking over. To the back of the alleyway was a dead end brick wall. The only other way out took him to the street, where they'd certainly be watching. He crept up to the corner of the building, glanced down the street—sure enough, there were the cars, and two men outside of them, looking at the door. One smoked a cigarette as he glanced up and down the street. Beyond them, down the street, was a subway entrance.

"Shit," Brett muttered.

Then he sprinted toward the entrance.

As soon as he made a break for it, they spotted him. He only had a few feet on them, but the adrenaline kept him moving—ten feet, fifteen feet, extending his lead. By the time he hit the top of the entrance, they were a few steps behind. He took the stairs at full speed, five at a time, feeling his feet fly out from under him, stumbling forward, plowing into a man holding a briefcase. The collision knocked him off his feet, and Brett was flying downward into the darkness.

He tucked his chin to his chest, turned it into a barrel roll, popped up onto his feet. They were still running down the stairs, taking them one at a time. He hopped the turnstiles, sprinting full out, breath failing him.

Brett knew he couldn't keep this up much longer.

He glanced behind him—they were gaining on him now. They'd jumped the turnstiles, and one was yelling into his earpiece. The backup would be there soon.

He took a sharp turn down another flight of stairs…

And found himself on a platform. To his right was a wall; to his left, the tracks. Beyond them, another platform.

Ahead of him was another flight of stairs.

He made up his mind, ran toward the stairs—and then saw a *third* agent descending them.

He was trapped.

The subway platform began to shake as the train arrived.

"General," shouted one of the agents, "just come with us. You know we have our orders."

Brett breathed heavily, bent down and put his hands on his knees. He held one finger to them—*All right, just catching my breath, guys*—and then looked up at them as the noise of the approaching subway train grew.

He counted down in his head. He could see the lights approaching down the tunnel now, the men closing in from both sides.

Just as the train began to pull into the station, Brett took a deep breath, crouched, took three running steps—and leapt into the space between the platforms. For a moment he hung suspended in the air, the train speeding toward him, the agents behind him stopping short at the edge of the platform…and then he landed, his toes gripping and projecting him forward. He fell to his hands and knees as the train whooshed behind him.

Relief began to wash over him.

Then the train stopped and the doors opened, and the agents began to charge through them.

He pushed himself to his feet and ran.

Ahead of him was an overhang over another tunnel. Exits stood to the right and left. The platform was filling with people now as the train unloaded, obstructing him in every direction. He shoved his way through the commuters, knocking them aside. He felt a hand grab his shoulder—he wheeled around and pushed the agent off, wrestled his own way forward again.

And found himself at the railing. Below him were tracks. There was no way he could get to the exits now—he was boxed in, and as he looked back, he could see the three agents shoving people aside, shouting.

Again he felt the rumble, this time beneath his feet.

No time to think.

Aw hell.

He put his hands on the railing and threw himself over it.

The drop was at least five feet to the top of the moving subway, and it knocked his feet out from under him. He fell directly onto his back, and watched the subway tunnel rush above him. It had to be moving at least thirty miles an hour, and there was little room to move atop the speeding train. He began pushing himself back with his feet and fingertips, moving toward the back of the car. He didn't want to get caught on top of the damn thing and get decapitated by a train light or sewage pipe.

His fingers ached as he gripped them on the dirty steel of the car; he yelped in pain as he stretched his knee just a bit too high and it scraped against the cement of the tunnel. Soon, though, he felt his head reach the edge of the car, and he swiveled his body so that he could drop his legs over the end of the train.

Then he hung on for dear life as the subway station faded into the darkness.

Brett emerged at the Prospect Park station. He turned up the collar of his coat as he walked—the weather had chilled. His breath misted as he walked, rubbing his bloodied knuckles. It had been a long night.

He made a right at Parkside Avenue, then a left onto Flatbush Avenue, then a right onto Winthrop. Then he looked down at the address. He was here. Mohammed's apartment was located in an old-fashioned brick building, water-stained, its stoop guarded by an iron fence. He tested the gate—it opened with a creak. The door to the building, however, was locked. He buzzed two apartment occupants before the third let him into the building just to get the buzzing to stop so late at night. He slipped inside the dim corridor.

Apartment 3A.

He had almost no chance of avoiding detection if Mohammed was listening, he knew—the complex just wasn't big enough, heavily trafficked enough. Sure enough, a woman from 2B opened her door a crack to get a look at him. He glared at her, and he heard her shut the door and lock it. His hand felt in his pocket for a weapon he didn't have. Instead, he clenched his fists and made his way up the stairs. He tried to quiet his steps, but the stairs were too old, too noisy for that. Mohammed would almost certainly hear him coming.

But the hallway remained totally silent, except for his footsteps. *Click. Click. Click.*

He felt sick to his stomach when he saw the door to 3A: it was already open a crack. The light shone from beneath it. He edged toward the door, placing his back against the wall. When he reached it, he nudged it open with his foot. It swung fully open without resistance.

There, on the couch, lay Mohammed. His throat had been cut. Blood pooled under his body, dripping onto the hardwood floor. His open mouth gasped for air that would never reach his lungs. Brett rushed to the body.

It was still warm.

Brett knew: the apartment wasn't empty. The door would have been closed had the killer had time to leave. They wouldn't want the body discovered too quickly—that would give away too much information. Brett quickly turned toward the bedroom—as he did, he saw a large, black-masked figure out of the corner of his eye. He didn't see the blade of the knife. It cut into his arm deeply as he moved to block it, slicing it nearly to the bone. He gasped in pain, then kicked out with his boot, directing his strike at the knee of the intruder. The big man screamed as the knee cracked, fell to his other knee, pushed forward toward Brett, knife poised in the air, ready to come down.

Brett only spotted the second man now—but he wasn't moving to help the burly assailant. He held a bag in his hand, and he was struggling to sprint for the doorway. Brett leapt to his feet, tried to tackle the man from behind . . . but all he got was the ski mask. He pulled it loose, had enough time to get a snapshot of the man's face—in particular, an ugly burn scar near his ear.

Then the burly man's knife was falling toward him again. Brett rolled out of the way; then, lying on his side, he kicked him full in the face. The man grunted as his head snapped back; he dropped the knife. He reached out and grabbed Brett by the throat, beginning to squeeze.

Brett rotated his body, stretching his neck out of the hold. Then he grabbed the left wrist with his left hand, holding it steady, then snapped his left elbow into the man's face. He could feel facial bones smash against his arm. The burly man collapsed, breathing bloody bubbles through his mouth and nose. Brett pushed himself to his feet, stepped on the man's wrist. Then he took off the man's ski mask.

"Mahmoud," Brett said. "Fancy meeting you here. Now"—he placed the knife against Mahmoud's throat—"let's chat, just you and me."

A few minutes later, after subduing Mahmoud, Brett dialed Ellen. "Honey," he said, "don't come to New York…I can't say for certain yet. Just *don't come to New York*. Something bad is going down."

NEW YORK CITY

BRETT HAD BEEN MISSING FOR more than twenty-four hours.

Nobody knew where he was. Meanwhile, she waited in her hotel for an audience with the president of the United States, who was said to be busy planning a major public address to announce his major new initiative. And so she stewed.

The call from Brett had sent her into a panic. If she headed to New York, she knew, she'd be headed into danger—Brett wouldn't have called otherwise. But if she refused, she endangered any possible détente between Governor Davis and Prescott. Prescott didn't take being blown off lightly, and he certainly wouldn't take it lightly in the middle of the largest border crisis in decades. In the end, she decided that the summons of the president trumped the wishes of her husband. *After all,* she thought, a bit maliciously, *if Brett can go halfway around the world for the bastard, I can go to New York.*

But what she found in New York wasn't the chaos she'd expected. Instead, the military had done a brilliant job of cleaning up the city. Businesses had opened up again. Traffic clogged the main arteries. The dredging of the Hudson had just about come to its conclusion, although the Coast Guard still patrolled the waters in heavy numbers. Military men and women seemed to throng throughout the city, occupying every coffee house, every restaurant. *This*, she thought, *must have been what World War II felt like.*

The effect was oddly calming. With armed men and women everywhere, she didn't feel nervous—she felt reassured. No terrorist would be shooting up a restaurant anywhere near here. And she had to admit she felt safer in midtown Manhattan than she felt in El Paso, Texas.

Still, Brett was missing.

She'd tried his cell phone over and over. She hadn't gotten an answer—it went straight to voice mail. That meant it was either dead, or he'd broken it. Either way, it put him out of reach. She didn't feel too worried, not yet—she'd been through far longer without hearing from him, with him in far more violent places than New York City. But his absence did disquiet her. And his words rang in her ears: "*Don't come to New York.*"

Ellen was no detective. That had never been her specialty, never been her job. That's why she called Bill Collier. Collier told her that they'd lost contact with Brett almost as soon as he hit New York; he'd been using his personal cell phone, and while the NSA had access to the metadata, the White House had cracked down hard on Brett. Any attempt to end-around the system would be met with severe repercussions.

Ellen, on the other hand, was Brett's wife. And, Ellen thought, after the Dianna Kelly incident, any jealousy she evidenced would be seen as reasonable. Brett was a hot item again. Hot copy. She didn't have much to go on in the way of gumshoe abilities, but that's what journalists were for.

She picked up the phone and called Jack Blatch.

The thickly built, mussed-hair little man from the New York *Daily News* with the Coke-bottle glasses grinned at Ellen across the table. "Are you sure you don't want a sandwich?" he asked, his face shiny with sweat. "The roast beef here is delicious."

"I'm sure it is," Ellen said.

"What brings you to New York again?"

"I'm here to see my husband."

"I didn't even know he was here."

"Neither did I."

Blatch whistled softly, a smile creeping across his face. "And now you, the good little wife, want me to bust him for you."

"Something like that."

Blatch leaned forward, wiping his forehead with a hand-kerchief. "So, what changed? He comes home, big hero, royal welcome, the whole thing. And now you want to bust him all over the front pages?"

"I don't know." She coughed. "I haven't seen him for months. You'd figure he might be a little more intent right now on getting home to see me. But here he is, in New York, and nobody knows where he's staying. I can tell you Prescott has no idea where he is."

"That so?" Blatch muttered, scribbling in a notebook. "So why come to me? Why not do it quietly?"

"Because the president has a vendetta against my husband, Mr. Blatch. You may be a lousy bastard and a vile little rodent, but you'll at least do your research before you smack him."

"And what do you want in return for this tip?"

"I want to know twenty-four hours before you run with anything. Mostly, I want to know about his phone records."

Blatch guffawed. "And how would I get those, exactly?"

"I figure you have your ways. You had to track down Dianna Kelly somehow. And those reports of yours on the call times were quite detailed, as I recall."

"Clever, clever, Mrs. Hawthorne. Or may I call you Ellen?"

"No, you most certainly cannot. Do we have a deal?"

"Only if you give me the exclusive reaction."

She nodded curtly. "You have my promise."

He laughed. "And I assume it's worth more than his?"

"That's what I'm asking you to find out," she answered, getting up from the table.

Blatch came through. Within five hours, he'd tracked down Brett's cell phone number and call log. Most of the calls went to Ellen, he said—a revelation that made her uncomfortable, given that with his access to the logs, he could presumably track her calls, too. But there were a few that looked out of order. He was still tracking them down. The last phone call, aside from his call to Ellen, went to an apartment in Washington Heights. He'd gone over there and knocked on the door, but nobody had answered.

She asked him the address; she typed it into her cell phone as he dictated.

"Oh, and one other thing," he said. "The phone isn't totally dead. It's going straight to voice mail because nobody's picking up, but the phone company tells me that the phone is on. That means I can track location."

"Where is he?"

"He's moving around. The last time I checked, he seemed to be up by the bombing site."

"Thanks," she said. "Keep me updated."

"I will," Blatch said. "Got my best guys on it. If he's with some floozy, you'll be the second to know."

As soon as Blatch hung up, Ellen grabbed her coat and headed to the door. Blatch may have been stopped by a closed door. But Ellen Hawthorne had had enough.

The apartment in Washington Heights did seem to be empty. At least nobody answered Ellen's knock. She didn't have the brute strength of her husband—she wasn't about to go around knocking down doors, not with her increased media profile since the Border Battle, as everyone in the press seemed to be calling it. Instead, she knocked on the building manager's door and told him she smelled the gas on in the apartment. Thankfully, Ellen noticed, he was drunk. He looked her up and down, decided she wasn't a criminal, and handed her the key. "Come back when yur done," he slurred. She nodded childishly and headed for the stairs.

When Ellen entered the apartment, she was surprised at the pictures: a slim, middle-aged black man wearing the *taquiyeh*. How did Brett know this guy?

Someone had searched the place—books were strewn haphazardly all over the floor, and the bookshelves had been flipped over, torn down to the ground. It wasn't until she searched the bathroom that she found Hassan.

He was facedown in the bathtub. Someone had stuffed towels under the doorway to prevent the smell of decomposition from alerting the neighbors to his death. His face was blue, bloated, swollen, white-edged. His eyes were open, staring at the drain. The water was red with his blood. His throat had been slashed.

She noted her own reaction to the body—she wasn't even fazed by it. El Paso had done something for her reactions to brutality, she thought grimly.

She knew enough not to touch him—the police would be suspicious enough about the situation, and the last thing she needed was to leave forensic evidence all over the crime scene.

But she *did* notice that the blood in the bathroom wasn't relegated to the bathtub. They'd slaughtered him like a pig, all right, but the blood trail began at the bathtub, then made its way up toward the mirror. He apparently tried to get to something at the mirror even as he bled out, then slipped and fell back into the already-full bathtub.

Ellen stepped carefully over the puddle of thick, greasy blood and, using a piece of Kleenex, carefully opened the mirror cabinet. At first, she noticed nothing out of the ordinary: bottles of aspirin, ibuprofen, vitamins. But something had led this small, wiry man to spend his last moment on the planet stretching for what was inside.

She began opening the bottles one by one. When she got to the aspirin, she paused—a bloody thumbprint marked the top. She tilted it over. Out poured a dozen pills…and a thumb drive.

On the way out of the building, she slipped the key under the manager's door. Then she called the police and left them a tip about the body of a black Muslim man in Washington Heights.

The thumb drive, it turned out, contained one video. She watched it three times before she began to make out faces. It looked like a young, slim Muslim man, wearing jeans and a long-sleeved shirt. He shook hands with another man wearing a white Islamic robe. As the video continued, a third man entered the frame: tall, spare, white-bearded. The third time Ellen watched the video, she realized she was staring at the face of Imam Anjem Omari.

Prescott finally called Ellen that night. They met at a conference room in the hotel—Prescott sat at one end of the long conference table, with Tommy Bradley at his elbow. They placed her at the opposite end. She felt like a little girl called into the principal's office. But realizing that's exactly how Prescott wanted it, she steeled herself for the confrontation.

She was surprised when Prescott grinned at her. "Have you seen your husband yet, Mrs. Hawthorne?"

That little riposte, Ellen quickly figured, meant they were tailing her. "Not yet, Mr. President," she said. "In fact, I'm not quite sure where he is." She figured Prescott must already know that—otherwise, he wouldn't have asked. He knew better than to ask questions to which he didn't know the answers.

"Well, why don't we bring him up here? Tommy?"

Her heart almost leaped out of her chest. She swallowed it. She wouldn't let them use Brett against her. "Why don't we attend to business first, sir?"

"Your choice, Mrs. Hawthorne," Prescott said amiably. "How do we come to an agreement about the situation in El Paso?"

"Some border security would be nice, Mr. President."

He laughed loudly; the tinny sound ricocheted around the paneled room. "Other than that, Mrs. Hawthorne."

"We may be at an impasse."

He leaned forward, a sudden seriousness coming over his face. "I'm sure you can do better than that. Look, see it from my perspective. We just faced the most serious terror attack in our nation's history. All I'm trying to do is rebuild. And all I need is some time, some calm in the country. You've seen the situation in Detroit. The world's on fire."

"Whose fault is that, Mr. President?"

"What did you just say?"

"I said, it's your fault, Mr. President." Ellen couldn't hold it back any longer. A husband gone for years. A state in ruins. And this man—this man!—claiming to be the victim? "With all due respect, we wouldn't have this situation on the border if it hadn't been for your cheap political tactics of nonenforcement, and then forceful opposition to Governor Davis's plans to do something to secure that border. The reason Governor Davis won't help you is that he simply doesn't trust you."

Prescott looked like he'd been hit with a tire iron. His face went red, his fists clenched. "Okay, Ellen," he said softly. "Our conversation appears to be at an impasse."

He stared at her, enraged. Then, he continued, "Now, would you like to see your husband?"

He signaled to Tommy Bradley, who got up and opened the door to the conference room. Two Secret Service agents ushered in General Brett Hawthorne. His face was bruised, his clothes were filthy. He looked awful. His hands were gashed and scraped, the knuckles bloody.

For a moment, Ellen felt miles away. Her husband blurred through her tears. Then she ran to him, throwing her arms around his neck. He stood there awkwardly, then raised his hands to her head, stroked her hair. She breathed in the smell of him. The wonder of him.

Then he saw Prescott's smiling face and came back to earth.

She kissed his cheek. "What did they do to you?" she whispered.

He gently pushed her back. Then he turned to the president, his hands open, pleading. "Mr. President," he said, "you need to call Imam Omari here, right now, and get some answers."

"And why is that, General? We've had this conversation before."

"Look, Mr. President. I spent the last day tracking down leads on one of the men I spotted in Tehran. A man named Mohammed. I tracked him down through my contact—he has him on tape talking with Omari. I got away from your boys long enough to find this Mohammed's apartment. I fought my way through two men, one of them a henchman for Omari. And then I forced him to talk. Mr. President, I think we're looking at a nuclear attack on American soil. I tried to track the bomb itself, but I lost the men down near the harbor when *your* men picked me up. I've seen this strategy before, in Afghanistan: they draw you in with one bomb, then use a second to kill those who help. I think what happened at the bridge was the preliminary attack."

Prescott paused. He stroked his chin thoughtfully. Then he said, slowly, "I don't believe you."

"You already knew," Brett mused, enraged.

"I did. And I don't believe your intelligence is better than my CIA, my FBI, my Department of Homeland Security. I don't buy this Jack Bauer routine you're putting on. I think you've got delusions of grandeur, and that you always did."

"Then why am I here?" Brett said.

"Because," said Prescott, "I want your wife to know that what happens next is up to her."

Brett's eyes narrowed. He had been threatened by some of the worst people on the planet, and he'd been threatened by this sorry excuse too many times. He took a step forward—and one of the Secret Service agents stepped toward him. "What is this?" Brett growled.

"Tommy, can you hand me that folder?"

Tommy Bradley shrugged almost sadly, then slid a manila folder to the president. Prescott hesitated just a moment, for the drama, then slid out three photos: one of Ellen in Hassan's apartment, one of Hassan's body, and the third of Brett in Mohammed's. When Brett saw the bloodied body of his friend, he groaned audibly. "Dammit, Hassan," he whispered. "Damn me."

"I'm not going to ask either of you what you were doing in the apartments of dead Muslims," Prescott said. "But these photos aren't good for you. They won't land you in prison, of course— we all know there isn't enough evidence for that—but they'll be enough to ruin your careers."

Ellen stammered, "But you know that we had nothing to do with that. If you were watching, you *know* who killed that man, don't you?"

"Actually, I don't. I just know that after we stopped watching him, he wound up dead. And as for your crime scene, General Hawthorne, I've got at least two witnesses who place you there around the time of death. They won't be great on the stand, but they'll play in the press."

Ellen felt the breath rush out of her. "Why—why are you doing this?"

"Because, Mrs. Hawthorne," said Prescott, "your husband forced me into this. So did you. The president of the United States is not just a job. It's a high office. The president of the United States cannot look ridiculous. He can't have two-bit jackass redneck governors spitting in his eye. And he can't have rogue generals portraying him as a weakling days after terrorists blow up the damn George Washington Bridge.

"So here's my offer," he continued. "We all walk out of here as best friends. Ellen, you tell the press that we've reached an agreement, and that the state of Texas will be removing its troops from the border. You apologize for the massacre in Mexico. And just so your boy Bubba has a fallback position, you can tell them that I've pledged to up the federal support on the border as soon as possible.

"As for you, General Hawthorne, you retire quietly back to Texas with your wife. You keep your damn mouth shut, because I'm tired of hearing it. And from now on, you've got nothing but praise for me in the media. Nothing. But. Praise."

Ellen looked up at her husband. Saw his jaw working. She knew him. She knew what he was thinking: that this president wasn't worth fighting for, that no matter what, he couldn't stop Prescott from his dangerous policies, that perhaps it *was* time to give up and go home. Perhaps, just perhaps, they could finally just be with each other. Her heart actually swelled with hope—hope that their someday had come, even if it had to come from the madness and bullheaded stupidity of Mark Prescott.

Brett's head fell to his chest. He opened his mouth to answer.

Before he could speak, Ellen found herself answering Mark Prescott. "Mr. President," she said, "I'm sorry, but we just can't do that."

Prescott swiveled his chair to face Brett. "How about you, General? Do you want to talk this over with your charming wife?"

Brett hesitated. Then he spoke. "Mr. President, can you give us a few hours?"

Prescott smiled and nodded.

He knew when he'd made a sale.

THE END OF THE BEGINNING

NEW YORK CITY

MARK PRESCOTT HAD GOTTEN HIS moment. But now the time had come for the next step: the actual launch of the Work Freedom Program. He'd spoken with the Chinese government, and they had confirmed their prior commitment to purchase another massive round of debt. His advisors had warned him that too much leverage to the Chinese would place the nation's finances at peril, but his own economists told him differently: the Chinese, they assured him, could afford to take a financial hit even less than the United States. By tying the two economies together, in fact, President Prescott would be doing a service for the financial future of both countries.

Now he had the opportunity to merge the legacies of Roosevelt and LBJ. The clamor for retaliation against Ibrahim Ashammi and other suspected terror networks had begun from the right—his "love" speech had staved them off for a while. But now he'd need something more. A collective effort. If there was one thing Mark Prescott had learned from history, it was the power of a grand vision, the power of a call to sacrifice.

Today, he would make that call. And he would do so with the military as a backdrop.

Using the military for the backdrop would force the militarists to back down—he'd already planned to talk about how he would no longer send Americans to die in foreign lands. He'd retaliate against aggression, and his retaliation would be uncompromising and powerful. But there would be no invasions, no military occupations. America needed to rebuild, and these men and women were just the heroes to do it.

The speech poll tested well. The aesthetics had been planned to the most minute detail.

Preparations for the event had begun nearly a day in advance. The military set up bleachers to hold thousands of troops from across the country. Prescott insisted that the most racially diverse troops be placed directly behind him for the cameras, and had them all prescreened for political sensibilities. He didn't want any frowning faces to take away from this victory.

Security was heavy, of course. The bomb squads were out, and all the surrounding buildings were covered by sniper teams. The president's security team did worry about the massive crowd expected at the event—the president would be greeted by thousands of cheering New Yorkers. He knew how well waves of applause played on television. Plainclothes officers would be patrolling the crowd to check for a *Taxi Driver*-type lone wolf attacker.

The forecast for the weather: mid-sixties, clear, not a cloud in the sky. Mark Prescott couldn't have planned it better.

Today, Mark Prescott would finally change America.

Brett and Ellen sat together at the president's hotel. They sat close, their foreheads touching, their hands clasping desperately, so hard the knuckles hurt. Ellen had sobbed quietly into Brett's shoulder after Prescott left for a few moments. Now they simply held each other.

"Brett," she finally said, "I thought I'd never see you again."

"Well, I'm sure you're not too happy to smell me again."

In spite of herself, she laughed. Brett always could make her laugh. "Seriously, honey, you know I want you to be with me more than anything, that I can't stand more of this separation, more of this chaos. I want to take Prescott's offer too. But we just can't."

He laughed softly. "I know."

"So why did you tell him you'd think about it?"

"You're too damn honest, sweetheart. You always were." He leaned forward and whispered into her ear, his voice deadly earnest. "Ellen, we need to get you out of here. We need to get you out of the city. Prescott is a damn fool. Omari had Hassan killed. He had Mohammed killed. They're planning something big, I know that. I saw one of their men run out of Mohammed's apartment with a bag. It took some prodding, but Omari's man told me they were planning something at the harbor."

"But Brett, why just me? Why can't you come with me?"

He shook his head. "Like you said, sweetheart, I just can't. I can't just abandon things. I can't."

She took his chin in her hands. "Honey," she said, "I never thought you would. It's why I love you." She leaned forward and kissed him. Then they stood, hand in hand. Brett knocked on the door. Tommy Bradley opened it.

"We're ready to talk to the president," he said.

"We'll meet him at the airport," said Bradley. "He's scheduled to leave from there as soon as his speech ends. Right this way."

The crowd began filing into the streets near the harbor two hours in advance. The security team had expected anywhere between five and ten thousand New Yorkers to turn out—but as the minutes passed, it became clear that double or triple that number had turned out. They needed something: a feeling of unity, a feeling of togetherness, a feeling of being a part of something optimistic again.

They came from all backgrounds: black, white, Hispanic, Asian. They were all ages: the elderly came in their wheelchairs, the young pushing strollers. They came bearing American flags and signs: "GOD BLESS THE USA" and "STAND STRONG" and the takeaway line from Prescott's *moment*, "TOGETHER WE WILL RISE." They stood in the heat, sweating, vendors moving through the crowds, tossing bottles of water and popcorn and dirty water dogs. The whole day had the feel of a mass picnic.

The throng grew, and then grew again. It poured out from the harbor area into the streets. It filled blocks.

Soledad casually slipped her way through the crowd.

Being dead certainly helped her escape scrutiny, she observed wryly. Aiden would have appreciated the irony. A few blocks away, she knew, Ricky O'Sullivan waited with the car. Her chances of escape were slim, of course. But she also knew that assassination attempts rarely ended with the assassin immediately detained: Oswald had made it to a theater; Booth had run for days. They'd catch her eventually, she figured, but they'd have to revise their estimate of her death first to identify her.

Aiden's death had changed her, hardened her, she knew. She could fob off the California water crisis as political bureaucrats playing games. She could even pretend that Ricky O'Sullivan had been railroaded by a race-baiting system. But the drone attack—that was on Prescott. She had voted for Mark Prescott the first time. His promises of a better America, a more caring America, appealed to her.

Then, it turned out, caring was just a cover for control.

The drone had targeted both her and Ricky, but they'd made it to the trees in time. The military must have miscalculated; for whatever reason, she and Ricky had been stunned to see headlines touting their deaths. They'd hunkered down in the woods for a few days; by the time they made it back to camp, the group had disbanded, disappeared.

That night, as they sat by the fire in a country that had tried to kill both of them, Soledad broke down and cried. It was the first time she could remember, at least since the death of her parents. It wasn't that Aiden had been so wonderful—there were times, she knew, she couldn't stand him. But he represented hope to her in a way difficult to quantify. She believed in the inherent goodness of the system, despite everything, and Aiden represented that: a system made of good people who, when push came to shove, would stand against the powerful on behalf of the powerless.

And then the powerful killed him.

Meanwhile, after Aiden's death, Ricky snapped back into the zombie state he'd been in before the rescue. He felt like a man apart, alone. The headlines about Soledad didn't surprise him—of course the media and many Americans would celebrate her death. It was the easiest thing to do. Better to cheer the downfall of a lone terrorist than to hold up her cause for understanding.

He had been stunned, however, by the triumphalism with which the media treated his own death. He'd been *acquitted*, for God's sake. He'd tried to serve his community. And there, on television, were faces from his hometown, Detroit, smiling at the news of his death. And there was Mark Prescott, telling the press that the killing showed that Ricky O'Sullivan trafficked in terrorism, and the killing closed the door on a "sordid incident sullying our national unity."

Something had to change. He knew it. Whether Soledad was right or wrong no longer mattered to him. Something had to wake people up.

They had turned their motorcycles toward New York City.

Soledad felt the handgun in her purse. It was a 3D printed plastic gun; she'd bought it from a gun enthusiast in Ohio. He'd been a nutcase, obsessed with weaponry, with an industrial-grade printer in his garage. Prior 3D printed guns had been made with a few key pieces of metal to absorb the explosion of the gunpowder in the bullet—but this guy had perfected a method of making specialized bullets with a thicker shell that could absorb the brunt of the explosion. That meant no metal in the gun at all, just metal in the bullet. The plastic gun could be hidden in the bottom of her purse and wouldn't set off a metal detector. And she could hide the bullet virtually anywhere. She chose to embed it in a pair of gaudy, dangling earrings.

That meant she'd have one shot.

She'd have to get within a few dozen yards of the president. But if she did, she knew, it would be enough.

Thanks to the foot traffic at the harbor, traffic had screeched to a standstill across the city. Brett and Ellen occupied one end of the limousine; Tommy Bradley sat across from them. For a few minutes, the White House chief of staff tried to engage with Brett and Ellen. When he realized they weren't in the mood for small talk, he went quiet. Now they stared at each other awkwardly. Eventually, Bradley took out his cell phone and began making calls, smiling apologetically as he did so.

Brett turned to Ellen. He whispered to her, "I need to go now, sweetheart." She looked up at him quizzically. He continued, "They won't let me go anywhere once we get to the airport. I need to get down to the harbor. But you listen to me: whatever you do, you get on the plane with Prescott. I don't know whether this attack will come at the event or not. But I want you out of this city." He paused. "I'm so sorry for this, Ellen. I'm so sorry for everything. We could have had a life together."

She looked at him, dead in the eyes. "Brett Hawthorne, I want you to know this: you are my hero. You always were. I am so proud to be your wife. I wouldn't trade my life for anyone's."

They felt the urge to kiss each other—then they remembered Bradley in the car, and hugged instead. "Take a bullet for you, babe," he said.

"Take a bullet for you, sweetheart," she answered.

Before Bradley or the Secret Service agent in the car could react, Brett reached for the lock, popped it open, and stepped out into traffic. By the time they responded, Brett had dodged through the cars, sprinted around the corner, and was gone.

In the car, Bradley glared at Ellen. Then he dialed. "Yes, Mr. President," he finally said, after the yelling subsided. "I'll take care of it. And yes, I've got Mrs. Hawthorne right here. He'll be back. I'll tell security to keep an eye out for him down there."

Brett reached the outskirts of the crowd just as the event began. Everyone in the huge throng could see the developments—Prescott's team had made sure to place enormous television screens throughout the area, projecting the events of the day for the overflow crowd. There, up on the dais, stood Imam Anjem Omari, giving an invocation. " 'Whoever kills a soul unless for a soul or for corruption in the land, it's as if he has slain mankind entirely,' " said Omari. " 'And whoever saves one life, it's as if he has saved mankind entirely.' So says our Holy Koran. And we all stand together against those who murder. Make peace, for Allah has proclaimed it so."

A polite applause rippled through the audience. Brett began to muscle his way forward, his eyes trained on Omari. The imam walked to the edge of the stage, then took his seat. Beside him sat Mahmoud, his nose bandaged. Brett began moving more quickly through the crowd now, weaving in and out. He was within 150 feet of the stage when the president rose to his feet for his introduction.

A video played on the screens flanking the stage: video of soldiers hugging crying family members of the slain, of Coast Guard members directing activity on the Hudson, and then, finally, of President Mark Prescott hugging the protester. Then his theme music began to play, a hard-pounding rock track, and he strode to the stage, waving to the crowd, grinning, giving the thumbs-up.

The crowd roared its approval.

It made Brett queasy. There were no pictures of the fallen in Afghanistan or Iraq. No pictures of the bombs going off under the bridge. President Prescott was a hero, the man who could bring America back together again.

He had no time to focus on all of that, though. Omari and his friend were whispering. Omari nodded, smiled softly, then glanced at his watch.

The president stood at the microphone, let the cheering wash over him. It felt as he always thought it would: better than the election, better than the inauguration. It felt as though all of America held him in its embrace. He raised his hands once more, and the crowd silenced, as if a conductor had told his orchestra to play pianissimo.

"My fellow Americans," he said, "we stand strong. We stand together. And today, we show the world, we will fight. We will win. And we will build.

"As we speak, I have authorized our air force to strike targets in Syria …"

Syria? Brett thought. *What the hell is in Syria?*

Prescott continued, "Our intelligence tells us that this vicious terror attack was masterminded in that war-torn country. We felt the brunt of their rage, and we took their best shot. Now they will take ours."

Screams, shouting, jubilation. Brett had never heard a crowd respond like this to any politician. "And," the president of the United States continued, "we will not stop there. We will build, as I promised we would. As of this morning, I have signed an executive order authorizing the Work Freedom Program. We have much rebuilding to do, and every American will play a part in that rebuilding!"

The roar redoubled.

Mahmoud, Brett noticed, had edged toward the stairs on the stage.

"We must build," said Prescott, "because America always strives for the highest apex. We dream big, and those dreams become reality. Look around you: they destroyed one of our bridges, but we have built thousands upon thousands of monuments to human ingenuity together. Only together!"

Brett glanced behind him—he could see a large man in a baseball cap, his head down, approaching his position from behind. An agent, no doubt. Brett began moving forward again. He was no more than seventy feet from the stage. Mahmoud had left the stage now, and seemed to be moving away from the dais.

Prescott gestured toward the skyline. "And we will build even higher. We won't just build monuments, though, to materialism.

We will rebuild ourselves. Better than we were before. More charitable. More giving. We will ask more from all Americans, and they will respond, because Americans always respond."

Brett was so focused on Mahmoud that he bumped into a smaller woman in front of him—pretty, close-cropped hair, in her early fifties. "Pardon me," he mumbled.

Then he saw her hand in her purse.

He'd seen that arm angle before. He knew what a person looked like before they pulled a gun from concealment. He could feel the threat before he even knew he felt it.

He responded instinctually. "Gun!" he shouted, grabbing at her hand. Before she could respond, he'd wrested control of it from her, but she managed to pull the trigger, firing uselessly into the air.

The crowd around them panicked, moving a thousand directions at once, women falling to the ground, men trampled. On the stage, Secret Service agents jumped onto Prescott to protect him, then hustled him off the stage as sirens began to wail and screaming broke out en masse.

Brett realized he was holding the gun a split second before he felt a large man jump on his back, slam him to the ground. The man put his knee to the back of Brett's head, driving it into the pavement. "Dammit, you idiots," he gasped, "it's not *me* you're after."

He glanced up at the face of the Secret Service agent on his back.

A thick burn scar marked his face near his ear.

Then everything went black.

Ellen had watched the proceedings aboard Air Force One. She watched the flustered anchors on the major news networks try to get a bead on the story, giving out unverified information, then retracting it. She knew Brett had no cell phone, so she had no one to call—instead, she waited.

It took nearly an hour for the presidential motorcade to come steaming onto the airfield at LaGuardia. The Secret Service rushed out of their vehicles, ran to the side of the presidential limousine, and created a phalanx around the president. Ellen watched as they brought Mark Prescott, his head covered, up the stairs to the Boeing VC-25. By the time they released him at the top of the stairs, he was cursing a blue streak, shouting. "Dammit, I want some answers! How could you let something like this happen? We *had* security, didn't we? And now I look like I'm cutting and running from the site of a terrorist attack?"

He spotted Ellen and ran over to her, his face red with anger. "Your goddamn husband …"

"My goddamn husband was saving your life," she said slowly.

Prescott laughed harshly. "Bullshit. He had a gun on him. He fired it. I want to know why."

"That's not his gun."

"How the hell would you know? You haven't seen your husband for months."

"I know my husband."

Prescott sneered. "Here's what *I* think. I think your husband showed up at that event because he's got a fixation with the imam. I think he's so suspicious of the imam that he actually thought the imam was going to try some sort of attack on the event. And he came to break it up." Prescott was working himself into a full rage, spittle flecking his upper lip. "I tried to reason with him. I tried to reason with you. But enough. I'll find whatever charges I need to find to press against him."

"Mr. President," she said, "you need to calm down."

"Calm down?! Have you seen these pictures? You said I was weak. *You said it.* Now, don't I look weak? Like I can't stand up to threat with the entire goddamn American military at my back?" He stormed past her. Tommy Bradley shrugged at her apologetically. As he followed the president, she grabbed his coat.

"Mr. Bradley, where are they holding Brett? He's got to know this is crazy, right?"

Bradley looked at her, shrugged. "I don't know anything," he said. Then he followed his boss.

She sat, stunned. From her vantage point aboard Air Force One, through the windows of the airport, she could see guests filtering through security. Security, of course, was heavy—every person and their baggage moving through a metal detector and an X-ray machine, bomb-sniffing dogs all around. She'd gone through the same routine herself before being allowed onto Air Force One.

Except for a man she didn't recognize at first, who emerged with his bodyguard from the presidential motorcade. The bodyguard carried a large duffel bag. Next to them stood a Secret Service agent; he carried a burn scar near his ear.

Secret Service quickly approached, but the agent drew them aside. After a brief conversation, they parted to let the men through.

Ellen put her head in her hands. She had no plan for Washington, DC—she and Brett hadn't had time to come up with a strategy. But she knew she would have to turn the president down. And she knew that the consequences could mean legal action, maybe even military action, against the Republic of Texas, against her, and against Bubba Davis.

When she looked back to the front of the cabin, she saw the two men from the motorcade entering. She didn't recognize the first. She felt a flash of recognition as she saw the second: Omari. As his colleague stuffed the duffel bag he'd been carrying in the overhead compartment, all she could see was Hassan's body, facedown in the bathtub. What was so important about that tape?

He knew Brett had seen it already—he knew Brett was tracking down the other man on the tape, clearly.

The safety announcements came over the loudspeaker. She buckled herself in, watching Omari and his man sit two rows ahead of her. Omari bowed his head, mumbling to himself. She couldn't catch the words—they were in Arabic, and she didn't speak the language anyway. The plane began to move.

The plane took off smoothly, flying to the northeast, then beginning to turn. Through her window, she could see the city fading behind her, leaving her husband behind, presumably in some cold cell somewhere. Air Force One continued to make a 180-degree turn, flying over the city. They'd gained altitude now, on the ascent as they moved south toward Washington, DC.

Then, oddly, the plane began to drop. The buildings of Manhattan grew nearer beneath the plane as Ellen watched curiously through the window. The voice of the pilot poured through the speakers: "Ladies and gentlemen, don't be concerned. The president has requested that we descend to a lower level over the city of New York in order to take publicity photos."

Publicity photos? Today? Ellen thought as the plane descended. As if the pilot were reading her mind, he continued: "The president wants to let Americans know he will not be cowed by any violent attempt against him. Thanks, and please ensure your seat belts are fastened."

Ahead of her, Omari still muttered in Arabic.

Then he unbuckled and stood up. In his hand, he held what looked like a cell phone, powered on. He said, much louder now, "*La ilaha illa Allah.*" Then again. The other man chanted along with him.

Suddenly it hit her: Mohammed had not sought out Omari for help. Mohammed had been a courier *to* Omari, bringing him a weapon. Brett had been right: they had planned the terrorist attack at the event, but the chaos had destroyed their timeline. *Oh, Brett*, she thought. *Oh, Brett.*

The plane circled lower as it approached the center of Manhattan. Ellen realized then what she had to do. Why, perhaps, God had given her no children to leave behind. Why she had been fated to marry a patriot and a military lifer. She was one, too: a soldier in a war. And she had to act now, before they hit downtown.

The other passengers looked around uncomfortably, paralyzed by a peculiar inability to overcome their political correctness. She unbuckled her seat belt and edged to the aisle. Then, she got up calmly and walked toward Omari. Before she could speak, Mahmoud cut her off, grabbed her hand, twisted it behind her back, then threw her to the ground. "He has a bomb!" she shouted.

Secret Service agents appeared behind Omari almost instantaneously; two agents pulled guns in the press cabin itself. Omari held up his phone. "All I want is to negotiate," he said. "President Prescott will speak to me. I know he will."

The agents froze. Omari had been invited by the president. This had to be an enormous mistake, something that could be worked out.

From the floor of the airplane, Ellen looked up at Omari. He was lying. She could see it. He was stalling for time. *No more time*, Ellen thought to herself. *No more talk, negotiations, games.* A line from her past crept into her head for some reason: *No loitering, cadet.* She almost smiled as she remembered.

"Take a bullet for you, babe," she whispered to herself. Then she pushed herself to her feet, launched herself past a startled Mahmoud, and grabbed Omari's phone.

Air Force One exploded at approximately two thousand feet. The daylight went bright, then brighter, a blinding green flash in the sky forcing people miles from the detonation to look away. The blast wave hit almost simultaneously with the light—those nearest the blast would never register it. The blast blew through skyscrapers, tearing them down sideways, their glass facades disintegrating almost instantaneously. It tore through Washington Heights, obliterated full blocks. It set the trees on fire through Fort Washington Park. Tenements blew apart like a house of cards. The shock wave exploded through the streets, disintegrating peoples' clothes, ripping the flesh from their muscles, tearing their faces open, turning them to ash nearest the bomb site; further away, debris from the buildings killed hundreds more.

Tens of thousands of military men and women still in the midst of cleanup at the George Washington Bridge were killed almost instantaneously; thousands more of them were wounded, doomed to radiation poisoning, burned beyond recognition by the nuclear wind in the aftermath.

General Brett Hawthorne saw none of it. He was staring at the wall of his cell near Battery Park when the bomb went off; he merely saw the sky grow light.

He turned to stare into the distance. He saw the mushroom cloud rise above the profile of the new Freedom Tower. "Oh, no," he whispered. "Oh, God, please, no."

Then he fell to his knees and buried his head in his hands, screaming silently.

EPILOGUE

WASHINGTON, DC

"GOOD EVENING, MY FELLOW AMERICANS."

The former governor of Michigan looked directly into the camera. She spoke from the East Room of the White House. The tears in her eyes were genuine; she forced them down.

"I know many of you may not know me; few Americans bother to learn the name of the vice president of the United States. But my name is Allison Martin. A few hours ago, I was sworn into office as the president of the United States.

"By now, I'm sure you have heard the news from New York City, where our nation's greatest city has once again been struck by the scourge of terrorism. I am also sure that you have heard that the president of the United States, Mark Prescott, was the target of that attack, along with hundreds of thousands of the citizens he loved so much."

Her green eyes, hardened by years in the political limelight, glinted. She had earned the lines around those eyes, the worry lines around her mouth. Allison Martin had fought her way to the top of American politics. She had done so not as a token woman on a vaguely inspirational ticket, but as her party's chosen ideological warrior. Allison Martin, they said, backed down from no one. She would keep Mark Prescott honest.

Her enemies had questioned her qualifications, her achievements. They had implied that her sex had elevated her to the second highest office in the land; they ignored her degree from Harvard, her law degree from Columbia. They had overlooked her.

Her speaking style was mechanical. She was unlikable. She did not have the charm of Mark Prescott; she did not inspire. She was, as she liked to think of herself, a grinder. She did not, she reminded her subordinates, tolerate losing.

"I would give my own life to have preserved Mark Prescott's. Mark Prescott was a visionary leader, a public servant for his entire life. He died serving the public, standing for you. He lived for unity, not divisiveness. He lived to bring people together.

"We will live for him, and for his memory. We will keep our commitments, and the commitments of President Prescott. The commitment to build. The commitment to love one another. Mark Prescott's visionary sense of Americanism will live on in our hearts, and in our policy. What Mark Prescott brought out in us, we will magnify; what Mark Prescott uncovered in us, we will allow to shine forth."

Her voice rose a pitch in urgency and tenor. "Mark Prescott was always honest with you. And I will be no less honest. Here is what we know tonight. We know that there was an assassination attempt on President Prescott today at New York Harbor; it was thwarted through the diligent work of our security on the ground. We do have a man in custody.

"Shortly after the attempted attack on the president, the president's security team moved him aboard Air Force One, where he was accompanied aboard by media and political figures. We have released a full list of those aboard the plane, all of whom lost their lives in today's tragic terrorist attack.

"The White House has been in negotiations with the State of Texas over Texas's refusal to abide by federal immigration law, and Governor Bubba Davis's unconstitutional use of state troops to attack a sovereign nation outside the borders of the United States. President Prescott had invited a representative of Governor Davis to New York City to discuss possible solutions. That representative, Ellen Hawthorne, is suspected of having smuggled and detonated a small-yield nuclear weapon aboard Air Force One.

"This aggression will be answered. As President Abraham Lincoln once did, I now appeal to all loyal citizens to aid the effort to maintain the honor, the integrity, and the existence of our national union.

"Now, life will undoubtedly change in the short term. Our intelligence shows that the highest levels of our government have been penetrated by those who sympathize with the extremism of Ellen Hawthorne and the State of Texas. This is a time for unity, not disunity, and we must steel ourselves for the battle ahead.

"There is also no question that America's capacity for rebuilding has been significantly damaged by recent events. Our estimates show the loss of tens of thousands of American troops. Our stock market has dropped precipitously; the value of the dollar has fallen off. But hope is around the corner. Tonight, we request that the American people stand together and find the best in themselves. Help is on its way.

"And we will help ourselves. Those who perpetrated this heinous act will be brought to justice. America will be made whole again. I stand with you, and we stand together.

"Let me end tonight with a quote from President Mark Prescott, spoken just a few weeks ago at the site of the George Washington

Bridge bombing. 'Love for each other,' the president said. 'Care for each other. Sacrifice for each other. And that's what I'm going to ask of all Americans now. Not anger, not lashing out, not blame or knee-jerk reactions. Love. Love your neighbor. Love your country. Stand together. And together we will rise. For in times like this, in times of tragedy and horror, it is love we most need.'

"We will love each other like never before. America, we are strong. Good night, and God bless us all."

The red light on the camera blinked off. Allison Martin looked at her reflection in the dark eye of the lens. Then she stood, ramrod straight, and walked briskly toward the Oval Office.

DETROIT, MICHIGAN

Levon spoke into the computer's camera. On the line, he could see from the list on the right-hand side of his screen, were the mayors of Indianapolis, New Orleans, Chicago, Philadelphia, Baltimore, St. Louis, Boston, Memphis, and a dozen other major cities. He'd talked with all of them repeatedly over the past few weeks, since the media and Mark Prescott had appointed him an emissary of peace, and since his big victory over Detroit Energy. Levon had reached out to others, too—"activist affiliates," he called them— who could influence the community to bring pressure against companies and government actors.

Now he sat alongside the mayor of Detroit in his conference room.

"Folks," Levon said, "I have known President Martin for a long time—we had dealings when she was governor of my state. She has asked me to speak with you all about basic security within your cities."

"We're at war," Levon said, "and that war is down south, as you know." Some of the mayors nodded; a few looked uncomfortable.

He pressed on. "That means that we've got to have order in our own cities. I know that you're all doing your best. But as you know, and as Mark Prescott said, police departments across this country have a long legacy of racial bigotry. With the current shortage of National Guard and federal military aid available, there's bound to be some unrest."

Levon looked at the faces of the mayors—most of them nodded along. "So here's what needs to happen, and here's what President Martin wants to happen: you're all going to set up civilian oversight commissions. These will be parallel to your city councils, and they'll have real authority, real *public* authority." He hoped his emphasis conveyed the threat. Just in case, he added, "If not, I can guarantee violence will happen. That's a guarantee.

"Now, don't worry—all of the leaders of these commissions will be in touch with me regularly, and I'll be in touch with President Martin. She has also asked me to work with the commissions to recruit for the new civilian national service corps she's planning, as well as help fill out the military's needs. So we'll all be working together a fair bit. Hope that works for y'all."

The dialect drew a few chuckles. Levon smiled. They could all chuckle. Underneath, they knew exactly what he did: they no longer ran their cities. Levon Williams did.

THE SOUTH CHINA SEA

The aircraft carrier sat moored to the man-made island atop the atolls of the Spratly Islands. The Chinese government had spent years dredging the coral reefs, turning them into military outposts in spite of international furor. The crew of the *Liaoning*, fully two thousand strong, had been trained aboard the ship and knew her well. They came accompanied by another seven hundred members of the air group. Beside the *Liaoning* sat a full flotilla of destroyers and frigates.

At 0400 hours, the flotilla, led by the *Liaoning*, began its over eight-thousand-mile journey to the West Coast of the United States. Admiral Chen De stood on the deck of the aircraft carrier, watching the greatest armed amphibious force ever assembled by his nation steam toward America. His orders had come through that morning. He knew that Chinese forces would be joined in the United States by coalition forces from Europe, Japan, Canada, and Russia. But by far the largest on-the-ground contingent came from China, which the new president of the United States had publicly labeled a friend and partner.

In the game of international politics, friendship and partnership only went so far, Admiral Chen knew. He had contingency plans, just in case something should go wrong. Such things were bound to happen from time to time.

AUSTIN, TEXAS

Pages sprinted around the Texas House of Representatives, bearing paperwork and messages from the legislators to each other. In the hallways, congressmen berated one another, cornering each other, trying to talk some sense into each other. Cameras clogged the corridors, reporters frantically attempting to sequester some unlucky rube politician and peg him or her down on the vote.

The impeachment vote against Governor Bubba Davis was underway.

Blocks away, Davis sat in his office, the drapes closed, the room dark. He stared into the darkness, thinking about Ellen Hawthorne. He'd watched the speech from President Martin, disbelieving—there was no way that the federal government, even *this* federal government, could actually believe Ellen Hawthorne responsible for the worst terror attack in the history of the United States. Could believe *him* responsible for that attack.

But they had said it. They had declared war. His bluff had been called.

Unless he wasn't bluffing.

Davis knew that governors all over the country were waiting, watching to see what the House would do today. He'd spoken with the governors of Mississippi, Louisiana, Alabama, Oklahoma, Arkansas, New Mexico, Arizona, Alabama, Georgia; he'd received calls from the governors of Nebraska, Wyoming, South Dakota, North Dakota, and Montana. He'd assured them all that he had nothing to do with the attacks in New York, and that President Martin had exploited the terror attack to reassert federal authority. All of them feared for the future of the United States, but they also feared the domination of their states by an assertive executive branch prepared to declare war on its own citizens.

The federal military still had tremendous resources, but the combination of Prescott's military cuts with the terror attack in New York had taxed them to their limits. If it came down to it, military action by the feds wouldn't be that easy.

The thought of American men and women aiming guns at each other made Bubba Davis sick to his stomach. He hoped, in a way, that the House would go through with it, remove him from office, put an end to all of this, replace him with someone who would back down. But if the feds could trump up such a pack of lies about Ellen, what would they do to him? He'd be put on trial for treason against his nation; maybe Martin would pardon the men and women defending the border, maybe not. All of that sounded better to Bubba Davis than the prospect of a war with his own government, a government he'd fought for overseas and defended with his blood.

But they wouldn't keep the citizens of Texas safe. Those citizens were Americans, but their rights didn't spring from the federal government—they came from somewhere deeper. That was the only reason Bubba Davis didn't resign and turn himself over to the feds for a trial. Polls showed that Texans were strongly divided on whether Davis should stay or go, but polls also showed that few believed Davis had been behind the attacks in New York.

The phone rang on Davis's desk. He let it ring twice. Then he answered.

He hung up, leaned back against his chair.

He was still governor of Texas. His state was with him. Soon, he knew, he would be at war with the federal government.

NEW YORK CITY

Brett sat in an empty warehouse—they weren't going to risk bringing him back to a known facility. Too high profile, too much media. He sat with his back to the wall—*just like the 'Stan*, he laughed ruefully to himself—his head in his thick arms. It was getting late; the sun was setting beyond the haze of the skyline, devastated once more by terror. He looked up, the sunlight reflecting in his red-rimmed eyes. "Ellen," he whispered. "Ellen, I'm so sorry."

He didn't even sense it when the door creaked open and an officer in full SWAT regalia strode into the room. He was tall, broad shouldered.

Piece by piece, he began undressing.

"There isn't much time, sir," he said. "You need to put this shit on."

Brett looked up at him. "What are you talking about?"

"You're leaving, General."

"How did you get in here?"

"You want to stick around here, that's up to you, General," said the officer. "But I have a feeling you'll be better off taking my advice."

Brett stood up and began putting on the police gear as the officer spoke. "General, you're going to walk out of here. Keep your face toward the wall as much as possible. Show them this ID. It's federal."

Brett looked at it. "EPA? What do they have to do with this?"

The officer laughed. "The ID serves the purpose. Used to belong to a friend of mine."

When Brett finished suiting up, the officer sat down with his back against the wall. "Only one of us can leave," he said. "That's you. No time to argue. Get out of here."

Brett nodded slowly as he clipped the ID to his vest. "Thanks."

"The car's down the street. Two rights, then a left. Black van, license plate 3X8FFSL. Get out of here." Then the man dropped his head to his chest as Brett opened the door.

None of the guards in the hallway gave Brett a second glance. The uniform took care of that. At the end of the hall, he took an elevator down to the street.

When he got to the street, he followed the directions to the van. As he approached, the passenger's side door popped open. He climbed in.

A woman sat behind the wheel.

Then Brett saw her face.

He grabbed a fistful of her hair, pulling her toward him as she screamed. He placed his hand on her neck, gripping it. "Why?!" he yelled. "Why would you do this? Who are you?"

Her left hand gradually came up—Brett found himself at the point of her muzzle. "Get the hell off me," she said.

Slowly, he let go.

"My name is Soledad Ramirez," she choked. "I'm here to get you out of the city."

"You tried to assassinate Prescott. What do you want with me?"

Soledad looked at him seriously. "Do you want to stick around? If so, get out right now."

Brett looked at her. "You're that terrorist."

"I prefer rancher. The government made me a terrorist."

"No," said Brett. "You made you into a terrorist."

"You're free to get out at any time."

Brett went silent. She started the engine. "For what it's worth," she said, looking straight ahead, "I'm sorry about your wife, General Hawthorne. I'm sorry for this country. I'm not sorry what happened to Prescott. None of that matters."

"Where are we going?"

"I figure you're the general. You pick."

Brett thought for a moment. Then he looked to the horizon again, to the murky cloud of ash blotting out the rising stars. He set his jaw in a look Ellen would have recognized instantly as unshakable determination.

"Let's head West," he said. "I'm going home."

ABOUT THE AUTHOR

Ben Shapiro is editor-in-chief of DailyWire.com, as well as editor-at-large of *Breitbart News*. Shapiro is the author of six books, including the *New York Times* bestseller, *Bullies: How the Left's Culture of Fear and Intimidation Silences America* (2012). Shapiro is also a nationally syndicated columnist since age 17, a graduate of UCLA and Harvard Law School, and the host of *The Morning Answer* on KRLA 870 in Los Angeles and KTIE 590 in Orange County.

Rush Limbaugh says Shapiro isn't just "content to have people be dazzled by his brilliance; he actually goes out and confronts and tries to persuade, mobilize, motivate people." Glenn Beck calls Shapiro a "warrior for conservatism, against those who use fear and intimidation to stifle honest debate. I've never known him to back down from a fight." Sarah Palin says that Americans should "consider Ben's advice about how we must stand up and push back twice as hard against this bullying." Sean Hannity says to join Ben Shapiro and "fight back!" against liberal bullying. And Michelle Malkin says Shapiro is "infused with the indomitable spirit of his friend and mentor Andrew Breitbart." Even the liberal *Washington Post*, in the aftermath of Shapiro's devastating destruction of Piers Morgan on national television, conceded that Shapiro is a "foe of extraordinary polemical agility."